Eva O'R<

Chocolates in the Ocean

Copyright © : Eva O'Reilly
Published: 26 December 2014

The right of Eva O'Reilly to be identified as author of this Work has been asserted by her in accordance with sections 77 and 78 of the Copyright, Designs and Patents Act 1988.
All rights reserved. No part of this publication may be reproduced, stored in retrieval system, copied in any form or by any means, electronic, mechanical, photocopying, recording or otherwise transmitted without written permission from the publisher. You must not circulate this book in any format.

This book is licensed for your personal enjoyment only. This ebook may not be resold or given away to other people. If you would like to share this book with another person, please purchase an additional copy for each recipient. Thank you for respecting the hard work of this author.

This book is a work of fiction. Names, characters, businesses, organisations, places and events are either the product of the author's imagination or are used fictitiously. Any resemblance to actual persons, living or dead, events or locales is entirely coincidental.

Find out more about the author and upcoming books online at www.evaoreilly.com or @OreillyEva.

Cover Design by BespokeBookCovers.com

Week One

The rain was lashing against the windows and the wind was buffeting my car when I left Copenhagen to take possession of my new home. In the back of my car were boxes and suitcases packed with assorted items I had convinced myself I could easily do without for a couple of weeks. My plan for the day was simple: get the keys, unload the boxes and go back to my apartment in the city. It really should have been a beautiful, July day. There should have been champagne toasts with family and friends, fragrant roses and a sense of new beginnings. Instead it was dark and cold and wet and lonely. All summer it had done nothing but rain. Instead of cosy evenings lounging by the water or sipping wine with my friends at cafés in cobbled squares, I'd been ensconced in my apartment with endless cups of green tea and the dreary task of packing my life into cardboard boxes. At least my furniture was staying put so I had no removal companies to clear paths for through the debris.

It was just after ten when I parked in front of my new house and hurried up the steps to the front door, my coat over my head. The vendors were waiting to welcome me and together we walked through the house, chatting casually as I took notes on how the central heating worked, where the fuse box was and where the spare tins of paint were kept for when the time came to fix the cracks in the walls. Now that the house was empty it seemed suddenly twice as big as before. I gazed up at the tall ceilings, made mental notes about which rooms to start work on first, and tried to remember what this house had been like when I had played here as a child. If I stood still and closed my eyes just a little, I could almost make out the shadows of me and my friends charging through the living room like rampaging savages on our way out into the garden.

About an hour later I said goodbye to the vendors and they ran down the steps to their car hand in hand, smiling for the first time that day. They waved to me as they drove off and I waved back and smiled. I stayed on the steps for a while, sheltered from the rain by the doorway, and watched their car disappear around the corner. Just as I was about to go back inside another car pulled up. I laughed when it turned out to be the estate agent.

'Your office is a two-minute walk away!'

'I know,' he shouted above the rain, 'but haven't you seen the weather?'

I stepped aside to let him in and he presented me with two bottles of wine; each with a picture of my new house on the label.

'House wine,' he said with a smile. 'Office tradition.'

'Thank you. I'm sorry I can't even offer you coffee.' Then I thought of the commission I'd just made him and stopped feeling guilty about being a bad hostess. 'Could you recommend a good builder? Maybe someone to take a look at the roof?'

'Sure. If you come by the office I can give you some cards.'

We looked around the house and he pointed out a few features I hadn't noticed before. I wondered if they did this for all their clients or just the crazy ones who showed up with more money than sense. The rain seemed to lessen for a moment so we ran out and got the boxes and suitcases from my car. I thanked him again for the wine and promised to come by the office later that day. I waved him off and closed the door and at last I was alone.

Alone in my new house.

Alone in my new house I leaned against the front door and breathed deeply. I listened to the rain and the wind and for a moment I closed my eyes and let the memories wash over me. I'd always loved this house. I'd been happy in this house. For a moment I wondered what had happened to the children I used to play with here. Then I opened my eyes and I grinned.

Excitement fluttered in my stomach like a thousand butterflies and my feet begin to move.

Through the hallway and into the living room I ran. The dining room. The kitchen. Bedrooms, bathrooms, upstairs and downstairs. Picking up speed as I moved, bounding and laughing by the time I reached the converted basement. Outside into the garden where it was still raining. I ran through the trees, shaking the branches and splashing through the mud.

Back in the hallway I opened the suitcases to find towels and a change of clothes. I put my wet things into a bag and then checked that all the doors and windows were securely locked. I closed the front door reluctantly behind me and got back into my car. I stopped at the estate agent's as promised and then I drove back to my other life with my wet clothes, two bottles of house wine and the keys to my new home. And the rain never stopped.

Week Two

It was still raining a week later as I walked around my apartment, filling more boxes and dreaming of what I was going to do with my enormous new house. It was only meetings with clients that kept me in the city. Every morning when I woke up to the monotonous drilling of the rain against the windows I wanted to pack up and leave. Everything was planned, everything was ready and there was nothing I loathed more than the wait. My decision was made, I was starting a new life. So the old one had better let go plenty quick-quick.

To pass the time I bought myself a colourful raincoat and bright Wellington boots and went for walks in the city I loved. I bought little things that I did not imagine would be easy to come by in my new life on the island. The special chocolate I used to make my signature desserts. My favourite wines ready for when my friends came to visit. Liquorice powder. Garlic and chili salad dressing that never touched a lettuce leaf in my house but got brought out on the rare occasions when I made French fries. Ground coffee from Starbucks. Vintage posters and prints for my walls. I tried to soak up the atmosphere, the memories, every delicious thing that had happened to me since I first came to Copenhagen from Paris when I was eighteen.

Then, one morning, I decided to get fresh rolls from the bakery and when I came out of my building the first person I saw was you. You. Standing with *her* outside the church on the other side of the street.

My hand still on the doorknob, I went quickly back inside not making a sound. I hurried upstairs, feeling like I was going to be sick.

You son of a bitch. I knew what you were doing. So many churches in this damn city and you had to choose the one across the street from me. Of all the places you could have gone to, you chose my neighbourhood to get married in. How would it have been, I wondered, to come out of my apartment on a beautiful sunny day, perhaps heading off to meet some friends for coffee or pitch a proposal to a client, and run straight into you, your blushing bride and six million relatives? You bastard!

I knew then that I had done the right thing. Leaving was the only option for me. People could call it running away, being cowardly, still letting you win, but I didn't care. I wanted to be far away from any place or anyone that would ever remind me of you. Any place that would ever remind me of the years I had wasted loving you, hoping for something to finally come right with us, believing so completely that one day, *one day*, we would get our chance again. All for nothing.

Rolls forgotten, my hands trembled as I fumbled for my keys and unlocked my front door. Once safely inside, I sank down on the floor and cried.

Week Three

The last box was packed and the car was fully loaded, everything was ready for me to head off at first light. I was standing by the kitchen window, a glass of white wine in one hand and the list of the last-minute things I had to remember to do in the other. Empty bins. Empty dishwasher. Leave note re. leaky radiator. Music was playing in the living room and the light of the summer evening was soft and warm. The rain had lessened to a drizzle and the air smelled fresh and new. Through the open window I could hear the noises from the courtyard below. The door to the laundry room opened and then closed. The lids banged shut on the bins. One of the neighbours was having a barbecue in the rain and I smelled charcoal and burnt sausages. I closed the window and took my glass and a small bowl of Spanish almonds and black olives into the living room. I curled up on the sofa and reached for the book I was reading. Just as I turned the page there was a knock at the door. I made a mental note to add 'doorbell doesn't always work' to my list. Putting my book down I went to open the door, expecting one of my friends for another last goodbye. But the person waiting for me outside was you.

When I woke up the next morning the space beside me was empty and you were long gone. I felt hot, almost feverish, with the beginnings of a sore throat. It was just before six and the birds were singing in the trees outside my window. The sky was a perfect pastel blue with the sun a giant yellow ball of heat. At some point during the night the endless rain had stopped. It would be the most perfect summer's day. A warm breeze would waft gently through the green leaves while families picnicked in the parks and built sandcastles on the beach. Girls in summer dresses would sit outside cafés with their friends, enjoying cool drinks while they gossiped the hours away and flirted with the boys at the next table. While bells pealed out a carillon of hope and joy, you would emerge from a beautiful old church, your blushing bride on your arm.

And me?

I would run.

Three months earlier, an April shower was tapping against my windows when a casual remark from an old friend on Facebook revealed that you had come back to Copenhagen and were getting married. At that moment I knew I had to get out. Without thought, without logic, I simply grabbed my handbag and ran out the door, the cup of coffee I had just poured still cooling by the sink.

Once in my car I just drove. Out of the city. Anywhere but here. For the first fifteen minutes I just followed random streams of cars and listened to inane chatter on the radio. After a while I found myself on the motorway, not sure which way I was going. At first I thought of driving up to the coast, I thought about taking a long walk on a beach somewhere. Then I saw the name of a town I recognised, an echo from childhood, and suddenly I knew where I was going.

The more I drove, the further away from the city I got, the brighter the day became. I filled up my car at a quiet petrol station in the middle of nowhere and the scent of fresh flowers drenched by the rain almost drowned out the smell of diesel. By the time I arrived, three hours later, at the place I hadn't even known I was going to, the rain had given way to what promised to be the first truly warm day of spring. I drove across bridges and watched the sun sparkle on the water. Denmark is made up of over four hundred islands and in the space of that morning my car had been on six of them. But when I crossed the last bridge, I felt like I had come home.

My father's family come from Langeland, a long, narrow island tucked away from more populated areas. When I was little we used to go there every summer and every Christmas. My great-grandparents had a little house by the beach where they lived until they were both well into their nineties. They died when I was twelve, within two months of each other. A developer bought their house and all the surrounding land and built little wooden holiday cottages now popular with German tourists. My grandparents lived in Rudkøbing, the one place on the island that can justifiably be called a town, albeit a small one. They had a little townhouse with an enormous garden where my grandmother grew peas, cabbages and strawberries. In the ten years since they had died my visits to the island had been very rare. I hadn't planned it that way, it was simply one of those things that happen when ties get broken and journeys take too long. I had never been there with you, although we'd talked about it many times. My grandmother had always said that once they were gone none of us would ever go back there.

I drove into Rudkøbing, following the road from memory and nearly squealing with delight at how little things had changed. Copenhagen seemed a lifetime away. My grandparents' house was just as I remembered it, red brick with a wooden door. Even the curtains were still the same. When I parked by the kerb and got out, the sound of the car door closing seemed loud and intrusive on the quiet street. I wondered for a moment whether anyone was home. Then I turned and looked at the house opposite. I saw the 'For Sale' sign tacked up outside and suddenly I knew exactly what I was going to do.

A moment later I was dialling the number of the local estate agent and twenty minutes later he pulled up next to me in a big black estate.

'Hello,' he said, locking his car and shaking my hand all at once. 'You must be Anne. I'm Steen.'

'Nice to meet you. And thank you for arranging this at such short notice.'

'No problem, the owners are both at work.'

We walked across the street and he unlocked the front door and launched into his sales spiel.

'Don't bother,' I told him with a smile. 'I've wanted this house since I was eight years old.'

'You know it?' he asked. 'I just don't remember seeing you around before. You don't live on the island, do you?'

'No,' I shook my head. 'But my grandparents lived across the street and I used to play here when I was little. I'm a little ashamed to say I can hardly remember the last time I came back here.'

'So why today?'

I just smiled and shrugged. I could have told him. I could have confided in this sympathetic stranger who was already praying for a sale and the big commission that would keep his job safe for at least another three months. I could have told him that I just couldn't bear the thought of sharing my city with you. That the thought of seeing you sitting with someone else in our favourite café was abhorrent to me. That I couldn't bump into the two of you wandering through IKEA hand in hand, picking out furniture for your new living room or, God forbid, nursery. I could have explained how, the moment I heard you were coming back to get married, all the restlessness and frustration I had been feeling for months coalesced and I knew it was time to run.

But of course I didn't tell him any of those things. I simply kept smiling as I ran my hands over the wooden banister and remembered dressing up as a princess and sweeping grandly down the staircase.

The house had been neglected for the last few years. The current owners had two sets of twins and their limited time and resources were apparent in the peeling paint, mouldy bathroom tiles and the overgrown garden. I didn't mind. I didn't even know what I would do with the house, I just knew I had to own it. I had to come here and live here and somehow everything would fall into place. For a moment, pausing at the doorway into the kitchen, I saw myself sitting by an old wooden table, grating chocolate while an enormous puppy lay at my feet. As we walked through the rooms, I stopped feeling restless and the nagging, searching feeling that had been hounding me for weeks began to lessen.

'What was the asking price?' I asked the agent and he told me without a glance at his file.

'That's ridiculous,' I told him. 'You need at least half that again to turn this place around. And I had a little look online while you were getting the keys. I know how much they paid for it. I know how long it's been for sale. And I know what's wrong with it.'

He nodded and I knew he agreed with me but, bound by professional ethics and the need for me to believe that his valuations were not governed by his client's unrealistic expectations, he said nothing.

We continued our walk through the house and I took copious notes and several photos. When we rounded the first part of the garden and looked at what used to be the largest vegetable patch in town, I wasn't sure whether to laugh or cry.

'Okay,' I said. 'This is what I will offer. Take it or leave it.'

He looked at me and shook his head. 'I honestly can't say what they will do,' he said, 'but let's go back to the office and I'll put it to them.' I told him I would go for a walk while he phoned the owners and they discussed it.

Looking at it from the outside, the house suddenly seemed much larger than it had ten minutes earlier. I sat down on the little wall by the pavement and looked across at my grandparents' house. If their ghosts had suddenly appeared and waved at me, I don't think I would have been at all surprised. I stayed there, swinging my legs back and forth, my mind empty of all thoughts except that profound feeling of peace.

Twenty minutes later I walked into the estate agent's office. He beamed at me and told me the house was mine. Quite in shock, I thanked him with a smile, left my details and signed the necessary paperwork. I walked outside, a little uncertain about my next move. Part of me wanted to drive straight home and start packing, another part wanted to run back to the house and kick the owners out right now, and a very large part just wanted to collapse on the pavement, laughing hysterically. I had just bought myself a house. And not a small house. A colossus of a building with a garden big enough for a pony. I had bought a house on an island I hadn't been to in ten years, an island three hours away from all my friends and my normal life.

The spring sun warmed my face as I stood there in front of the estate agent's office. The air was fresh and on the other side of the road someone was teaching a child to walk their dog. As I looked up and down the street, so many memories came flooding back to me. I remembered walking here, hand in hand with my grandfather, on our way to the playground. I remembered running here breathlessly one summer evening, puffed up with the responsibility of being sent to the chocolate shop for evening truffles, holding on tightly to the shiny coins in my hand. As I looked around, I picked out houses I had known. Places where my grandparents' friends had lived, places where my friends had lived. There was one place I had to visit before I left, so I started walking towards the shops. I found a florist, bought the largest bouquet I could find and then headed up the hill to the graveyard to tell my family that I was coming home.

The little family plot was well-tended but I was little ashamed that it had been so long since I had been here. Even though I kept my great-grandparents and my grandparents fresh in my memory, even though we paid the church to take care of the plot, we should have come here more often. I laid my flowers down on the damp earth and stood there silently for a while, looking at their names on the headstones. Then I sat down and began to talk. I told them all about you, about the house and what I had just done, about how restless I had been. It was the first time I said it out loud.

I'm tired of living in Copenhagen.

Sitting there uncomfortably on the gravel, I found the words to express the frustrations I had been feeling. I continued talking, not caring who heard me or whether they thought I was nuts. I spoke as if my family was really there, sitting right across from me just as they used to at the kitchen table, and we were having coffee and pastries.

When I eventually got up from the path my legs were stiff and my back ached. So it seemed like the sensible thing for the town's newest resident to do would be to go for a walk and reacquaint herself with the sights.

Spring was definitely in the air so I bought myself an ice cream by the harbour and went for a walk along the marina, looking at the names of the boats bobbing up and down on the waves. I stood by the beach where we used to take my grandparents' Great Danes for walks and looked at the bridge I had driven across a few hours before. It was like something that had happened in another lifetime. Walking back through the park, I sat on the swings and watched a little boy and his mother play in the sandpit while their dog lay on the grass next to a pushchair filled with shopping bags. Everything seemed so very familiar. Even the shops had not changed much. The bookshop was where it had always been, so was the toy shop. The chocolate shop was gone, but the supermarket was in its usual place. It was as though time had rolled back twenty years and I was a child again in a world filled with endless opportunities. On my way into the supermarket I bumped into a young man with a guitar case on his back and a big bag of potatoes in his arms, and the warm smile he gave me when I apologised seemed to affirm that I had done the right thing by coming here.

I'd always loved Rudkøbing. I remembered clearly the first time that I was allowed to go exploring by myself. It was an Easter holiday and my grandmother noticed I was practically expiring from boredom while I sat alone in the corner at her friend's birthday party, every other guest at least forty years older than me. She gave me some money and told me to go get myself an Easter egg from the chocolate shop. When I got back I asked if I could go out again for an hour. And then another hour. Soon I was leaving the house immediately after breakfast and staying out till lunch. I'd leave again almost immediately afterwards and only come back for dinner. Wandering the cobbled streets, playing on the swings in the park, I learned how to day-dream, how to create worlds in my imagination. I learned to love the quiet little town for its peaceful atmosphere and for the sense of independence it gave me. Exploring became an adventure. One minute I could be a princess in dragon-guarded tower, awaiting the arrival of my knight in shining armour, and the next my new friends and I could be government agents on a top secret mission, sneaking around corners and spying on strangers from behind trees.

From the moment I had crossed the bridge, everything that had happened that morning had become a blur and it was as though a weight had been lifted from the day. A line had been drawn in the sand, dividing the life I knew from whatever new experience I was reaching out for. Maybe that old feeling of serenity was why Langeland had stood out so vividly in my mind as I drove. Langeland was filled with happy memories. Memories that had nothing to do with you.

I knew that what I had just done was insane by most people's standards, but the moment I saw the house was for sale, the desire to leave everything behind and start all over again was simply too strong to resist.

And now it was three months later and I was frantically throwing yesterday's clothes into plastic bags and ignoring the scent of your cologne that wafted up from the pillows to haunt me. Whatever it took I had to be out by the time you stood up in that church and said your 'I do's. The last thing I wanted to see when I drove out of the courtyard was your wedding party.

The woman who was going to rent my apartment was taking it fully furnished and equipped. Recently separated from her husband and desperate to move out of her sister's spare bedroom, she was on the phone to me ten minutes after my ad went live on the rental site. Suddenly it seemed as though everyone was trying to ditch their baggage and flee their old lives. I'd given her my spare set of keys the day before and she would be arriving with her suitcases later. Another reason to leave early. I didn't want to see someone else move into my home and start using my things.

Since my suitcases had been loaded into the car the day before, all I still needed to pack were the last few bits and pieces. Our used sheets had to go, so I stripped the bed. The wine glasses we drank from, those long-stemmed ones you once bought me for my birthday, were washed and put away in their box for the journey.

My throat hurt and even after a cool shower I was feverish. The last thing I felt physically equipped to handle was a long car journey at the end of which would be an empty house filled with nothing but boxes and suitcases. But the last thing I felt emotionally equipped to deal with was the thought of being stuck here while your wedding guests spilled out of the church and onto my street. So I threw the bags into the back seat, placed a big box of tissues next to me, checked one last time that my apartment was properly locked and nothing left behind, and then drove away without looking back.

As I crossed the Great Belt Bridge the sun was sparkling brightly on the water. I sang along to the radio, ignoring the sick feeling in my stomach and the thought that I had actually let you drive me out of my home. Would you look up at the windows as you passed by in your morning suit? Would you remember last night? Would you regret it? Would you wonder if I was sitting up there on my own, listening to the church bells and crying? Or would you even care?

The song on the radio changed and the lyrics surrounded me with their message. I pushed the accelerator down still further, increasing the distance between us with every passing moment. They were singing about running away, protecting yourself from harm. It was what I had done three months ago and it was what I was doing now. Running away. I'd given you nearly thirteen years of my life. I couldn't give you any more.

When I arrived at the house three hours later, I practically crawled inside and collapsed on the pile of duvets that I'd brought two weeks earlier. My throat was raw and every part of my body ached. Unable to face the thought of unloading the car, I wanted to lie down and close my eyes for just a minute. I slept for over eighteen hours and when I awoke the birds were singing again.

According to the statistics in the local newspaper, Langeland is an island with a dwindling population trying valiantly to market itself as an attractive place to live and work. The only problem is that there isn't much work to be had any more. But for me, waking to my new life, it was a safe haven of childhood memories, a place filled with summer holidays and Christmases by candlelight. It was long summer days that never ended, when you made friends quickly and played outside in evenings that never grew dark. It was not school, or work, or normal life. It was gently rolling hills, fragrant green woods and sandy beaches by warm seas. Ice cream and cakes every day, perpetual holiday, adopted pets and that never-ending feeling that the world was an exciting place and that tomorrow would be full of adventure.

I don't know if I had been thinking clearly when I'd bought the house. I just knew the time had come for me to get out of the city and live another life. For years I'd been translating and editing novels, film scripts and PhD theses and, while I loved helping other people realise their dreams, it was more and more as though I no longer had any of my own. Just before the start of the property boom a friend and I had managed to buy two small derelict apartments that we planned to renovate. Halfway through the project, she pulled out and moved to Australia with her boyfriend, selling me her share for a nominal sum that would be enough to help them start their new life down under. One apartment I sold, one I rented out to a succession of students. Medical students were my favourites. Their course lasted years and they paid well. That income, combined with payment for my translations and the rent I would be getting from my own apartment, left me feeling secure enough to embark on this fool's errand on the island. While I awaited the lightning bolt of inspiration, I'd keep my business running smoothly during the day and spend my evenings painting bedrooms and taking long walks through the town.

The house had been built a hundred years earlier as the residence for the chief surgeon long before the island's working hospital was turned into council offices and doctors' surgeries. It was spacious enough for the family and the requisite number of servants. Naturally it came with a beautiful ornamental garden where the mistress of the house could entertain the other prominent wives during the long summer days. Also, behind the garden, a large vegetable patch that was still being used when I used to come to the house.

For the last forty years the house had been home to various families, usually with at least three or four young children. I had played there. I had picked cherries in the garden, rolled in the grass and, for the first time, seen framed posters on the walls instead of paintings and photographs. That had seemed incredibly grown-up and chic and I couldn't wait until I was an adult and could do the same. I remembered a big wooden table in the kitchen. The tabletop was at least three inches thick, and we would sit there with our sandwiches and milk before rushing madly through the rooms and out into the garden again.

The family I had purchased it from had obviously been unaware of the enormous challenge and burden such a large house would be. Their frustration and neglect were obvious from the peeling wallpaper and their shoddy attempts at repairs. The garden had been allowed to run wild and had we been in warmer climates, I wouldn't have ventured into the grass for fear of snakes. I could imagine the petty squabbles that had arisen between them, the endless recriminations because nothing was being done right and the final realisation that it was the house or them. No wonder they had agreed to my offer. It had nothing to do with getting out of an uncomfortable mortgage, it was their marriage and their family that were on the line.

As I lay listening to the birds my sore throat was gone and I felt better than I had done for months. At some point my mattress of soft quilts had shifted and I had ended up half on the floor. But I didn't mind. I felt great.

In one of my boxes was a new kettle and some mugs. I made myself a cup of green tea and opened the doors to the garden. The morning dew was heavy on the grass and the little spiders had been hard at work spinning their webs in the wilderness. How did I, who could barely keep basil alive, possibly think I could manage something as enormous as this? The very thought of it made me laugh out loud and I realised that a large lawnmower would probably have to be at the top of my shopping list. Along with shears, seeds, gardening gloves and all sorts of strange implements I'd never imagined would have anything to do with me. Occasionally I caught myself wondering what the hell I was doing and whether I hadn't just wondered into someone else's life by mistake.

But on that quiet, July morning, while my new neighbours were still asleep, I walked through the damp grass in my colourful rubber boots and dressing gown. My empty tea cup dangling from my fingers, I allowed myself to think of you.

I wondered if you had enjoyed your wedding. I wondered if you had also had a sore throat yesterday and had coughed and sneezed your way through your vows. I wondered if the bride had fallen flat on her face on her trip up or down the aisle. I imagined the guests' horror if your best man had messed up his toast and revealed exactly where you spent your last night as a free man. I wondered if you were now on your honeymoon, soon to be sunning yourselves on some Caribbean beach or sipping morning cappuccinos in an ancient Italian square filled with statues of great men. And ... oh God! ... I wondered again and again till I was almost sick with it, how you could possibly have gone through with it. How you could have stood there with her and said those words, promised yourself to her for all eternity, when just twelve hours before you had been in my bed, in my arms and we both knew that your whole future was a lie.

The last drops of my tea fell like tears from the cup and onto the grass. And I leaned my head against the withered trunk of an old apple tree and cried.

I was eighteen the day we first met and had my whole word turned around, never to be the same again. Newly arrived from Paris, revelling in my independence and my studies, I was trying to make new friends. The autumn sun was warm on the windows as I sat chatting to people I would never see again. I remember so clearly that moment when you walked into the room and I looked up at you for the first time. I knew you then. I recognised you. I had never seen you before, but my first thought was, 'Oh! *There* you are!' And we just stood there, gazing at each other, locked in one of those rare moments when the whole world seems to hold its breath. It was barely two months later, on a dark, cold evening in November that the inevitable happened.

It had lasted two months. Two months of bright, exciting days filled with adventure as we walked hand in hand through the gently falling snow. We kissed by the harbour, passing little restaurants where torches burned brightly on the pavement outside. We bought a cheap plastic toboggan and went sledging in the park by the zoo. Alone in my tiny little apartment, we experimented with odd pasta dishes and ate them by candlelight before making love till dawn. And then I ended it for strange reasons I couldn't even remember. And I had regretted it ever since.

What had we had since then? Why had we kept coming back to each other, like those little dolls that always come back upright when you push them over? Passion that would not die? Love that would not speak? Missed signals, missed opportunities and always – always – the chance to return to square one and start over. Over and over, year after year, always trying and yet always failing. The air was electric every time we met. The tension unbearable, the desire palpable. But somehow, every time, it was never right for us. There was always something in the way. Always something, because we were both scared to death of each other. Both scared to reveal a depth of emotion that we feared the other would not reciprocate. Both scared to admit what we both knew. That there could be no other, ever, for either one of us. That we belonged together so completely.

Thirteen years later and I had sent you off to marry some other woman. A woman I knew you did not love. Or loved only with the complacent, petty emotion that we could conjure up for others. The kind of feeling that never lasted. Because always, with the inevitability of the turning tide, would come the comparison. Every man who was not you was not enough. The passion was missing, the desire did not last. The most secret, most sacred part of my soul cried out for you, and you alone. Every time, without fail, I knew when you would walk back into my life. And every time, without fail, you knew when I was on the verge of contacting you. So many things that could have been. So many sweet men and women who fell by the wayside. Of course your marriage would not last. But I'd be damned if I'd stay and watch it run its course in my city.

Here I was safe. Here you could not touch me. Here there was nothing to remind me of you unless I chose to let it. I was going to shut the door on you, on us, and let it stay shut. This is not, I told myself again and again, some tragic love affair that is meant to be. This is just a stupid, adolescent passion that should have run its course years ago.

You are not meant for me. Nothing is meant to be. I believe that.

I do.

If I said it enough times, it would have to be true.

I was looking forward to furnishing my new home and I didn't want to waste money by buying essentials quickly and cheaply only to want to replace them two months later. So I slept on an inflatable mattress, used some of the removal boxes as tables and put large cushions on the floor in the living room. There were five bedrooms and a bathroom upstairs and one bedroom on the ground floor with an en suite. I was considering knocking two of the upstairs rooms together, once I figured out what I was going to do with the monstrosity I'd saddled myself with.

Every morning I walked in the garden while the birds sang in the trees above my head. Every morning the last drops in my tea cup spilled like tears onto the grass. But I did not cry again. I walked along the beach for hours, losing myself in the quiet rhythm of the waves. I watched the clouds scuttle by over my head when the wind grew stronger in the afternoon and I skimmed stones across the water. And every time I thought of you, I dug my nails into my hands until marks like tiny crescent moons appeared on my palms. But still I did not cry. I started taking my camera with me whenever I went out and, in the bright light of the summer afternoons, I found picture postcard images in this town I had thought I knew so well.

During those first few days I cleaned the house from top to bottom, even getting down on my knees to scrub the last stubborn stains off the floors. I bought a lawnmower and garden shears and found it surprisingly soothing to push the machine up and down in endlessly straight lines. I stood on the steps in front of the house looking across at what used to be my grandmother's well-tended front garden and I knew she would be so sad to see her house now. Every morning I considered sneaking across the street with my new shears and doing some violence to the weeds. I collected colour charts and paint samples and felt wild when I tentatively experimented with bright colours on the walls. Every evening, when the light mellowed, I walked up to the graveyard and sat on the grass by my family plot. With my back against the hedge, my long hair tangled up in the leaves, I told them about my days, my plans for the house, the e-book I was proofreading. There was calm and peace and, for the first time in months, I was truly happy.

Week Four

I had been in the house for about a week when my friend Lisbeth came to visit me. We'd become friends after meeting in the library in my first year at university about a week after I'd first ended it with you. I'd had puffy eyes and had still been struggling to get through the day without bursting into tears. Lisbeth had found me hiding in the bathroom because I'd caught a glimpse of someone I had thought was you. She'd asked me what was wrong, we'd gone for a coffee which had evolved into dinner and a bottle of wine and we'd been friends ever since.

The fact that there was no furniture and nothing but boxes and paint samples in every room made the house appear empty, but she loved it. The evening she arrived we bought a disposable barbecue and I found two old folding chairs in the garage. It reminded me of the weekend five years ago when you and I had driven up to the coast and spent the evening on a secluded beach. We'd barbecued sausages, waved across the water to Sweden and sipped coffee from an old flask you'd found in your mother's kitchen. Later, when the air grew cooler, we'd cuddled under a blanket and kissed under the stars. We'd made plans that night to walk to Sweden if the sea froze in the winter, just as it had once in the eighties, and I'd clung to the notion that this time we would still be together when winter came. But when the leaves turned that year, I was alone again.

Lisbeth and I sat outside, eating off trays on our knees, our glasses on the ground beside us. She was fascinated by the garden, the open space and the old trees. When I described how the back part of the garden used to be filled with rows and rows of vegetables, she didn't believe me.

'It's like the old days! I remember you telling me about this house once but it's so weird to actually be here. And now I find it was just like you said. I don't remember knowing anyone who actually grew vegetables before.'

'Who are you calling old?' I looked at her and laughed. 'Just think of how many people are trying to grown their own vegetables now. You can't swing a cat on social media without hitting a picture of home-grown this and home-made that.'

'Good point. You're going to be so trendy. Soon you'll have your own little segment on morning television and then he'll come crawling back to you.'

'Sure. 'Cause the way to a man's heart is through dirty fingernails and earthworms. But I do like the idea of growing my own vegetables and eating things fresh from the garden.'

'Really?'

'Yes.' I took another sausage off the barbecue and added some more spicy sauce and salad to my plate. 'I'm so hungry these days. Must be all the physical work. When I was little,' I continued, wiping sauce from my lips with my napkin, 'my grandmother grew her own vegetables in the back of her garden too. Everyone around here did. And I used to love going down there to fetch fresh peas and strawberries. It was part of why summer here was so nice. And of course I'll never use pesticides so my produce will be organic. So okay, you're right, I'll be very trendy.'

Lisbeth laughed and poured herself another glass of wine. 'I could see that. Fresh fruit from the trees, vegetables from the garden. Soon you'll be making preserves and selling them from a cart outside the house.'

'Yeah, right. I don't think I'll go that far. But you know I love cooking.'

'I know. And I hope to enjoy much more of it once you start growing your own food. Will there be cows and maybe a sheep or two? You could add fresh milk to the strawberries and knit throws for your sofas. When you get some.' She winked at me. 'But seriously, this place is great. It's so peaceful. No wonder you ran here. And don't say you didn't run away, because I know you too well.'

I shook my head. 'No, I guess I did. Although it wasn't all about him.'

She looked at me with a quizzical, slightly incredulous expression.

'I'm serious. For the last few months I've been feeling so restless, so hemmed in by everything in the city. I wanted to get out, do something new, be somewhere new. I just didn't know what to do or where to go. But when I found this place, I knew where I wanted to be. Now I just hope that I can find out what it is I want to do.'

'What you're doing now still pays the bills, doesn't it?'

I nodded. 'But I want to do something different, something more. I need challenge, adventure. I was bored. Like I'd got everything I could out of that life.'

Lisbeth took another sausage off the barbecue. 'Well this house should definitely prove a challenge. I wish I'd had somewhere like this to run to when my marriage fell apart.' She sighed and then shrugged off the regret. 'So, do you think he married her in the end?'

'I guess so. I guess if he hadn't I would have heard. At least I hope I would have.'

'I'm sure he would have come back if he hadn't got married.'

'I don't even know why he came that night.'

She smiled at me and squeezed my hand. 'Because he loves you.'

I smiled and shook my head as I looked out over the garden. 'I used to think so. I used to hope so. I used to feel it so strongly. I used to be so sure.' I wanted to say something else, but she and I had analysed you and me to death so many times that even I was sick of it now. Maybe it was time to stop thinking so much. Sometimes I wondered if I would have forgotten about you long ago if we had stopped talking about you. But when it came to girl-talk you were such a fascinating subject.

I used to *know* that you loved me. Deep down inside, in that place where there are no lies and no fear, I just knew. But after everything that had happened the week before, all I was now was confused. So I just shrugged my shoulders and looked at the last rays of the sun falling between the trees. I wondered where you were and what you were doing. Again and again I wondered the same thing: did you think of me?

When I woke up the next morning Lisbeth was already up and had even been to the bakery for fresh rolls and pastries.

'Wow!' I said. 'Aren't you normally the one who loves to sleep till noon at weekends?'

'I stopped being able to do that the moment I became a mother. But I guess this country air just does something special. I didn't even wake up in the night and I *always* wake up at least twice. But when I woke up this morning I remembered what you said last night about how you and your grandfather always used to go to the bakery in the morning. It seemed like a nice idea. I don't think I've done that for years. It's always muesli and fat-free yoghurt.'

I laughed and started to make coffee while Lisbeth laid the table and found butter, jam and honey. 'Part of the point of being on holiday is to enjoy doing something different to what you do at home,' I reminded her. 'But I'm not on holiday and what I need now is some furniture.'

She nodded. 'Yeah. I didn't want to say anything but this refugee chic that you've got going here has a very limited lifespan.' She winked at me and I stuck my tongue out at her. 'You definitely need a bed, a sofa, a table and some chairs.'

'Wardrobes and bookcases would also be nice. Right now my clothes are all in suitcases.'

Lisbeth buttered a roll and smothered it with jam. I poured coffee for us both and put pastries on the table. 'We'll have breakfast and then we'll go shopping for furniture. I'm in the mood to go and spend some money.'

'Sounds perfect. You'll want a comfortable bed in case he shows up.'

'I'm not even going to comment on that.' Instead I picked up a cinnamon pastry thick with chocolate icing and tried to ignore Lisbeth's further insinuations. It promised to be a warm August day filled with sunshine. Just perfect for starting over.

I took Lisbeth to Odense and we spent the better part of the morning window shopping. Lisbeth bought presents for her daughter, Emma, who was being spoiled at her grandparents while Lisbeth was here with me. She was four now and loved nothing more than dressing up. For her last birthday I'd bought her a ninja outfit and she'd spent most of the evening sneaking through Lisbeth's apartment, pressing herself against the walls while attempting to enlist our help for a secret quest.

'I'll get her a book,' I said. 'Look, how about this one?' It was a book about costumes and Lisbeth nodded.

'I'm bringing her some of her favourite chocolate. It's the exact same kind we get at home when we have our special movie nights, but she'll think it's extra special because it came from here. And she'll like this tiara for when she wants to dress up like a princess.'

I smiled. I couldn't imagine being a single mother like Lisbeth. I admired her tremendously. Emma was a loving, intelligent, funny little girl who was kind to everyone and never threw tantrums or made you want to mutter 'spoiled brat' under your breath. Whenever I spent time with them I always thought it was amazing how Lisbeth could manage to raise such a lovely child on her own when many parents I knew didn't do half as well even with two of them on the job.

We had smoothies and paninis for lunch before getting down to the serious business of furniture shopping.

'I just don't get,' Lisbeth said to me while we ate, 'why you don't just bring the furniture from your own apartment.'

'Because I'm renting it furnished. I wasn't sure what I was going to do down here so I didn't want to spend a lot of money on removal men. Practically everything there is from IKEA, there's nothing special or expensive. Moving it all the way over here would cost just as much as buying new furniture. And the woman I've rented it to is in the middle of her divorce and they're busy fighting over who gets the sofa. Until they figure that out, she can use mine. It's so old now anyway. It's much easier to let short term if it's furnished.'

'I suppose that makes sense. So what kind of furniture were you thinking of?'

'Comfortable. Stylish. Things that I like. That's a good thing about being single, you don't have to be concerned about anyone else's taste.'

'Tell me about it. Remember how Kristoffer wanted minimalist designer? Do you know how hard it is to be minimalist designer with a baby?' We laughed as we remembered him running around picking up toys because they destroyed the purity of the empty space. 'Now he lives in a loft furnished with a futon and uses a pallet as a coffee table. And twitches when Emma brings toys.'

It took me three hours to find a bed and a sofa that I thought were comfortable and to arrange delivery of them for the following day. I also selected a bookcase and a coffee table. I told Lisbeth I would just have to eat in the living room until further notice. There was a new kitchen in my house's immediate future and what I wanted most was an old, wooden table, with a really thick tabletop, just like the one I remembered from childhood. I thought it would be nice to have a bench along one side of it, where I could pile colourful cushions and sit and read magazines and sip tea. But with what I had now ordered I could sleep comfortably, I could relax, and I could work.

'Once the furniture has arrived tomorrow we'll go round the island and see if we can track down any antique tables.'

'Okay. But I want to go back to the bakery for more of those pastries.'

'You have pastries in Copenhagen.'

'I know. But I never eat them there. Now I'm on holiday.'

The next morning we went shopping in Rudkøbing and Lisbeth bought me a lovely bouquet of flowers for my new coffee table. We ate pastries as she insisted and sent a postcard home to Emma. I couldn't remember the last time I'd sent a postcard to anyone. While we were standing in line at the post office Lisbeth nudged me and winked.

'Do you see that guy over there?'

'Which one?'

'The young one. The one who's staring at you.'

I looked up. 'Don't be silly. No one is staring at me.'

'He is.'

'He's a boy.'

'He's not a boy. He's just a little younger. And he's cute.'

'You're blind,' I said. 'He's gorgeous,' I giggled and winked at her.

'See,' she smiled at me. 'Plenty more fish in the sea. Cougar.'

I laughed and sneaked another look. I was sure I had seen him somewhere before. Then he smiled as he looked at something on his phone and I remembered him as the young man with guitar case and the potatoes who I had bumped into the day I bought the house. We cast a few more glances at him while we waited and then talked about him all the way back to the house. As we arrived, the van with my new furniture was just pulling into the driveway.

With the help of the two delivery men it didn't take us long to unload the van and get everything safely put away in the right rooms. I offered them coffee once we had finished and, since the sun was shining and they didn't want to get my new sofa dirty, we sat on the steps in front of the house. They were curious and obviously thought I was insane when I told them about how I had gone out for a drive and come back with a house.

After we waved them off we decided to skip the search for a table and start putting furniture together instead. We spent the afternoon giggling and gossiping, putting books on shelves, turning my vast, empty spaces into the beginnings of a comfortable home.

'Do you remember,' Lisbeth said as we moved the sofa for the third time, 'when you first bought your apartment?'

'I do. Remember how we spent the first evening trying to paint by candlelight because the guys digging up the road accidentally cut through all the electricity cables in the street?'

Lisbeth laughed and nodded. 'Yes. And I remember having to re-paint a lot because we kept missing spots. You two seemed so happy that night. Remember how we sent him out for pizza, got everything ready to paint the hallway and then forgot to move the paint when we went to open the wine.'

'Yeah. And he came back with the pizzas, opened the door and stepped straight into the paint.'

'I remember how much he laughed. I really thought you were going to make it work that time.'

'I did, too.' I looked out the window and smiled. 'That was a lovely evening.'

Lisbeth let out a giant sigh as she put her end of the sofa down. 'Okay, is this a good spot for it? Because I don't think I can move this thing any more today.'

'Better than the others at least. I'll try it this way for a while and see how it goes.'

'Great. Now what's for dinner?'

Week Five

It took us two days of driving around the island, but we managed to find the perfect wooden table for my kitchen. Looking at the scratches and stains on it, I found myself wondering about the people who had owned it before me. How many birthday presents had been laid out on it, how many Christmas dinners had been served?

'I'm amazed we found one so quickly,' I said to Lisbeth when we were getting the breakfast things ready.

'I know,' she nodded. 'And so cheaply.'

'I guess this kind of furniture isn't really in style at the moment. Maybe everyone wants modern these days?'

'I don't know. I read somewhere that the furniture my grandparents used to have is coming back into fashion. You know, stained oak dressers and dining chairs with needlepoint.'

'Seriously?' I tried to remember my great-grandparent's furniture and couldn't imagine ever having anything like that in my home. Everything so dark and upright. 'Nah, that must be some dodgy antique dealer trying to make a quick profit by pretending there's a new trend on the way.'

Lisbeth put the plates on the table. 'I couldn't imagine it either. I'd feel like I had wandered into an old people's home. Or stepped back in time to a family Christmas lunch in the living room of an elderly relative.'

'I know,' I laughed, 'it's ... ouch!'

'What is it?'

'It's nothing.' I walked over to the fridge and started to get butter, jam and juice out of the fridge. 'It's weird and kind of embarrassing to talk about, but my breasts are just so sore these days. Do you know, I actually had to hold onto them to get out of bed this morning, they hurt so much? Guess it must be some weird hormone thing, although this is definitely a first. My period's a little late, I'll bet that's what's causing it.'

'Uhm hmm.' Lisbeth looked and me critically, her eyes narrowed and she smiled strangely, the look on her face a cross between someone about to tell me that the aliens had landed and someone who was going to hand me a big parcel and let me unwrap it.

'What? Why are you looking at me like that? What?'

'Didn't you say yesterday that walking past that pizza place made you feel sick?'

'Yes. So? It was disgusting. Greasy and icky and ... just horrible. Oh for God's sake this really hurts. And stop staring at me like that!'

'Darling,' she took my hand and grinned wickedly, 'sore breasts, late period, nausea ...' She trailed off and looked at me like I was an idiot. 'Don't you get it?'

'Get what?'

'I almost hate to have to tell you this. I think you're pregnant.'

So that's what they mean when they say it feels like time stands still.

Two minutes later Lisbeth had thrown on some clothes and was running out the door, heading to the supermarket to get every brand of home pregnancy test she could find. I sat in the kitchen with my head in my hands, numb and in shock. Maybe if I didn't move I could turn time back five minutes and none of this would be real. Yes, none of it would be real. I would still be asleep in my new bed and all of this would just be some bizarre dream. I poured a glass of milk – no green tea when you're pregnant! – and walked out into the garden.

Oh God.
Oh God.
Oh God.
Oh God.
Oh God.

How could I be pregnant? 98% effective and I turned out to be part of the sorry 2% it didn't work for. I couldn't even win 50kr in the lottery, how could I beat the odds to create a baby?

Oh God.
Oh God.
Oh God.
Oh God.
Oh God.

And my baby's father is on his honeymoon!

Oh God.
Oh God.
Oh God.
Oh God.
Oh God.

Even so, I couldn't stop a tiny smile. Pregnant. A baby. Your baby. Our baby.

Oh God!

I'm pregnant. Well, I thought, and gave a wry smile, at least I have space for a baby now. I sat down on the terrace steps and tried to imagine myself running around on the lawn playing football, badminton or just lying back on a blanket, reading a favourite story aloud in the sunshine. This enormous house that I had found for myself would be home to a little baby. A little person who would learn to walk, talk, feed themselves, dress themselves. A little person who would one day grow up and head off into the world and whom I would love and worry about every day of my life.

Oh God.
Oh God.
Oh God.
Oh God.

Oh God.

Two hours and three pregnancy tests later, it was confirmed. I was no longer going to be alone in my big new house. I thought of you and me and everything we'd shared and everything we'd missed out on. I thought of a little version of you. Someone with my dark eyes and your dark blonde hair. Please be a boy, I thought. Please, please be a boy. I want a son. I want a son.

All day long we planned and I dreamed. We went through all the rooms to decide which one should be the baby's room when the time came and how there had to be a way to fit a baby gate onto the stairs. I entertained a delicious, unrealistic fantasy that everything would work out all right. Somehow, now, one day, it would be you and me. The way it was always supposed to have been. The way we planned it. There had been a time when you and I had talked about having a family.

Oh yes, I glanced at myself in the bathroom mirror as I hurried back downstairs, tomorrow I will wake up to reality and be terrified at the thought of what all this really means. But right now I want to dream. Good God, I've just sent the love of my life off to marry another woman. The least I'm allowed to do is be a little happy I'm now carrying his child. Let me be happy today. I will regret and worry tomorrow.

'Let's celebrate,' I said to Lisbeth.

'Okay. But no champagne for you.'

'No, no. God, now I wish I hadn't had those two glasses of wine last night!'

She smiled. 'I'm sure you'll be fine. Emma was conceived during the Christmas party season and she turned out perfectly normal.'

'Do you miss her?' I asked.

'Every minute,' she answered. 'Sometimes the pressure of being a single mother drives me to distraction, but the second I know I won't see her for a few days I miss her so much I want to run back and hug her tightly. You'll see,' she laughed, 'it'll be your turn before you know it.'

I smiled again and just about resisted the impulse to put my arms around myself. 'Let's go for a drive round the island and find somewhere to stop for lunch.'

'Sounds great. But don't forget all those things you're not allowed to eat now. No more rare steaks for you. And no more carrying furniture!'

I tried to laugh but didn't recognise the weird sound that came out of my mouth. I fought down the panic rising in my chest and balled my hands into fists. Let me be happy today. I will regret and worry tomorrow.

It seemed to me the most beautiful day there had ever been. The sky was a clearer blue, the fields were a deeper shade of green. People were smiling everywhere we went. We took the small roads around the island and ended up in the small village of Tranekær. If I'd wanted a picturesque setting to remember this day I couldn't have picked a better spot if I had tried. Not only was the village filled with thatched cottages, a red castle stood proudly on a hill surrounded by a moat. As we parked the car and got out I tried to be a tour guide for Lisbeth.

'This used to be the castle stables until they turned it into a restaurant. My great-grandfather was a stable boy here. When we came here when I was little, he used to get such a kick out of the fact that people were paying to eat food in the stalls he used to muck out. And you'll see how ornate they are. The horses lived better than the labourers.'

She laughed and wanted to know if it was possible to see the castle.

'No,' I said. 'It's only open to the public a few times a year. But we can pay to walk in the grounds. A lot of artists were commissioned to create sculptures for it for the millennium. It's worth a look as long as the weather is nice. And from what I remember about your pregnancy, I guess I should walk as much as I can while I still have the energy.'

'Very funny. Just remember I looked like a bloated hippo because of water retention, not because my only pregnancy craving was for chocolate. Which it was, but that's not the point.'

'Cravings haven't hit me yet but I am hungry. Let's eat first and walk afterwards.'

'Okay. I'll check the menu for you and see if I can remember all the those things you're not allowed to eat.'

We went inside and sat in a booth named after whichever horse used to be stabled here. Although Lisbeth swore she could still smell hay and manure, all I could smell was fried food, summer and too many tourists wearing too much perfume.

'Why don't we sit outside? Take advantage of the good weather while we have it?'

We found a table next to a family with two babies and Lisbeth laughed and said something about how my reaction when they started screaming would let me know if I was truly ready for children.

'I always say to my friends who are getting broody that when you get to the point where you can sit in a restaurant, listen to a crying baby and wonder what might be wrong with the poor little thing rather than wanting to throttle both baby and parents, then you're ready. Until then, don't throw away the condoms!'

'Was it like that for you?'

She nodded. 'Unfortunately not quite for Kristoffer. He was very good at being father of the year when everyone else was around, but at home he still wanted his single life. So even as a married woman I was a single mother. That's why I'm much happier divorced.'

'And Kristoffer?'

'Plays football and goes out with the guys every weekend and so never manages to find the time to collect Emma. So I've stopped telling her that he's coming because she got so disappointed when he never showed up. If he can't be bothered to make the effort, that's his problem. The weekends are the only real time she and I have together anyway, so I'm not letting him spoil those anymore.'

'Do you ever miss him?'

'Lord, no. I know we were happy once, but if it weren't for Emma I wouldn't mind never having met him. I consider my time with him a waste of five years of my life.'

'That's a shame. You were happy once.'

'We were. But we should never have moved beyond dating and seeing each other at the weekend. Everything changed for us the day he moved in. I think it's like that for a lot of couples. You love each other and you think the relationship should evolve, but not all relationships are meant to evolve towards marriage. But once you've tried to make them, it's damn hard to admit it was a mistake.'

'At least you got Emma.'

'Yes. She was worth it. Every fight, every argument. Even when we started hating each other, one of her fierce little hugs was worth it all. Worth more.'

That night I couldn't sleep. While Lisbeth was happily grunting and talking in her sleep on the sofa, I alternated between sitting in the kitchen and roaming through the dark rooms restless and unsure of myself.

Single mother.

That's what I would become.

Single mother with no support network since my parents were still living in Paris and I had just been dumb enough to move to a remote island and leave all my friends behind.

Oh God.

This house and this new life were a huge mistake. I would have to go back home immediately. At least back there I knew people. I knew my doctor. As part of my new life I had imagined friends coming to visit me for long weekends, I had not imagined those visits accompanied by 2 a.m. feeds and nappies all over the place.

I remembered Lisbeth in the weeks and months after Kristoffer left and she was alone with Emma. I remembered how many times she ended up having to take Emma everywhere because there was no one to babysit. I remembered other friends who, even with husbands, always seemed to end up literally holding the baby while the men went off to play football, handball and have guys' nights out. I remembered how relieved all those women were when the grandparents showed up to give them a few hours to themselves. Just a few hours to meet friends, do some shopping without worrying that someone was getting sticky fingers on the merchandise or about to wander off on their own. A few hours to just lie at home and do nothing. Or do laundry. I wondered what the hell I was getting myself into. Was I ready to be a mother? A good mother?

But I had no choice. I had nine months to get ready. Because at the end of the day I knew I could never give up on your child. Our child. What was the point of everything we had meant to each other if I just upped and threw it all away because it wasn't convenient? And I could never carry a baby for nine months just to see it for a moment before giving it to somebody else. I'd always wonder, always worry that they weren't looking after it well enough. Weren't encouraging it to do well in school, follow its dreams and make sure it was happy, safe and well. If I were going to have a baby, it was going to be mine. If it had been any other man's I could have considered an abortion. But not yours.

You were the man I loved. You were the only man who had ever managed to inhabit my dreams. During those times when we had been together, when I had allowed myself to be swept away by your dreams, I had imagined what the future would be like if, one day, we managed to work it all out. So I could never get rid of your baby. I had already pictured it too vividly in my mind.

I don't know if I was nervous, relieved or just plain terrified once I knew irrevocably that this was going to be a reality. Then of course there was you. Should I tell you? Oh yes, that would be a great way to mess up your new marriage. By the way, sweetie, remember what we did the night before your wedding? Yes? Good. Well, you knocked me up. I'll be expecting regular child support and you're going to have him/her on alternate Saturdays and we can talk about Christmas and summer holidays later.

I don't think so.

After Lisbeth went back to Copenhagen (promising to come back frequently with Emma so that I could get used to having a child around), I ordered pregnancy books, signed up to several websites that promised information and support during this radiant time of my life, and booked an appointment with my new doctor. Mostly, in between work and arranging things in the house, I drew up lists and tried to make plans for my future. I found, as the hours wore on, that it became easier and easier to accept that my days of being alone were definitely over.

What I would do with the house I had bought was hovering over all my thoughts like a big, black cloud. For the first time I admitted to myself that it had perhaps been a bad, impulsive decision and that it probably wouldn't have been that hard to have seen the two of you together at Café Norden or in IKEA. Sure, it would have hurt like hell for a while but I'm sure I would have got over it. Then, of course, I was quick to remind myself that I had also grown weary of the city and had been anxious to get away, explore new options and be challenged again.

'I could just have bought twenty square metres in Paris,' I said aloud to myself one morning while the kettle was boiling and I was wondering when I might expect morning sickness to hit for the first time. 'I could have simply traded one city for another, then at least I would have had my parents to help when all this happened.' At one point I did consider just selling the whole thing again. Then I looked out into the garden.

The morning sun was inching its way across the grass. Two white butterflies were circling each other just outside the window. The beds I had weeded were now a riot of colour. The air was already warm and I pictured myself sitting on the grass next to a blanket with toys hanging from a mobile and a chubby baby arm trying to swat them. I walked outside, took a deep breath of the clean air, and stood looking up at the house. It needed a new coat of paint and several roof tiles were in need of repair. Paint was peeling from most of the window frames; they needed to be stripped, repaired and repainted. The iron balustrade needed paint and the front of the house was just as bad.

'What a dump,' I laughed out loud. 'No wonder I got you for such a knock-down price.'

I needed a plan. With my job, maternity leave was not going to be an option and I needed something that would keep me happy and busy for the next nine months. And keep the bills paid afterwards. My need to do something new was still very real. Baby or no baby, I desperately needed some kind of change. I thought about the island and what other people did. You couldn't swing a cat on Langeland without hitting a gallery or an artist. There were German tourists galore but I didn't really fancy the idea of a bratwurst bed and breakfast. Industry had departed, more and more houses were standing empty.

'There must be something,' I wondered out loud, 'something that ...' I froze with my hand on the doorknob. What was it Lisbeth had said? That first night we sat talking about you, before I knew I was pregnant.

I wish I'd had somewhere like this to run to when my marriage fell apart.

Somewhere to run. A haven. Somewhere to lick your wounds and figure out where to go before you had to face the world again. Somewhere with no sympathetic relatives or friends waiting to tell you why you should never have been with the rat-bastard in the first place, and how relieved everyone is that you've seen sense at last. Somewhere to stay until you're ready to hear those things, until you become yourself again.

I ran upstairs.

Five bedrooms and a large bathroom. Plus one downstairs for me and the baby.

In the converted basement, an old bathroom, two bedrooms and what was meant to have been a games room.

I could bake cakes, cook and maybe turn one of the rooms into a studio. If magazine articles were anything to go by, every woman discovered a passion for art during major crises in her life. People could relax, go for walks, draw, paint, write, do anything they wanted to. I could make a deal with some therapists, spiritual healers, sculptors or whatever else the island had to offer. Somehow, people would find themselves again. And hopefully, in the midst of all that, so would I. Back in the kitchen, I grabbed a notebook and began to jot down ideas and make lists of what I would need. The hours seemed to fly by as I sat writing notes, rifled through my cookbooks for the perfect comfort food recipes and strode around the kitchen, making tea and voicing my ideas out loud. It was big, it was exciting, it was a terrifying project but it felt like just the thing I had been waiting for. I forgot about dinner, I forgot about time. When I eventually thought about going to bed, it was just after two o'clock.

Once I had a plan, I stopped worrying that I had made an enormous mistake in buying the house. I couldn't sleep at night, I was so excited and filled with ideas. Now when I wandered through the rooms, it was with a light step and a smile. I was up at five every morning and didn't want to go to bed because there were so many things to plan and do. One of the first things I did was to get myself a large noticeboard, lots of magnets, and Post-its in every available colour. For someone like me, to whom a trip to the office-supply section of the bookshop was better than a visit to the sweetshop, starting a new project was like Christmas come early.

    The one thing I still hadn't decided was how to tell my parents that their first grandchild was on the way. And that, just to make matters a little more interesting, its father had married another woman the day after it was conceived. It didn't seem like something you could share over the phone. Maybe the answer was simply to go and visit them in Paris so the moment to tell them would come naturally when they asked me why I wasn't drinking my wine and coffee. But I needed a more substantial future for their grandchild before I started sharing the good news. It was for my own sake I was stalling, I wanted to be sure I was completely ready and committed before I started breaking the news to people.

I didn't for a moment think my parents would be upset at the thought of their first grandchild coming into the world in such an unconventional set-up. My mother, a fan of the romantic and dramatic, would probably applaud it, but 'abandoned-mistress-single-mother' was not a role I had ever seen myself cast in.

My mother was a firm believer that only relationships which were in some way out of the ordinary could survive to withstand the daily drudgery of living together and arguing over whose turn it was to clear the table and dust the shelves. She was eighteen when she went to Paris to visit a girlfriend who was working as an au pair. She met my father at the Christmas get-together at the Danish church. Neither my mother nor her friend were in any way religious, but since it was Christmas they both felt the tug of home and longed for candles and dark afternoons with mulled wine and Christmas biscuits. So off they went into the Parisian afternoon.

My father was working for the Danish embassy, his first posting abroad. My mother still says it was as though time stood still when they both reached for the last cup of mulled wine. Their fingers brushed against each other and they looked up into each other's eyes. They've managed to avoid too many mundane arguments and, judging by the dreamy look on her face when she tells the story and then looks over at my father, have never once doubted that the other is, and always will be, the only one for them.

I remembered that day when I met you. I was eighteen and you were twenty-two. It was beautiful, crisp autumn day in September. The leaves hadn't started to turn. The sun was warm on my face. Here we are now, nearly thirteen years later. Oh God.

My parents spent the rest of my mother's holiday together. When my father came back to Denmark for Christmas, they saw each other every day. A week later she was pregnant. A month later they were married. My mother transferred her studies to Paris and decorated my father's little loft apartment with the bright colours the world suddenly seemed full of. When she grew too big to manage the climb up six flights of stairs and the idea of dragging the pram up and down every day became too daunting, both sets of future grandparents helped them buy a first-floor apartment in the Latin Quarter and came to visit often.

My mother would still look at me sometimes and say, 'You haven't heard the last of him.' I guess she was right. And now a part of you would be with me for the rest of my life.

The garden was rapidly becoming one of my favourite spaces. I loved it in the peaceful morning light when the dew made my slippers wet and the birds sang in the trees above my head. It was during those hours that my memories of you were the strongest. There was a fallen tree trunk towards the back of the garden that I began to use as a seat. Cradling my warm cup in my hands, I would sit there and look up at my big new house and remember those times when I had believed that we would have a home together.

It didn't seem that long ago that we had managed to stay together for about six months. We'd spent a weekend in Paris with my parents, we'd practically lived together in my apartment, and when we'd curled up in bed at night we'd started to talk about the possibility of a real future. You'd even started joking about what our children's names were going to be. Some mornings it hurt to remember these things and some mornings it gave me strength. I needed to remember that I had meant something to you, that together we had shared something beautiful, that I was not carrying some stranger's child. But you'd still married her. You might have spoken of that life with me but she was the one you were sharing it with. When that thought occurred to me, I picked up a stick and threw it at one of the other trees. Usually I missed. Then I would look up at the house and try to decide what to do first.

I had asked the builders to come and give me a quote for the roof, the bathroom and all the other essential bits. After I'd finished laughing at their initial prices, we sat down and negotiated over coffee and cake. My mother was right, it was amazing how far you could get with a smile. Or perhaps, once I started making pointed comments about how nice it was to be able to look at my grandparents' house and how many visits I paid to the graveyard, they stopped looking at me as an out-of-towner and started giving me the local prices.

I knew the roof was the biggest issue and the one that needed addressing immediately. There was, as the builder pointed out when we walked through the garden, no point in making up fancy rooms if the roof tiles blew off in the night and the rain came in.

'I'll have two men out here on Monday,' he said.

Which in builder speak, I thought, means a week from Thursday at the earliest. So when two men with ladders and lots of scaffolding showed up at seven o'clock Monday morning, I was beyond astonished.

Week Six

The two men crawling all over my roof were called Bjarne and Alexander, which they informed me of when I stuck my blurry head out the front door to see who could possibly be knocking at this hour. I had been ripping pictures from IKEA catalogues and making guest room collages until three in the morning. and had not realised that I would be expected to look presentable four hours later. Rather embarrassed to be greeting them in my dressing gown and slippers, I quickly excused myself on the pretext of making them coffee. While the kettle was boiling I splashed some water on my face, combed my hair and threw on some clothes. I'd nearly choked when the one who introduced himself as Alexander turned out to be the young man with the guitar case, the one Lisbeth and I had whispered about in the post office.

By the time I'd got dressed and had made the coffee they had finished inspecting the front of the house and moved round to the garden. Alexander ran to open the door for me when he saw me through the window struggling with the tray. Bjarne stared intently at me over the rim of his coffee cup, then he smiled. 'I have the feeling I know you from somewhere,' he said.

'It's possible,' I said. 'My father's from Rudkøbing, I used to come here as a child.'

'That's it! Is that who you have a picture of in the kitchen windowsill? I think my younger brother was in the same class as your father in school.'

'What's his name? I'll ask him when I talk to him tonight.'

We talked about the house and the work that would be needed as I gave them a brief sketch of my initial plans. Bjarne loved the idea of someone returning to the island rather than running away from it. 'Let's hope the weather holds,' he said. 'After all that rain we're due a good bout of real summer. And once we start taking those old tiles off, it would be really helpful if it stayed dry. Speaking of staying dry, could you tell me where the bathroom is?'

I told him and when he'd gone Alexander asked me if I'd looked at any other houses. I laughed and confessed that this was probably the biggest impulse buy I ever had or ever would make. In return he told me that his move to Langeland had also been somewhat impulsive. He was really a musician but had found that building work was a good way to pay the bills while composing his first album.

'I moved down here earlier this year because a friend offered me the use of his studio while he went to America for a year. It was one of those late night offers that you always kind of expect people to take back again in the morning, but he didn't. So I packed my bags and headed out. As long as I keep the house from falling down he's happy. But I like it here. Even if it is a big change from Copenhagen.'

'Yes, I know,' I said. 'I just didn't want to be in the city anymore. It was time for a change. When I came down here something just clicked. It might turn out be one of those relationships where you move away and discover how much you love each other, but right now I don't want to go back.'

'We want different things at different points in our lives, maybe this is just the point where you don't live in a city,' he said and I nearly laughed. Then I caught myself and realised how old it would make me sound to laugh at the life experience of someone so young. Besides, for all I knew he could have lived through twenty lifetimes. Who was I to judge what a stranger had experienced? 'For instance,' he continued, 'one day when I have kids I don't think I'll want to be in the city.'

I didn't say anything to that and decided to change the subject. 'So how did you come across this job?'

'My uncle has a company that does renovations. Roofs, bathrooms, kitchens, all things like that. I used to work with him during all my holidays so I could get money for my music. It gets pretty expensive when you want to start recording. When I told him I was coming down here, he called some friends who called some friends and three days later I had a job.'

'So it really is about who you know?'

'So they say. But I think it's amazing how you decided to come down here.'

'Actually,' I said, 'I think I saw you the day I came down and first saw the house. You had your guitar case on your back and a sack of potatoes in your arms.'

'That was the day I first moved in. My friend was still living here and just as I got off the bus he texted me and asked me to bring potatoes.'

'That sight just stayed with me. The guy with his guitar case and an arm full of potatoes.'

'Hey, how often do you see that in Copenhagen? But I remember. Newly arrived, not quite sure where I was going and then this beautiful woman smiled at me and my potatoes.' He winked at me and I this time I laughed.

Bjarne came back outside and I took the coffee cups back to the kitchen. Secretly I was relieved to get away before Alexander started asking me more questions. My present situation seemed too complicated to share with someone I'd only just met, even if he was the first person who had seemed interested in getting to know me since I'd got here. It might be nice to have someone around who might turn out to be a good friend. If he also happened to be really good-looking, I'd just call that a bonus. Alexander had long, elegant musician's hands, green eyes and tousled brown hair.

Back in my bedroom, I looked at myself in the mirror as I did every morning to see if there were any visible signs of being pregnant. Maybe that morning I might have taken an extra hard look to see if I'd looked like a complete disaster all the time we had been talking. I found it hard to believe that it was still the same person looking back at me. Same woman in her early thirties with dark eyes and long wavy hair, so dark brown it was almost black. I didn't look like a mother. Half the time I wasn't even sure I looked like a grown-up. I shook my head at my own reflection and then went into the bathroom for a long hot shower.

Alexander was putting up the last bit of the scaffolding when I came outside a few hours later to go shopping.

'Where's Bjarne?' I asked.

'On the other side of the roof,' he answered, 'seeing just what needs to be done over there.'

'How long is all this going to take?'

'Depends on what we find. I have to be honest with you, that's pretty much a standard answer.'

'So just a way of telling me that you don't really know how much it will end up costing?'

'No. But in all fairness, we've been uncovering some pretty bad roofs lately.'

'Okay, okay. Just try not to fall off.'

'I will. I mean I will try not to fall off.'

I laughed and went off to the supermarket.

It seemed a long time since someone new had made me laugh.

That evening I was sitting in the living room absentmindedly reading a book and listening to the Beatles on my iPod. I was wondering what you were doing. I wondered what kind of home you were building with her. Was it in some beautiful old building in the middle of Copenhagen with hardwood floors and stucco ceilings? Or maybe one of those of brand new apartments overlooking the harbour? Perhaps even a house outside the city with a big garden where your other children would play one day, spending their summer afternoons running around the lawn with a couple of dogs. Bet my house is bigger than yours. I hope you get subsidence. I'd been so sure you wouldn't go through with it. I'd been so sure I would hear from you again.

But I couldn't bring myself to hate you. We'd been through this too many times for me to hate you. If I should hate anyone, it should be myself for allowing this to happen over and over again. It was the same game we'd been playing for years but this time it had resulted in a very unexpected yet, I couldn't deny it, very special accident. Despite my apprehensive terrors, part of me was looking forward to being a mother. I was thinking about afternoons in the park, bedtime stories, first day of school, teddy bears, drawings on the fridge. Although I never would have imagined it, the thought of being on my own with a baby did not seem scary. Maybe I'd listened to too many stories of women whose husbands never did anything to help, had sat next to too many families on the train where the mother kept the brood from running amok while the father played with his phone and only came to life when the snack trolley rolled past. Why not just skip all that and go straight to the part where we've brought down the curtain and the fat lady has sung? Looking on the bright side, I was at least saving myself the expense and heartache of a messy divorce.

I got up, leaned against the window and looked out onto the lawn. It seemed blue in the dusky light of the evening.

A mother. I was going to be a mother.

A single mother.

I would certainly have an interesting story to tell when I arrived as the lonely freak to every school function and the other parents asked me where my husband was. Because, Lisbeth had assured me, they would.

Bjarne and Alexander crawling over my roof stopped me from feeling sorry for myself when I couldn't stop thinking of you. I was never quite sure when one of them would suddenly appear at my window and that prevented me from wandering listlessly through the rooms or bursting into tears when the thought of the two of you together made me want to scream. How could you have done this to me? After all these years, how could you have married someone else? How could you not have come back to me to finish what we started all those years ago? And having known that, how could you have come back one last time, and how could I possibly have let you into my bed?

So many missed opportunities. So many lost chances. All those things that should have happened but never did. So many lost years, so many tears, so many hearts broken and mended. Over and over again for thirteen years. Broken dreams, broken promises. But I knew I would love you till the end of my life. That no matter what happened in the years to come, it would be you I thought of when my life was over.

Broken hearts mend. My experience with you had taught me that. But the pain is almost unendurable. My experience with you had taught me that, too. There is an agonising moment when realisation stabs you in the heart and you know that what you desired, what you loved, is forever beyond your reach. The moment when the future you had believed within your grasp slips through your fingers like sand. And it comes not once, but over and over again. It is those moments that are the hardest to get through. When there's nothing to do but grit your teeth and wait for the pain to end. The knowledge that you were forever gone from my life but that I would be reminded of you every single day was sometimes more than I could bear.

Little things, inconsequential memories, kept coming back to me. Coffee at our favourite café, the one I could not have borne seeing the two of you in. Walking hand in hand by the harbour. That afternoon we walked across Kongens Nytorv, the square by the Royal Theatre, and you took my hand for the first time. The evenings we spent talking in my kitchen. The afternoons we fell asleep on your sofa, wrapped in each other's arms. The endless nights when we threw ourselves at each other as if we could never get enough. All those times you told me you loved me. The summer you wrote me letters that I would read aloud to myself in the warm evenings when I wandered through the empty rooms, missing your touch and counting the days till you came back to me. And more than anything else, the feeling that, no matter what happened, you would always come back for me. The feeling that now was gone.

Several days later, after countless cups of coffee and lots of getting-to-know-you conversations, Alexander knocked on my door with fresh rolls and pastries. While I made coffee, he rummaged through my kitchen looking for plates and cups. I noticed how well-tended his hands were, looking nothing like those of a man who spent his days surrounded by brick dust and plaster.

'It's the musician in me,' he said when I commented on it. 'If my hands get ruined I can't make music. That's the most important thing to me. This is just to tide me over in the meantime.'

'So why building work?'

'I know I can do it well and I enjoy it. But mainly it's a compromise. If I lived in the city I could go back to working in an office. But I found it so draining and I always ended up being the last one to pack up and go home, so there was never any time for me at the end of the day. And it either meant living in a tiny apartment where the neighbours complained every time I switched on an amp, or living far outside the city where the commute ate up all my spare hours. I like the freedom of being out here. I like that when I go home tired it's because I've done something physical, not because I sat in front of a screen all day.'

'I can see that,' I said, taking a sip of coffee and buttering another roll. 'There is a real difference between the way I feel after a long day in front of boring documents and a day of painting a room.'

'I like being able to see results,' Alexander continued. 'I like that here I can see that I am helping you to build a home and that what I am doing is making a difference to your life.' He looked up at me for a moment and smiled. 'And hopefully some day soon I'll get myself a record deal and I can dedicate myself to my music. But I'd like to do something like this too. Like what you're doing,' he added.

'What I'm doing?'

'Buying this old place and bringing it back to life. You'll bring people to the island, you'll help local businesses. It's something worthwhile.'

'Are you a philanthropist?' I smiled at him as he poured another cup of coffee, clearly considering his answer.

'Not really. I certainly wasn't brought up to do charity work. Not to say that I was brought up not to give a damn about others,' he laughed and reached for the sugar. 'I find that being here makes me appreciate the simpler things in life. Sorry, that sounds like a tourist brochure.'

He passed me the sugar bowl and I smiled at him. 'I understand what you mean. I find myself appreciating things much more here. Good food, sunrises, birds singing. Of course it helps that I can hear the birds here because there are no cars honking or people yelling into their phones on the street.'

'I notice that too. Especially where I live. This place is like the big city in comparison.'

I smiled and stirred sugar into my coffee. 'It was really nice of you to bring breakfast.'

'You're welcome. You keep making us coffee and bringing us cakes and biscuits, it seemed only fair. Actually it's the one thing I miss about working in an office.'

'I know what you mean. I've had a few company clients over the years and it was nice to sit in their offices sometimes. There was always some kind of breakfast rota or someone bringing in cake for no reason.'

'Especially in the summer when everyone else was on holiday and only a few people were holding down the fort.'

'Exactly. Someone would go for ice cream and it just made the day a little nicer. But at the end of the day I prefer my way. I can enjoy the beautiful day and work through the night instead.'

He laughed and we compared the companies we had worked for as we finished off our breakfast.

'But what about Bjarne?' I asked as we got up.

'There's plenty left for him. I didn't know he was going to be late today.'

I nodded and started clearing the table. Alexander helped by putting away the butter and milk then went back outside and up onto the roof. I wondered about him as I wiped the table free of crumbs. I wondered what he did when he wasn't working. I was sure a twenty-two-year-old guy must have more in his life than music. Did he have some sweet girl waiting for him back in Copenhagen or, I uncharitably thought, some blonde bimbo with tacky hair extensions? I smiled at the sight of his legs disappearing back up the scaffolding as I walked through the living room to the downstairs bedroom where I was halfway through sanding down the skirting boards. I had my first doctor's appointment in two hours. Once it was official there would be no going back. So help me, I would have to tell my parents.

Week Seven

The first onslaught of morning sickness sent me scurrying from my bed in a desperate bid to reach the bathroom. Lying trembling on the bathroom floor while the world kept spinning around me was the moment I realised two things very clearly. One, there really was a tiny person beginning to grow inside me. Two, choosing the ground floor bedroom with the en suite bathroom had been a really smart move. It took thirty minutes before I was well enough to stand up, brush my teeth and rinse my mouth. Wrapping myself in my dressing gown, I crawled to the living room and collapsed on the sofa.

As I lay there, I remembered my appointment with the doctor and the little apple seed I had seen on the scanner. The tiny little dot that, until this morning's mad flight to the toilet bowl, had been the only evidence of a new person growing inside me. I missed you at that moment. I felt your absence then as it would be for the rest of our lives. A cloud to darken even the most beautiful days. The vast, unbearable sense of the life that should have been and everything that would never happen. The life I would live alone. The birthday parties you would never attend, the Christmases you would never spend with us. The ice creams in the summer, the mugs of hot chocolate in winter. Playing games, building Lego, reading bedtime stories. You should be here.

I vaguely remembered Lisbeth once telling me that morning sickness was a sign of a strong pregnancy. Something about how morning sickness was caused by good hormones and the more sick you were the more hormones there were. Actually I was sure she'd said, 'I don't know if it's true or if it's just some nonsense they made up to make you feel better when you're sticking your head down the toilet at all hours of the day and night. For God's sake don't believe it only hits you in the morning. With Emma I woke up at seven and couldn't function till eleven. And then it usually hit me again in the evening.'

It must have been three hours later when I heard Alexander and Bjarne start their daily preparations outside. Unwilling to face either them or the coffee pot, I grabbed my cashmere throw and burrowed under it. Telling people who knew our story was one thing. Telling complete strangers was something else. I didn't want them sitting in judgement on me. I didn't want their pity. I needed to get my story straight in my own mind before I could tell people. I wanted my defences lined up because I knew, deep down, that the more of the story I ended up telling the more I would have to justify and explain. There was just no good way to admit to people that I had slept with a man less than twelve hours from the altar, no matter how much history we had shared. I also needed to decide what to do about you once the baby was born. What would I tell him or her about you when the questions came? Even before then, shouldn't there be some sense of a father in their life? Even a distant one who was a memory if not a presence? I knew Bjarne and Alexander would ask me if I was all right if they saw me comatose on the sofa and I didn't want to lie. But I wasn't quite ready for the truth either.

It was nearly lunchtime when I snuck off the sofa to have a shower and get dressed while they were up on the roof. Then I made them some coffee and went outside. The wind was cool on my face and there was a misty rain in the air that seemed to wash the sour taste of the morning away. I thought I detected a hint of surprise that I had not been out to see them earlier. I wondered if they had caught a glimpse of me through the curtains and wondered why the lazy cow was hiding on the sofa in her dressing gown even though half the day was gone.

'Are you okay?' Alexander asked me as he took the cup I handed him. 'You look a little pale.'

'I'm fine,' I lied. 'I just couldn't get to sleep last night so I ended up working instead.'

'Too many empty house noises?'

'Something like that.'

I sensed he wanted to ask me something more so I hurried back inside before he could.

I spent the rest of the day at the kitchen table looking at colour charts and bathroom brochures. For the first time it really hit me that I had a schedule to meet. Whatever I wanted to do with this house I could not amble along, taking years to select just the right rug and leaving rooms half-furnished. If I was going to do this, I would have to be ready by the time my little mini-you or mini-me arrived. For a moment I was quite ready to give up on all my mad plans. Who was I to think that I could create some kind of haven for people getting over broken hearts and trying to move on with their lives when mine was still stuck in the middle of a love affair that should have been over years ago?

God knows I wanted to forget you. And God knows I'd tried so hard to do so over the past thirteen years. There had been other men that I'd believed myself in love with, but every time, without fail, you crept back into my thoughts. I offered endless reasons, superb justifications, but at the end of the day it had to be you or no one. I told myself countless times that I obviously had commitment issues and that you were just a convenient escape route whenever things with another man got too serious. I told myself that you were just a romantic dream that I cherished when other relationships capsized under the swell of the mundane. I didn't know what it was about you. From that first moment, it had to be you.

I kept a big black box under my bed filled with old photographs, letters, notes, birthday cards. Things my grandmother sent me when I went to university. Pictures of me and my friends in Paris, sunsets in Brittany. The only pictures I had of you and me together were ones that we took as a joke one afternoon in a photo booth at Copenhagen's main station. You'd very carefully torn the strip across the middle so we both got two photos. I wondered sometimes whether you had kept yours. I kept my half in that box together with old letters and printouts of emails from you. You had loved me once. I wasn't just imagining it, you had told me so. In print and in person.

Sometimes when I needed to remember that, I would open the box and curl up with some of my fondest memories. Maybe one day I would decide to light the barbecue with them. Maybe one day they wouldn't matter to me anymore and could simply rest, no more important than all my other memories.

I looked out the window as a leaf wafted against the glass, deep green in the last week of August. I got up, opened the door and a crisp breeze blew through the house. I smiled. If I really sniffed hard, I could almost believe that I could detect a hint of autumn in the air. The season of backyard bonfires, decaying leaves on forest floors, hot chocolate in cosy cafés on lazy afternoons. Another wave of nausea hit me as I leaned against the door frame and let my memories run free.

That day in September thirteen years ago when I first met you was imprinted on my memory. It was one of the last warm days of the year. I'd been to the cinema with a potential new friend. When we got back to her rooms on campus she made us coffee and we sat in the kitchen talking to some other students. That was when I first saw you. You walked in and stood in the doorway. I think I forgot what I was saying. The way you stood there looking at me, I knew it then.

I smiled as the nausea passed. When I looked back and thought of you, I was happy. The sky was bluer, the birds sang more clearly. Was the memory enough for me? Didn't I want the happy marriage, the 2.4 children and the house in the suburbs? Or the apartment stuffed with designer furniture and a husband with a fulfilling career who supported me in my choices while I ran my own business, changed the twin's organic nappies and still managed to wow him in the sack every night? Was I that different? Didn't I want normal things like everyone else did?

When I looked back to the romantic dreams of my childhood, none of them involved a husband. Of course there was to be a dramatic, tragic love affair that ended with terminal tuberculosis in a Paris garret, and somewhere in there was the vague notion of children, but I'd never considered a husband except as a reason to get dressed up in a stylish white dress. In fact the only husband I had ever considered having was somebody else's. Being a mistress sounded much more romantic than being a wife. Far from the dreary monotony of the boring lives I imagined married couples leading, I dreamed of adventure and passion. I never knew where that notion came from because my parents' marriage had been anything but boring and there was no question when I looked at them that it could work.

What I had really wanted, more than a husband, was a dog. Lots of dogs. I had wanted somewhere I could find inspiration. Somewhere I could bake cakes. An enormous house that I could decorate as I saw fit and dream in whenever I wanted. A haven where I could be myself. A garden where the leaves would flame in the crisp autumn mornings and where my friends could sit on the terrace and sip chilled white wine on cool summer evenings. Somewhere big enough for an enormous Christmas tree and filled with cosy corners to sit in and read.

Alexander waved to me from the garden as he walked past with a wheelbarrow filled with something or other, and I smiled and waved back, trying to stop myself from laughing out loud. What I had here was my dream from childhood and I hadn't even recognised that I'd stumbled into it. The only difference was that I was having a baby instead of a puppy. But here I had laid the foundations for the life I had always dreamed of.

The one thing I was not sure of was whether I could live the life of my dreams alone. Children love dogs, don't they?

That night I couldn't sleep. After hours of tossing and turning, I got up and went into the kitchen. I guessed it would never be too soon to start practising for sleepless nights and I wondered what kind of 2 a.m. garbage was on television these days.

There's a special kind of peace in a house at 2 a.m. The kind of private peace you only get when no one else is around and there is absolutely nothing to do. At 2 a.m. it does not matter if you are the only one awake. At 2 a.m. no one will come and tell you to do your taxes, wipe the kitchen table or fold the laundry. If you are awake at 2 a.m., it is okay to be alone.

I remembered a friend I had at university who went abroad for a year as part of an exchange program. She had looked forward to it throughout her entire first and second year but when she came back she admitted it had been the worst year of her life. She explained how nothing compares to the complete loneliness that hits you when you are all by yourself in a place where nobody wants you and nobody cares. I remembered her saying that the dark nights were her friends. Because in the darkest hours of the night there is no shame in being alone. There is no one to tell you that you are doing it wrong. In the darkest hours of the night whoever you are is right for you.

In the dark hours of this night, I roamed my cavernous, empty house and thought of the life that would now never be mine. I thought of you and her and the life you would build together, and somewhere a small part of me began to hate you. I thought of Alexander, asking me if I were all right because I appeared outside later than usual, and I thought of you, who slept with me the day before your wedding and hadn't spoken to me since. I looked back on all the years you had been a part of my life and I wondered if our relationship had ever been anything but a figment of my imagination. A crutch. A safety net that I clung to because you were familiar.

How ironic if that should be true. That I had been the one using you. The thought made me laugh, and my laugh sounded loud and hollow in the empty rooms. I thought for a moment that I might be afraid of my large house, so dark and silent in these cold hours of the night. Still unfamiliar to me, would it one day wrap itself around me like a second skin so that I knew every creaking floorboard, every shudder of settling furniture. Would it, one day, become a real home?

I made myself a cup of tea and stood looking out over the garden. The trees moved gently in the breeze and I opened a window to let in the night air. So clean, so far from the city. I stood at the window and cradled the cup in my hands. In the city, there would be cars driving past my window. There would be people calling to each other as they made their way home from a bar. In the city 2 a.m. is not a time for peace and quiet reflection. No city ever sleeps. New York isn't as special as it thinks it is.

When I was younger and used to go out with my friends on Friday and Saturday nights, the greatest thrill was coming home early in the morning, watching the sun rise over the harbour and finding the baker who was willing to open up early and let us buy a few freshly baked rolls and pastries. There's something so magical about the dawn. It's a whole new opportunity, fresh, with no mistakes in it. I've never believed that you can start your life over on the first of January every year, but I honestly believe that you get another chance with each new dawn. Whatever awful things you've done the day before, you can always try to make amends the next day. Whatever chances you lost, whatever dream you didn't follow, you can always try again when the sun comes up to dance once more on the water.

I took my tea into the living room and curled up on the sofa. I was glad now that it had been my first priority and that I'd remembered to bring the soft, cashmere throw I'd once bought in a small boutique in Paris. I wondered what the divorced woman was doing in my apartment and whether she'd been able to find ways to start putting her life back together. I wondered if I was doing the right thing.

Being the altruistic cake-baker who offered people a safe haven while they put their shattered lives back together was a wonderful, heart-warming idea. But was it really the life for me? Was I really the kind of person who would put my daily plans on hold to bake cakes, organise yoga classes and make beds for strangers? Wasn't I more the kind of person who would stay in a five-star resort and expect people to make beds for me? I enjoyed the freedom that my work offered me. If I went through with this idea, I would be tying myself down indefinitely.

It was Alexander knocking on the garden door who woke me up. My first thought as I saw him through the glass was that I must look like hell. I waved at him, ran my fingers through my hair and opened the door.

'Good morning,' he said.

'Good morning,' I replied, fighting down the day's first wave of nausea and trying not to breathe in his general direction.

'Are you all right?'

'Fine.'

He laughed. 'My ex-girlfriend told me never to believe a woman who says she is "fine". Any other word is okay, just not that one.'

'I'm pregnant.'

I don't know what forced the words out of me. Certainly I hadn't intended telling him, a virtual stranger, and certainly not like that. I nearly clapped my hands in front of my mouth as if the sentence had run away from me and I was trying to get the escapees back inside the fence.

'Pregnant?' Alexander said. 'Uhm ... wow ... congratulations? But I thought ...'

'Yes?'

'I thought you were single. Sorry, it's probably none of my business.'

'No, no, I am. It's a very long story.'

He looked uncomfortable for a moment and stood scraping his feet against the ground. 'I should get to work. I just wanted to check you were all right.'

'I'm fine.'

We both smiled and I left the door open to air the room out.

I didn't know what to say but, just for a brief moment, I thought I'd seen a look of regret in his eyes when I'd told him I was pregnant. In same way that there might have been regret if I'd told him I had a boyfriend. I ran to the bathroom with a little smile on my face. I remembered that he'd said ex-girlfriend. Which of course wasn't to say that there wasn't a current one. Oh yes, you were the great love of my life. So naturally I was planning on flirting with the handsome young musician who was mending my roof.

Two days later the bedrooms were ready for their first coats of paint and the house smelled of freshly baked buns and cakes. Bjarne and Alexander were on the roof and my parents were on their way from the airport. I'd been trying to work out the best layout for the house since it had dawned on me that I'd be needing a proper office as well as a bedroom for the little one. Although, as Lisbeth had pointed out, it wasn't something he or she would be needing immediately, with only one downstairs bedroom it would need thinking about. I couldn't imagine my guests would be thrilled at the idea of a crying baby waking them up in the middle of the night while I charged upstairs for feeding and changing. Part of the house would have to be set aside as my personal space. The idea of sharing my home with strangers was at once terrifying and rather exciting. The thought of helping people mend their broken hearts and find themselves again was intoxicating. The thought of maybe ending up with guests I didn't like and then having to sit next to them at dinner was not. But running through the hallway when the doorbell rang it dawned on me that it was more than large enough for a desk and a bookshelf for files and records.

'Welcome!' I threw open the door and hugged my parents. My father dragged the suitcases inside while my mother stole a quick glance at my stomach to see if I was showing yet. I shook my head and smiled at her before she enveloped me in a fierce hug.

The conversation we'd had on the phone when I'd told them about the baby would always stay in my mind as a reminder that family is what matters most. There had been no recriminations, no regrettable outbursts about how I'd ruined my life or just what kind of a callous slut I was to sleep with an engaged man. There was only support and the underlying excitement that they were to be grandparents. Whatever they really thought, whatever they said between themselves, they were kind enough to keep hidden at home showing only love and comfort to me.

They left the suitcases in the hallway and we went through to the kitchen. When I was a child and we came back to Langeland for visits, freshly baked buns were always waiting for us. I thought this would be a good time to revive the tradition. The sun was shining through the windows and the rooms were warm and welcoming, as though it really were the summer holidays again.

After we'd finished our coffee I took some outside for Alexander and Bjarne. Within ten minutes, my father had changed clothes and joined them on the roof, swapping stories about the things he and Bjarne's brother had got up to at school. My mother and I remained in the kitchen and I showed her all my room collages and the lists on the noticeboard.

'I'm going to assume there's at least one notebook crammed full of ideas,' she said with a smile. 'And I imagine it will soon be full, so I brought you another one. From our latest collection.' She opened the handbag she had left by the kitchen table and handed me a beautiful leather-bound notebook.

I stroked the soft cover and flipped through the pages. 'Thank you. It's beautiful.'

'You're welcome. Now, I want to see all the rooms and hear all about your plans. I think it's a fantastic idea.'

'I think it will be an exciting new adventure. I like the idea of helping people and I'd quite happily be in the kitchen all day experimenting with new dishes.'

'I know.'

I nodded and smiled. We walked upstairs.

'So,' she said when we got to the top of the staircase, 'how did it happen this time?'

By now I'd lost track of the times I'd relived that night in my mind. I'd stored it away with all my other memories of you, pressed like wildflowers between the pages of my life. That evening when I had stood by the window listening to the sound of the neighbours' barbecue, thinking I would spend my last evening in Copenhagen alone.

You didn't say anything when I opened the door, you just stood there looking at me. I stepped aside to let you come in, you shut the door with your foot. Then you framed my face in your hands, looking at me intently as though you wanted to freeze my face in your memory. Then you kissed me. Without thought for what might come next or why I should have kicked you out and slammed the door, I kissed you back. You lifted me up and with my legs wrapped around you, you carried me into the bedroom. We didn't say a word, we just let ourselves be swept away. Afterwards, we lay in each other's arms for what seemed like hours. Then you rolled over and kissed me again.

It was a long time afterwards when we sat up in bed together, sipping wine and talking quietly.

'What's with all the suitcases and boxes in your car? Are you donating old stuff to charity again?'

I considered telling you the truth. But that would mean admitting that the thought of you getting married made me sick to my stomach. So I just nodded. 'Yes. Something like that.'

'I saw you last week. When we were outside the church. I'm sorry.'

'Sorry for what?'

'If it had been up to me, I wouldn't have picked that church. But every time your name gets mentioned it turns into a screaming row.'

There was so much I wanted to ask you. So many things I wanted to say. But the words all died in my throat so I kissed you instead. You put your arms around me and held me close to you. All I really wanted to do was cry.

My mother squeezed my arm and smiled. 'I still say you haven't heard the last of him. Will you tell him about the baby?'

'I really don't know. Right now I'm not sure what I'm going to do.'

'Well, you've got at least nine months to work it out. Or I guess it's eight by now.' She sighed. 'I can't say that sleeping with him was a good idea. Especially the night before his wedding. But then the two of you have always been a bit of a mystery. I don't pretend to know what the future will bring either of you. You could argue that he has the right to know and that a child should have a father. On the other hand I think the baby will probably have a better, certainly less confusing, life here alone with you.'

We looked through the rooms and she suggested that, ideally, each room should have its own en suite. 'No woman likes sharing a bathroom with strangers. Half of us don't even like sharing them with our husbands.'

I laughed. 'I guess that's a good point. But if I decide to drop the idea later it will make it difficult to sell, don't you think?'

'Already thinking of selling? You just got here!'

'Not now! But I have to consider these things. I may hate the idea of running a hotel and then I'll have done a lot of expensive renovations for nothing. I have to think of my budget as well. I've got a meeting with the bank next week.'

'So four bedrooms for guests up here and one, eventually, for the little one. How about downstairs?'

One set of previous owners had attempted to turn the basement into a small haven for their teenage kids with two bedrooms, a games room and a bathroom. Next to the bathroom was a small utility room. When I was little and used to come to the house, it had been a spooky place filled with the strange shadows and creepy silences you get when a place becomes a dumping ground for a family's assorted junk. What could still be seen, amidst the faded board games and old winter coats, were the remnants of a wine cellar and a space for storing preserves.

'You might not have all the rooms filled up at once so I guess they can live with sharing a bathroom or two.'

'I'll make it so luxurious they won't mind sharing.'

'Put a real bath in one of them.'

'A real bath?'

'Yes. A tub. There's nothing better than a long, relaxing bath when you need some time to yourself. Especially during the winter or if you just need a break from the world. And it sounds like that's what you want to give people here. A break from the world.'

'That's a good point. And one of those enormous rain showers in the other one.'

'Have you got any samples and colour charts?'

'Loads. Let's go back to the kitchen and I'll get them out.'

My father had made more coffee for Brian and Alexander and the three of them were now wandering around the side of the house assessing the windows. My mother smiled and opened the first book of bathroom tiles.

'He's very cute that young builder of yours.'

'He's a musician apparently.'

'Single?'

'I'm not sure. He mentioned an ex-girlfriend but no current one.'

'You should find out.'

'Come on,' I laughed. 'Haven't I got enough on my plate already? Besides, I'm too old for him.'

'I'd say not even ten years. That's fashionable now, isn't it?'

'Very funny, mum.'

For the next few days we toured memory lane, stripped floorboards, sanded skirting boards and found a lovely old desk in a barn outside Odense. Alexander offered to take his friend's van and go and pick it up for me. Within five minutes of shaking his hand my mother had wormed all the information she wanted out of him. Completely single, the youngest of three brothers and uncle to three nieces and one nephew. Parents married almost thirty years. Creative, ambitious and caring and with a good sense of humour was her final verdict.

'Mum, I'm pregnant with another man's child. I don't think any man will be interested in me right now. Even if I wanted to find one.'

'You never know.'

'I don't want to know right now. I've got a new life to plan and enough to worry about without adding a relationship with a musician ten years my junior to the mix.'

I had to smile, though. On the one hand she was convinced that you would come back to me and on the other she wanted me to find someone else. I guess she just wanted me to be happy. In whichever weird way that was.

'Your parents are nice,' Alexander said to me as we drove to pick up the desk. The only difference I had been able to detect in his behaviour towards me since I told him I was pregnant was an increased solicitousness. He wasn't at all happy about the idea of me helping to carry the table or being exposed to paint fumes.

'They are. I don't get to see them as often as I'd like.'

'So you grew up in Paris?'

'Yes. My dad's been with the Danish embassy there since just before he met my mother. '

'What about your mother?'

'She spent their first years in Paris studying. While she was pregnant so it took a little while longer to finish her course.'

'What did she study?'

'Design. So Paris would have been the best place in any case. She works with accessories.'

'Handbags and things like that?'

'Yes. Lately it's all about iPad covers.'

'So where is this desk going?'

'In the hallway. I need a desk for work and a modern one just wouldn't go.'

'I guess not. But putting an iMac on top of it is acceptable?'

'Of course. Beautiful things always look good wherever you put them.'

'Like you.' He smiled at me. 'Not to say you're a thing.'

I blushed and didn't quite know what to say. He kept his eyes firmly on the road. But the silence between us didn't seem awkward. Then, after a few minutes, I asked him about his music and that kept him talking until we arrived at the barn.

When we got back Bjarne and my dad were waiting to help get the desk into the hallway. While we had been gone my dad had sanded and waxed my new kitchen table and as we all stood around admiring it, it became clear that the renovation of that room should be first priority. I had thought it looked shabby chic. Now it just looked shabby.

'Off to IKEA?' Alexander asked.

'Yep. Can we borrow the van again?'

'I'll come with you if you like.'

There's something special about a man who's willing to go to IKEA with you.

Week Eight

A few days later I'd learned the secret of coping with my morning sickness, which basically meant that I started taking digestive biscuits with me everywhere. The very thought of even attempting to eat anything else made me want to throw up. We'd painted two of the upstairs bedrooms and Bjarne had chased a flock of pigeons out of a hole in the roof. One of his old colleagues came to take a look at the garden and give me a quote for weekly maintenance. From what I could tell there were a lot of bushes to trim and leaves to rake. Since I had started to worry that if I got down on my knees in the garden again I'd tumble over and never get up, I was positively grateful to him for offering to take the job off my hands.

'Give him the job,' my mother urged me. 'You'll have enough to do without the garden and he's an elderly man who could use the extra income.'

My head spinning from the nausea, I agreed to his quote, handed over a huge chunk of responsibility and he promised to start the following day. The most exciting thing from my point of view was that he promised to bring the vegetable garden back to life and asked me to start thinking about which plants I wanted.

'Strawberries,' I said without hesitation, 'and peas. Oh, and some more blackberry bushes. I'll have to think about the rest.'

'I'd suggest potatoes,' he said. 'Everyone loves new potatoes.'

Everyone except those of us who have bought into the idea that carbs are our enemy, I thought. But I would have guests to feed who would be lonely and miserable, and one thing I'd always found to be true was that good food helped make everything easier.

I remembered a night years ago that my mother and I had spent at an out-of-the-way hotel in a little French village.

We had been on our way to visit a friend of hers in Bordeaux, had left the motorway too soon because of a diversion and, of course, by the time we realised we needed somewhere to stop for the night all the signs saying 'Hotel Chateau-This-and-That' had long since disappeared. The car nearly went into a ditch as we tried to do a three-point turn on a tiny country road. By the time we found a village we were dirty and tired and would have put up with anything. The hotel was the strangest place we'd ever stayed but the restaurant we found further along the street provided us with one of the best meals either of us had ever had. What I remembered most about it was the sight of the proprietor outside in the garden cutting the fresh herbs he needed to prepare our meal. And the fat black cat who showed up to mark his territory on them two minutes later.

I went to IKEA with my parents and Alexander on Friday afternoon. Alexander and I drove in his friend's van, my parents following behind in their rental car.

'How are you feeling?' he asked me.

'Not bad,' I answered truthfully. 'Once I get past lunchtime I'm all right until about eight in the evening. And see, I didn't say "fine," did I?'

He laughed and smiled at me.

Yes, he was sweet and yes, he was kind and good-looking. But he shouldn't have been the one helping me to decorate my new home. He shouldn't have been the one asking me how I was coping with morning sickness. It should have been you. You should have been the one by my side. And however sweet and interested Alexander might seem, he was a twenty-two-year-old who deserved better from life than what I could offer him. So I looked out the window and listened to the music he chose in silence. I could feel him turning to look at me, probably wondering why I had gone quiet.

'Feeling sick again?'

'A little bit. It's not your driving,' I tried to laugh.

'Just lie back and shut your eyes for a minute. Did you bring any biscuits?'

I nodded and got one out of the emergency supply in my bag.

'Must be tough, never knowing when it's going to hit you.'

'It is. It's supposed to pass in a few weeks. Then I have about three months of feeling good before a whole lot of other discomforts hit me.'

He laughed and changed the music. He chose the very song I'd listened to over and over again the day you got married, the day I drove to Langeland to run away from the sight of you, her, and your wedding guests. A song about running away, about trying to find a safe haven. I dug my nails into the armrest and turned to Alexander.

'Could you play something else?'

'Don't you like it?'

'Oh no, I do. It's just ...'

He looked at me and smiled. He knew perfectly well that there were so many things I hadn't told him. I knew perfectly well that he desperately wanted to know. 'I know we haven't really known each other very long,' he said, 'but if you need someone to talk to ...'

'Thank you.'

'So what's the plan for today?' he asked, changing the subject.

'New kitchen.'

'Guess you'll need some help fitting it?'

'My parents are here for another week but we can always use an extra pair of hands.'

'That house of yours is a big project.'

'I know. It will keep me busy for at least a couple of years.'

'Is that what you want? Something to keep you busy?'

I thought about this for a while before I answered. 'I wanted somewhere new. Something new to think about. A new challenge and a different life. I was bored in the city. Can you believe that? But I wanted clean air and trees in my own garden, not in a park. Now the whole world has turned upside down. Now there's someone other than me to think about. I have to consider childcare, schools, dummies without phthalates, things I'd never dreamed I'd be thinking about at this point in my life.'

'It's a lot to take in all at once.'

'Especially when you're all on your own and hadn't planned for it at all.'

'I know ...' I could sense his hesitation. 'I know it's none of my business, but ...'

'But where's the father?'

'Well ... Yes.'

'You're right,' I said. 'It is none of your business.' But I smiled at him while I said it and hoped he wouldn't think I was shutting him out or being impolite. 'I'm not being rude. I will tell you about it one day. Just not right now.'

'Okay.'

Over coffee Alexander asked me why I'd chosen an IKEA kitchen. After the table I'd bought he'd pictured me heading off to some eccentric designer who would recreate the sort of French country dream you normally only see in the magazines.

'No,' I said, 'I am on a budget. Besides, I love IKEA. And if I have a house full of grieving women who are going to be sneaking down to snack in the middle of the night I want something I can easily repair and replace. Eccentric designers tend to charge extra for that.'

'Maybe you should get a dog. You know, like a kitchen alarm. Plus they're great companions and it might be good therapy for the women.'

'I like that idea,' my dad said. 'But get a real dog, not one of those awful yappy things that get carried around.'

Alexander smiled at me and, with his spoon, discreetly pointed across the room where two women were sitting with Chihuahuas in their handbags. I tried not to laugh.

'A Great Dane. Just like Thor and Odin. They were my grandparents' dogs,' I said to Alexander.

One thing I'd never admitted to anyone was that every so often I'd sneak off to dog shows just to be surrounded by wagging tails and big, soulful eyes. Friends who needed someone to look after their dogs while they went on holiday knew that I'd be at their house before they'd even put the phone down.

'Just remember that puppies grow up,' my mother said. 'Especially Great Danes. And you're having a baby.'

Alexander nodded. 'The baby might be a girl. All little girls love ponies, don't they? A Great Dane would be the next best thing.'

We all paused for a minute and for some reason tilted our heads to allow the mental picture to sink in. Then we all laughed. I had to admit that the thought, albeit slightly ridiculous, was a little appealing. Alexander looked over at me and winked.

'Just warn them about the kitchen alarm,' my father said. 'A Great Dane looming out of the darkness might seem a little frightening.'

When we got home my mother cooked dinner for the four of us while my father and Alexander unloaded the van. She sliced mushrooms and spring onions while I tried to block out the smell and resisted the urge to run to the bathroom. The pile of flat-pack boxes in the hallway kept on growing and to avoid looking at the food I began to unpack some of the new glasses, placemats and napkins I had bought. I set the table and lit some candles, mentally picturing my lovely new kitchen with its wooden worktop and smart new units. There would be herbs on the windowsill. Once I could face the thought of food again, I would fill this space with the delicious scent of freshly baked bread and garlic and basil and more delectable chocolate cakes than even I could imagine. I would find the time to prepare all those dishes I had always longed to try but never found the time to cook.

'Do you think I'm nuts?' I asked my mother as she crushed garlic and rubbed salt and pepper on rib-eye steaks.

She shook her head and laughed. 'No. I don't think this is most well-thought-out decision you ever made, but I don't think you're nuts. If nothing else, it's wonderful to be back here again. Your father certainly couldn't be happier. I do think you need to decide on whether or not you are going to tell him about the baby. Not your father. The baby's father.'

I sighed. 'I know. But right now I don't know what I want to tell him. If anything.'

'I'm not going to ask if you don't think he has a right to know. I've never pretended to understand the two of you and I've never interfered. If I hadn't met your father when I did there would probably have been someone like him in my life.'

'Someone you couldn't let go?'

'For whatever reason. Maybe it's true love. Maybe it's the chance you never took. Maybe it's just an old habit that's safe and familiar. Do you love him?'

I nodded. 'Always. At least I think so. I know it doesn't make sense. I know it's ridiculous. I know it's wrong.'

The steaks sizzled as she dropped them into the frying pan. 'Maybe you two are meant to be together. You'll see him again. But that's as far as I can see. For now focus on you and the baby.'

I finished setting the table and went to tell the others that dinner was nearly ready.

'Excellent,' my father said. 'We've just finished unloading. I'll start ripping out the old kitchen tomorrow.'

'I'd be happy to come and help,' Alexander said.

'Thanks,' I answered, 'but it's the weekend. Don't you have plans of your own?'

'Not really.'

'I don't want to take time away from your music.'

'That's okay. I'm a little stuck at the moment. And a kitchen will be a nice break from the roof.'

My father smiled at him and filled his glass. 'We'll start at ten if that's all right?'

'Earlier is fine with me.'

'Even better. Just come round when you can then.'

I managed to enjoy the meal and successfully keep the nausea at bay. That night I slept soundly and didn't once feel the urge to get up and wander aimlessly through the empty rooms.

The next morning I lay in bed and listened to the sounds of the birds outside my window. I felt the warmth of the early sun and was grateful there would be at least one more day with no rain on my patchy roof. Then I turned over and within seconds was off on another mad dash to the bathroom. When I staggered back, I collapsed on the bed before I noticed that I'd received a text from the woman who was renting my apartment back in Copenhagen.

Hi, Anne. A man showed up last night looking for you. He seemed very surprised to see me! He didn't know you'd moved so I didn't tell him where you were. I said he could call you, hope that was okay. He said he had your number. He was very tall and quite cute ;-) Hanne

I closed my eyes and tried to breathe deeply. It was you.

You!

You'd come back for me.

For a moment I closed my eyes. All nausea vanished as I experienced the familiar of rush of knowing that you were back in my life again. Now surely you would call or text. I'd tell you everything and it would all work out. I tried to imagine what had happened. You'd loathed your honeymoon and had realised it just wasn't going to work out. You knew that I was the one you loved. I danced into the shower. When I came out, I even managed a cup of tea and two pieces of toast. I found myself humming as I boxed up the few things I had put in the kitchen cupboards. When Alexander knocked on the door a few minutes later my mother let him in and gave him coffee and I gave him a big smile.

By lunchtime the old kitchen had been dismantled and Alexander was ripping up the lino. The original floorboards had turned out to be in a much better state than I could have hoped for so they were just going to be sanded down, not replaced. The machine was waiting in the hallway and my father was staring at it like a small boy in front of the Christmas tree. I could see this project taking longer than the weekend. After we were politely asked to move aside for the fifth time, my mother and I decided that we were only in the way, so we went into town to do some shopping and get lunch for everyone.

'Alexander is very sweet,' she said.

'Yes, mum,' I sighed.

'I know, I know. I'm not interfering. I'm just saying. And he obviously likes you.'

'Mum, I'm two months pregnant with someone else's child. Alexander is twenty-two. Even if he were ready for that kind of baggage, it wouldn't be fair. I'm too old for him.'

'But do you like him?'

'Of course I like him. He's very sweet and helpful. And yes,' I could see her about to interject, 'he's very attractive. But I'm not interested in a relationship right now. I have a lot of other things on my mind. So can we please stop having this discussion? I don't have anything good to offer at the moment.'

'Don't be ridiculous. Of course you have a lot to offer.'

But I really couldn't see that. A single mother-to-be in her early thirties, self-employed, with a monster of a house and far too used to her own company was not the right woman for someone like Alexander. Or anyone else for that matter. And then there was you. You were going to come for me. I knew it. You had been to my apartment. You'd be in touch. You'd come and find me.

'How about pizza?'

'Sorry?'

'Pizza,' my mother said. 'How about pizza for lunch?'

'No. It will have gone cold by the time we get it back home. I know it's not a long walk but still.'

'That's true. Sandwiches then. Why do you keep looking at your phone?'

'Oh. It's nothing.' For all my parents' loving support about the baby, I couldn't tell them about the text and that I thought you'd be in touch soon. Because if it didn't happen, I'd never hear the end of it. There had been so many times in the past when I had believed completely that you were on your way back into my life only to have the dreams torn apart a few days later. Right now I needed to believe that you would come for me. I needed a few days to dream in a world where I wasn't making a huge mistake and where my baby would never know its father.

Week Nine

My new kitchen was up and running, my parents had gone back to Paris, Alexander and Bjarne were back on the roof, and I had heard nothing from you at all. I felt like such an idiot. Wandering through the quiet rooms, I cursed the day I had ever met you. I found myself reconsidering the idea of having the baby. Why should I spend the rest of my life paying the price for a faulty condom and your hormones being in overdrive the night before your wedding? I'd be much better off with just a puppy. Who was I to think I could be a good mother? My whole life was being turned upside down by some selfish bastard who didn't even care enough to try and find out where I was when he found someone else in my apartment and me gone without a trace.

As I put away plates and cutlery in my new cupboards I found myself wanting to slap you. I'd like to get hold of you and sit you down and scream at you till I was hoarse. I'd get that bloody Great Dane and as soon as it was fully grown I'd bring it over to your new house, have it sit on you and leave big dirty paw prints all over your floors. And I just hoped you'd have been dumb enough to choose white carpets. Slamming cupboard doors was a miserable outlet for my frustration. Since I didn't want to break anything in my beautiful new kitchen all I could do was close them slightly less softly than usual. Wasn't there a wall somewhere that needed to come down? Swinging a sledgehammer and imaging that I was aiming for your head might make me feel better. Yesterday I'd gone to the golf club instead and beaten the hell out of the balls on the driving range. On the bright side, it had really improved my swing. I'd also met some friendly people and had a game scheduled for next week.

You had been doing this to me for years. Time and time again you had waltzed into my life and turned my world upside down. You were always full of promises and dreams, you mourned our lost chances and then you vanished again as quickly as you came. For days, for weeks, afterwards I'd float through life on a cloud. I'd dream of the future you'd sketched and I'd believe the honeyed words that had dripped with sincerity and remorse. But the spell always broke when months had passed and I'd heard nothing. What I hated the most was how many times I'd let you come back to do the same thing to me over and over again. What kind of life could you ever give our baby? Would you disappear when it was time for birthdays, bedtimes, school plays? Why not save myself the bother and my child the heartbreak? Dreams might have been good enough for me, but my baby deserved more. You were nothing but a liar. A fantasist. A scared little man who couldn't face his own emotions. Well, you could get lost for all I cared. You were never going to mess up my life again. But even that I had said so many times before. I was trapped in a circle and seemed unable to break free.

Angrily I blinked back tears before I looked up and noticed Bjarne and Alexander standing in the garden pointing at something I couldn't see. I went outside expecting to see a large crack, subsidence or another flock of pigeons.

'What's up?'

Bjarne turned to smile at me. 'Just looking at how much work we have left to do.'

'And?'

'I think another few weeks should do the trick. Which is good, it will give us a chance to get everything finished before the weather changes.'

'That's great.'

'I'll get someone in to look at the bathrooms if that's what you want to do next.'

'You won't be doing that?'

'No, I just do roofs. But Alexander will still be around to help out.'

'Okay,' I smiled at them.

Alexander laughed and said, 'If that's okay?'

'Of course,' I laughed. 'I need someone to help me eat the desserts I plan to make with all those apples once they ripen. And once I can face the thought of food again.'

'Still feeling bad?'

'I'm so hungry,' I told him while Bjarne went back onto the roof. 'But even the thought of food makes me want to throw up. The only thing I think I could eat is McDonalds.'

'So go to McDonalds.'

'I should. My doctor says I should be putting on weight and all I've done is lose it. But McDonalds is three islands away. It's a long way to go for a meal on a plastic tray.'

He laughed. 'When you put it like that it does sound far. Three whole islands. So how about I take you? My treat? Call it a thank you for all the great food and coffee you keep us supplied with. We can go this evening when we finish up here.'

'All right.' I smiled at him and nodded. 'Thanks.'

'I'm impressed,' Alexander said later that evening while we sat at plastic tables and looked out at the car park, empty and depressing in the dusky light of the early evening. 'I've never seen a woman eat two large burgers and all those fries.'

'I'm starving,' I laughed, 'and finally I've found food that doesn't make me want to throw up.'

'Would you like a sundae?'

'I'd love one. But I can't,' I said when Alexander started to get up.

'You can't? Too much of a good thing?'

'I wish. No, it's a pregnancy thing. Apparently it's something to do with the machine. If it's not cleaned properly some dangerous bacteria can grow and they can be harmful to the baby. Or fatal. Either way, another big no-no. I get a little confused sometimes with all the prohibitions.'

He nodded and sat back down. 'I remember my sisters-in-law when they were pregnant. Two of my nieces are just three weeks apart. I remember the problems we had in the beginning when we all tried to get together for dinner. One of them couldn't stand this but the other one wanted nothing but. You can imagine.'

I laughed. 'I'm just glad I don't have anyone to cook for. Apart from the morning sickness I have to remember not to drink green tea, not to have too much coffee. I can't have rare meat, I can't have prawns, I can't have too much fruit or sugar, I can't have sundaes, I can't have soft cheeses. No alcohol of course. And it just goes on.'

'Must be tough.'

'It sounds worse than it is when you list everything like this. But it's all right. I just keep a list on the fridge and try to plan my meals around that. Even though I can't face the thought of any of them. But there's a lot you can do to help give your baby a good start. At the moment the biggest problem is that everything makes me sick.'

'Well, I'm glad I could help feed you.'

'Thank you. The last time a man took me to McDonalds I was … well, your age.'

Alexander made a face at me.

When I got back home I lit some candles and sat in the living room with my laptop, translating an online course. It was dark outside and Alexander had gone home. When I had finished I closed my eyes and tried to imagine what it would be like this time next year. There would be a little baby asleep in my room. There might be a large dog curled up next to me. Somewhere in the house one or more strangers might be putting their lives back together. Somewhere out there you would be building a life with your wife, and you would never know that on this little island you had a child. Never know what you had missed out on. Never have to know something that would tear apart your sweet new life. Think of it as me doing you a favour.

My phone rested on the cushion next to me. I looked at it as if it were a bomb. So easy. So easy to text you, call you, yell at you. But too late to tell you all those things I wanted to say. Too late to say that if we could just sit down and talk to each other like adults we would be able to stop playing games and finally make it work. Too late for all those things. I closed my eyes and sighed.

I sat in silence for a while as the gentle light from the candles danced behind my eyes. One more time I conjured up the image of the two of us together. Then I shook my head, put work away and started looking for puppies. Seven months until the baby arrived. New house, new career. It would be criminal to let that enormous garden go to waste. I'd been dreaming about a dog for as long as I could remember. I'd never wanted to get one while I was living in the city because I wanted a large dog. A real dog. Not, as my father had said in IKEA, one of those yappy things. Why not live all of the dream? Why not do everything I had dreamed of? It was my life. One of the benefits of being alone was that I needed no one else's approval for anything.

You only get one life. It was up to me to do what was needed to ensure that mine turned out to be a happy one. I would build a world for myself and my baby that would make us happy even without you in it.

The next morning Alexander found me in the kitchen writing down phone numbers of kennels who had just had or were expecting puppies.

'So you're going to go for it?'

'Yes. I've always wanted a big dog. Now at last I have the room for it.'

'Does this mean you're going for the small pony?'

'Yes. If I'm going to get a big dog, I might as well get the biggest. Besides, they're good with children and won't fawn all over my guests. My grandparents had them and I loved those dogs. They were the sweetest, gentlest little things. Well, hardly little, but you know what I mean.'

He nodded. 'I love dogs. Mind if I come with you to check them out?'

'Not at all.'

'Great. We'll be on the roof.'

'Coffee will be out in ten minutes.'

'I'm glad I get to stay on and help with the rest of the house,' he said. 'The service here is wonderful.'

'Wait till I start baking again.'

He laughed and went outside.

I got up and started making coffee. Then I went outside to see how the apples and blackberries were coming along. I hadn't had the chance to cook with fruit fresh from the garden since my grandfather died. I was considering making jam.

There was something so different, yet so peaceful, about my life here compared to the one I had left behind. In the city I was out nearly every weekend. Theatre, cinema, shopping. Here I went for walks along the beach or in the woods. The only person I really spoke to on a regular basis was Alexander. But one day the house would be finished and he would be gone. It would probably get a little lonely.

I remembered one holiday, the year before I went to university, which I had spent most of in the kitchen experimenting with new menus and fun creations. I had loved those days. Those relaxing, wonderful times when I would immerse myself in chocolates, creamy sauces, delicious salads and all manner of dishes that I would inflict on my family and friends night after night. But there was something so soothing about it. At a time when life was about to change completely, it brought tremendous peace and solace to me. One of my teachers taught me that cooking was not merely a utilitarian exercise, but a sensuous delight. That no matter what happened in our lives, at regular intervals we all needed to sit down and put food in our mouths so we might as well enjoy it.

I also remembered a summer when Lisbeth and I had borrowed a tiny little house by the coast from a friend. We'd been full of plans for an active holiday, with plenty of delectable food. We had planned to walk to the harbour and bargain for fresh fish, see all the surrounding sites and really learn how to barbecue. We were going to take our pastel blankets to the beach along with freshly baked bread and organic juices. Instead we'd spent most of the holiday talking about men in the garden, eating rice cakes and cucumber sticks. When I looked back, I realised it had often been like that. I'd always excelled at dreams and plans. It was when it came to realising the dreams that I often fell short. Daily life and the normal routine were too quick to bury my good intentions under a mountain of missed deadlines. But not this time. This time I was determined. I wouldn't simply talk about making jam, I would do it. If I enjoyed it, I would keep doing it. Little changes would creep into my routine and I would make damn sure that if I left this house I wouldn't look back on it with a large pile of regrets, remembering all the things I'd promised myself I'd do but had never found the time for.

After I'd taken coffee and biscuits out to Bjarne and Alexander, I immersed myself in my cookbooks. Phantom menus did not give me nausea although the thought of what to have for lunch still made me rush to the bathroom. I spent the rest of the morning organising my desk and mapping out my work for the rest of the week.

When I woke up the next morning I was too sick to do anything. I lay comatose on the sofa all day cursing pregnancy hormones and wishing for the first trimester to be over. When evening came and Lisbeth and Emma knocked on the door, I was taken completely by surprise.

'He's been to my apartment,' I told Lisbeth later that night once Emma was asleep and we were curled up on the sofa with cups of tea.

'And?'

'And then nothing. According to Hanne, he came round the other night and obviously didn't expect to find her there and me gone. She didn't tell him where I was, just that I'd gone and she was renting the place.'

'And you haven't heard anything?'

'Nothing. Not one word. Not even a text. Not even one wondering where I was or why I lied to him about all those boxes in the hallway.'

'Maybe ...' Lisbeth shook her head. 'I'm not defending him. But if he turned up and found you gone, maybe he assumed you didn't want to be found. That if you had wanted him to know where you were then you would have told him. Would have told him that you were going. He might be sitting there thinking you don't want to see him again and that's why he's not getting in touch. He might want nothing more than to know where you are. He obviously wanted to see you again. He probably guessed that Hanne would tell you that someone had been looking for you and since you haven't called, thinks you don't want to see him. Maybe he's just respecting what he thinks your wishes are. God knows you two were never good at communicating. You always knew when the other one was going to show up, but rarely what each other was thinking.'

'Oh God,' I sighed and ran my fingers through my hair. 'So what do I do? I can't get in touch without telling him about the baby.'

'I don't know what you can do. You might call him and find it all comes to nothing. Maybe he just wanted to check that you are okay because he's ecstatically happy in his new marriage and feels guilty that you're the one alone.'

'Great. Thanks.'

'Why don't you sleep on it? You'll feel better tomorrow. We'll go and get some fresh air and take Emma round the island.'

I nodded. Sleep was what I needed. Lisbeth said she would clear up, so I went to my bedroom and got undressed. But I couldn't sleep.

Lisbeth's words had made me think differently about your silence even though part of me wondered why we couldn't just stop trying to find excuses for you. Why had she never just said that you were an idiot and I was a fool? I wrapped myself in my dressing gown and looked out into the dark garden and up at the stars. I wondered if you were looking up at the same stars. Sometimes I sensed your presence so clearly it was almost palpable. It wrapped itself around me, like something tangible I could cling to.

The passion. That complete, abandoned passion that I'd never known with any other man. How it took me by surprise almost every time. No one else could ever make me feel that way. There was no one else I was so comfortable, yet so sensual, with. No one but you. I wasn't sure whether to laugh or cry, so I lay down on the bed and covered myself with the duvet.

Get some sleep. Everything looks different in the morning. And never write to a married man in the middle of the night.

Emma was thrilled with the big house and the enormous garden and had explored every inch of it the next morning before her mother was even out of bed. I managed to suppress my nausea sufficiently to make her breakfast and then sent her off to say hello to Alexander and Bjarne.
'Do they live here too?' she asked when she came back.
'No,' I said and smiled. 'They do work on the house for me. They're mending the roof. Remember when your dishwasher overflowed and a man came out to make it work again?'
She nodded.
'Just like that, except with a roof. So they don't live here, they go home at night.'
'You live here all alone? But it's so big.'
'I'm having a baby so it won't be just me. Did Mummy tell you that?'
She nodded again and looked at the table. 'May I have another bun, please?'
'Of course. Would you like it toasted?'
She nodded.
'With Nutella?'
'Yes please! And can I have some more milk?'
I sliced a bun in half and toasted it for her, spread Nutella on it and poured a large glass of milk.
'I've started gymnastics now,' she told me.
'Yes, I heard. Have you made nice new friends?'
'Yes. My best friend there is called Isabella. And there's a boy called Simon. He's missing two teeth.'
'He must be a little older then.'
'Yes,' she nodded secretively. 'He's six. Lots of the other children have lost teeth. I don't think I'll ever lose mine.'
'Of course you will. You just have to wait a few years.' I smiled at her and told her about the first tooth I lost. I re-

membered just in time that the tooth fairy is the one who leaves the coin under the pillow.

'Good morning,' said Lisbeth.

'Good morning,' I said. 'Breakfast?'

'Please.'

'Would you mind making it yourself? I need to go stick my head in the toilet.'

'Sure,' she laughed and opened the fridge to get the milk out for coffee.

We took Emma to the restaurant in the old stables and then went for a walk in the castle grounds. I tried to believe that I could detect the first hint of autumn in the air, but the day was unseasonably warm and everyone was still in their summer clothes.

'So,' Lisbeth said while we watched Emma run on ahead, waving a stick like a sword, 'are you going to write to him?'

'I don't know.'

'Don't make it all about the dream.'

'What do you mean?'

'I mean, just be careful that you're both not clinging to the idea, the dream, some beautiful, unobtainable fantasy that keeps you warm at night when you're lonely.'

'I ...' For a second I didn't quite know what to say. Was there any truth in what Lisbeth said? Was it easier to just cling to the dream rather than to just get up and go for it? Do everything we could to be together and then – God forbid – never see each other again if it didn't work out? Was that why she walked down the aisle with you instead of me? Or were you just a cheating little rat like the rest of them? I sighed and shook my head. 'Right now I don't even know what to do tomorrow, let alone the next day or the rest of my life. I can't work anything out. And your over-analysing everything and coming up with new scenarios every minute isn't helping.'

'You could call him, right now, and tell him everything. Tell him you're pregnant. Tell him you still love him. And then what will happen, will happen.' She looked at me. 'Scares the hell out of you, doesn't it?'

I nodded. 'What if it's no? What if he doesn't want us? Or wants the baby but not me? I'm not giving up my child every other week so that they can play happy families. Or what,' I sighed and threw a stick at a tree, 'what if it's just another one of those times where he makes promises and never keeps them? I don't think I could pick up and move on again right now. Not from that. Not when it's like this.'

'What if it's yes?'

'Then he should come and tell me. He's the one who got married. I don't want to spend the rest of my life wondering whether he only came to be with me because I was pregnant. I want to be wanted for myself.'

Lisbeth picked up another stick and gave it to Emma who came charging at us from between two trees. She smiled as she watched her daughter run through grass. 'Make your decision and stick to it. Stress is bad for the baby. You're going to have someone else to think about soon and you'd better believe that they will come first in everything you do.'

'I know.'

'No,' she smiled at me, 'you don't. You know in theory but you have no idea what it's really like. I once heard someone say that you fall in love with your children. The same euphoria, the same incredible rush of emotion. Sometimes it just overwhelms you till you think you can't bear it. You will do whatever you have to do in order to protect them and keep them safe. Things you never had the strength to do for yourself will become so easy once it's their happiness at stake. Every priority is going to change. And you'll finally understand just how much your parents love you. But all things considered ... how is he going to feel the next time he sees you, because there will be a next time, and he finds out that you never told him he was a father?'

We walked on in silence while Emma charged ahead, still waving her stick and battling imaginary demons.

Later that afternoon we baked buns and played card games on the terrace with Emma. She wanted to climb onto the roof with Alexander and Bjarne and I laughed as Lisbeth looked up at the scaffolding and turned a strange shade of green.

'Not this time, sweetie,' she said and took her hand. 'You need to have longer legs to climb up that scaffolding.'

'That's true,' Alexander said and jumped down. 'Do you see how far apart those little ledges are?' He pointed at the scaffolding and Emma nodded. 'Your legs aren't long enough for them yet. But when they are I'll help you climb up. Okay?'

'Okay,' Emma laughed and ran back to the terrace. 'I'll bring you some buns.'

We stayed on the terrace till Bjarne climbed down and he and Alexander got ready to go home. 'See you Monday!' they called as they were leaving and Alexander smiled and waved.

'He's cute,' Lisbeth remarked.

'So everyone tells me.'

'I liked him,' Emma said. 'He showed me the apple trees.'

Lisbeth shuffled the cards while I poured more tea.

'Have you been taking your folic acid?' she asked.

'Yes. I manage to time it so I don't throw it up straight away. I'm so tired of feeling sick every day.'

'Just a few more weeks and you'll be out of that phase.'

'Thank God for that.'

'Can I help lay the table for dinner?' Emma asked.

'Yes,' Lisbeth replied. 'But not right now, sweetie. We've just finished our buns. Dinner is quite a few hours away. And don't get too excited,' she said to me with a wink, 'it will be many years before yours can help out.'

When we went inside Lisbeth began to make dinner and I watched Emma put the place mats on the table. She had a look of intense concentration and her tongue firmly between her teeth. She found cutlery and napkins and asked for help getting plates and glasses.

'Thank you, Emma,' I said and she smiled. I saw the look of happiness on Lisbeth's face and knew that what she had said earlier was true. I had no idea what being a parent was really going to be like. But hopefully, I thought, neither did anyone else who did this for the first time.

Week Ten

After Lisbeth and Emma went back to Copenhagen I was a little lost and alone in a house that suddenly seemed very empty. Alexander was the person I spent the most time talking to and he was very good at suggesting food that I could eat without feeling sick while I waited for some exotic craving to kick in. I was hoping for something a little out of the ordinary like strawberry and champagne jam or sweet potato ravioli. Something less banal than chocolate or cinnamon pastries. When my grandmother was expecting my father her craving had been for liquorice. My great-grandmother used to tell me stories about how all her friends in town would bring their sweet ration to my grandmother so she could feel better. After she died and we went through her cupboards to sort out her things, we found packets of liquorice hidden in the oddest places. I wondered then what they would find when I died. Pictures of you? Messages I had never been able to send? Chocolates I didn't want to eat for fear of gaining weight?

    I remembered the night she died. I remembered sitting in the hospital, holding her hand and waiting for the end. Calling you at three o'clock in the morning to tell you it was over. Breaking down and crying in your arms outside the hospital later that morning when you came to take me home. It was such a beautiful April morning and I wondered how the sun could shine so brightly when the world had just ended. I think she would have liked my plan for the house. She loved good food. She loved having friends and family to stay and planning treats for them.

By now I had got used to the noises that the house made. Floorboards creaking, furniture settling. The mornings were slowly getting a little darker and I was lying in bed reading. Burrowed under the covers, I enjoyed looking up from the page to watch the light glow on the freshly painted walls. Outside the rain was lashing against the windows and I could hear the wind whistling through the tarpaulin still covering part of the roof. I really hoped that Bjarne and Alexander had done their job properly. There were puddles on the terrace and the temperature had dropped. I sighed, yawned, got out of bed and ran my fingers through my hair. I thought that I was starting to notice a little bulge. Either I'd had too much chocolate or I was already starting to show. I remembered how Lisbeth kept telling people, 'Nah, not pregnant, just fat.' Then she'd laugh.

Walking to the windows to look out over the garden as soon as I got up had become routine for me now. This was the first time since my arrival that it really rained. I've always loved the sound of rain and how fresh and new everything smells after a summer storm. When I was a teenager my best friend and I used to take advantage of the rain to stay in all day, watch films, drink tea, eat sweets and dream about the boys we had hopeless crushes on. Then, later, the only one I could ever dream about was you.

I got my big box of old letters from under the bed. I read the ones from you again but this time I read them with a smile. I saw the big loops of your hopeless handwriting and I knew that I loved you. That deep down, I always would. Even if it never worked out. I was bound to you. Even as I heard the words forming in my mind, I felt utterly pathetic.

Sitting there on my bed with letters and photographs spilling onto the covers, I began to wonder about my life. Looking back through the years at decisions I had made, things I had done, I wondered if it were not simply just a matter of fear. I was afraid. Afraid of being loved, afraid of tying myself to another person. Which was why I had run away from you all those years ago. The world of dreams was easier to navigate than the pitfalls of a real relationship with a living, breathing person. Each time I got hurt, each time I got bored, I shut myself off a little more. Only the dream of you remained alive, because dreams could not hurt me. When each dream died, another one could rise up to take its place. Perhaps it was the same for you? Perhaps you had been brave enough to see that dreams were not enough and that you had to break the cycle and find someone real. I just wish, I thought as I lay back on the bed and a stack of photographs cascaded over the edge, I just wish you could have made that real person me.

    I got up from the bed and hunted through the cupboard I had reserved for winter clothes and found my warm dressing gown. Wrapped in that, I settled myself on the sofa with the one cup of real coffee that I allowed myself a day and picked up the catalogue from the bathroom company. I'd thought about you enough for one morning, now it was time to do something sensible. I was trying to work out a deal with a little company on the outskirts of town. There didn't seem to be much point in trying to bring people back to the island if I couldn't at the same time help support its existing workforce. At some point I would also need a cleaner, a website, a newsletter and some kind of marketing. This was the advantage, I thought, of having run my own business and cultivated all those networks for so many years. I already knew who to work with. I just hadn't told them yet.

Two hours later Alexander arrived. Since we'd known the rain was coming and work on the roof would have to be put on hold, I'd made an appointment to go and look at puppies. I packed my usual supply of digestives and also included a banana in an effort to try and eat healthily.

    'Ready to go?'

    I nodded, turned off the lights in the hallway and locked the door behind me.

    'How are you feeling this morning?'

    'All right at the moment. But it still hits me every time I get up. And then again in the evening.'

    'Did you go back to McDonald's?'

    'Once. It's still quite a way to go and it's not exactly the healthiest option.'

    While I checked the directions one last time, Alexander rummaged through my CDs and picked the same one I had been listening to when I drove down here the morning of your wedding. That day when I drove as though demons were chasing me. Reckless, fearless, unable to endure the thought of you standing next to her at the altar when less than twelve hours before you'd been asleep in my bed with your arms wrapped so tightly around me.

'Is this one okay?' he asked.

'Fine,' I said. He smiled at me. Then he reached back into the glovebox and found something else.

We arrived at the kennels two hours later after a long drive filled with music, comfortable silences and small talk about the house. Deep, booming barks alerted the owners to our arrival and they came outside to greet us and usher us inside. Alexander looked a little apprehensive but I felt like a kid at Christmas.

The owners of the kennels were Sisse and Lars, a husband and wife team with three children. One of them was a six-month-old baby girl who was asleep in a Moses basket on the sofa while a Great Dane lay beside her, resting it's head on her legs. The dog looked up as we came in but made no move to bound over and great us.

'Would you like coffee or tea?' Sisse asked.

We both asked for tea and Lars moved the Moses basket out of the way to make room for us on the sofa. The dog got up too, then came back to sniff us and say hello. Stroking his silky ears, I knew that this was the right decision. I had to have a dog and now I was able to provide a good home for a dog of the size I wanted. I had never been one of those women with a desperate need to have children, but I knew it would have broken my heart to have lived all my life without having had at least one dog.

'Have you had a Great Dane before?' Sisse asked me while Lars went to the kitchen to make the tea.

'No, never,' I answered. 'But my grandparents had them. I always wanted one of my own but this is the first time I've had the space for one. I have a house now with a garden. I used to live in an apartment in Copenhagen.'

Sisse nodded. 'You can have them in apartments, you know.'

Alexander looked shocked. 'Really? But they're huge!'

Lars came back with a tray filled with cups, a teapot and a large cake. For once I found my appetite perking up.

'They're not wildly active dogs like Labradors, for instance. They are actually a companion breed. But it's not good if you live higher up than the first floor. Stairs aren't good for their joints. And you still need a big apartment. Bigger than average.'

'I used to be on the third floor,' I told them. 'That was one of the reasons I never got a dog. No matter how much I wanted one.' I beamed down at the dog at my feet. 'Now my bedroom is on the ground floor. I don't plan on using the first floor that much, personally. And I work from home so it's not a question of leaving him alone for eight hours a day.' I got out my phone to show them the pictures I'd taken of the house and the garden but what greeted me on the screen was a message from you. 'I ... I took some photos of the garden and the house to show you.' My voice sounded breathless and I couldn't stop a smile from breaking out. I hadn't even read the message but just the fact that you were getting in touch again was enough. I could sense Alexander's eyes on me, puzzled by the strange turn my mood had taken.

'That looks lovely,' Lars said. He looked at both of us. 'Do you have any children?'

I laughed nervously and I noticed that Alexander blushed.

'No,' I said, 'we're not a couple. We're just ...' I looked at him and smiled, realising the truth. 'We're friends. But I am expecting a baby in the spring.'

'When?' Sisse asked.

'April.'

She frowned. 'That will give you about seven months alone with your new dog before the baby arrives. But it will still be a puppy at that time.'

'I know,' I said. 'I know it may not be the ideal situation but, trust me, none of this is.' I laughed a little. 'If I end up waiting until I think the baby is old enough I'll still be wondering about it in three, five, ten years from now. I finally have the chance to do something I've always wanted to do.'

'And I'll help walk the dog,' Alexander said, and I smiled gratefully at him. I had come so close to realising a dream that I didn't want to see it shattered now because my timing wasn't good.

'They are wonderful with children,' Lars said, 'as you can see.' He pointed to the Moses basket where a giant paw was now resting on the blanket. I could hear the baby gurgling in her sleep.

'Your dog will insist on its own space on the sofa,' Sisse cautioned, 'so I hope it's not too expensive.'

'No,' I laughed, 'which is good since the baby will probably just spit up all over it anyway.'

'Excellent,' Lars said and poured the tea and offered cake. I decided to risk provoking nausea and accepted with a smile. Alexander smiled at me and I looked over at the dog and the baby. Yes, definitely the right decision.

The puppies were the most adorable creatures I had ever seen. They were sleeping next to their mother when we came in, except for one little puppy who immediately came over to inspect us. Sisse told me I could pick him up, so I did. He licked my nose, gently bit my finger, then lay down on my lap and went to sleep.

'I think he likes you,' Sisse said and smiled.

I nodded and looked down and the little blue bundle in my lap. This was my dog. No doubt about it.

Sisse sat down beside me and told me about their kennels, their other dogs and about the breed in general. I sat quietly, enraptured, while she talked. The other puppies stirred a little when their mother moved over to sit with us. She licked her sleeping puppy and put her head in my lap next to him. We all make choices, compromises in our lives. Right now I knew that I would gladly give up everything life in the city had to offer me just to wake up every morning next to one of these giant dogs who wanted to be walked, loved and played with.

'They seek companionship,' Sisse said. 'They're extremely sociable dogs. But they are usually shy around strangers. Let the dog make the first move. You did it just right when you came in. And if you're going to live alone then you couldn't ask for a better watch dog. They've lovable and friendly but they look scary as hell when you see them roaming around the house or garden. I always feel perfectly safe when I'm here on my own. No burglar would dare come here.'

She excused herself to check on something and I was left alone with my potential new puppy and my thoughts. My phone was in my bag in the living room so I couldn't even read your message. I knew what I had to do. With your marriage you'd walked out of my future. So now I needed to stop dreaming that one day you would come back for me. I had to stop being afraid, I had to create a future for myself that I didn't keep putting on hold because of a dream that one day you might come for me. Otherwise I'd wake up one day with a future that had never materialised and wonder where my life had gone.

'I shall find a good name for you,' I said and stroked the puppy's head.

Alexander and I drove back to Langeland a few hours later. My phone lay in my bag like an unexploded bomb. Whatever you had written, even if it was just 'Hello, how are you?' I wanted to read it and react to it on my own.

'Do you want to stop at McDonald's?' he suggested.

'Actually yes, I'd love to. My treat this time.'

We talked about the puppies, the dogs, the baby. Alexander marvelled at how they managed to keep the house looking comparatively neat with all those dogs and three children.

'You really think you can manage a puppy and a baby and a new business?' he asked.

My eyes flashed as I looked at him. 'Yes.' By now I'd spent so much time weighing my options that the last thing I wanted was for someone to come and unravel my certainty so I'd have to start convincing myself all over again. I didn't want to have to re-examine my choices and find myself thinking again about decisions I had made in the past. Like the very first time I had let you go. The mistake I still brooded over, all these years later. Because no matter what had happened since, the first time things went wrong it had been my fault. I had thought enough about that this morning. I didn't need regrets right now, I wanted to be happy.

It was still early when we got back to Langeland so Alexander invited me to come and see his studio and hear him play. His friend's house was very cosy with white walls and exposed beams. I looked at the floor and the kitchen.

'You don't clean much, do you?' I laughed. The dirty plates and glasses stacked in the sink and the dust accumulated in corners and on tables were a perfect testament to the fact that a single man in his early twenties lived here.

'No,' he sighed and shook his head. 'I guess I'm not very good at that. With work and my music, it always seems like something that can wait till tomorrow.'

I really needed to use the bathroom but I was almost afraid to ask.

The studio was in a room built onto the end of the house and accessed through a very solid looking door in the kitchen.

'His wife insisted on that to keep the sound out,' Alexander explained, 'but then she left.'

Good thing, too, I thought. She'd go berserk if she came home and saw the state of her kitchen.

Alexander asked me to turn on some lights while he picked up a guitar and turned on some amps and other strange looking equipment that meant nothing to me. The only thing I recognised was an iMac. Not quite the starving artist I thought to myself, and grinned at him.

There was a large squashy armchair in the corner and I curled up in that as Alexander began to play. The soft notes wrapped themselves around me in the wet, September evening as I looked at the young man in front of me. He played things I knew, things I didn't and in the end a few bars of something he told me was his own composition. When he stood there in front of me, looking at me with those penetrating green eyes and sang of love unrequited I realised two things. He really was a very talented musician. And he really did have feelings for me. But I had no idea what to do about them. So I sat in silence and let the music wash over me, knowing that soon I would have to go home and that saying goodbye would be awkward. Then I realised something else. At some point work on the house would be finished and I would have to say goodbye to Alexander. I didn't want to do that.

When I got home it was dark and the house seemed damp and clammy. I put the kettle on, took out my phone and read your message. You had written:

I hope you're OK.

That's it? You find a complete stranger in my home, two weeks pass and all you can come with is, 'I hope you're okay?'
      I got a cup out of the cupboard and slammed the door shut. You have no idea, I thought with a shake of my head, and headed into the living room. I tossed my phone onto the sofa and went back to the kitchen. I drank my tea in silence and with a murderous expression in my eyes.

That night I tossed and turned, trying to compose the perfect reply to your message. I came up with:

Fine thanks.

How the fuck do you think I am?!

Drop dead.

I'm fine. I just needed to get out of the city for a while. (btw I'm also pregnant with your child, have bought a huge house and am getting a puppy.)

Good. But there's something I need to talk to you about.

I'm great! Hope you're enjoying married life :-)

Why did it have to be so hard? Why hadn't I just been honest with you when you asked me about those boxes and suitcases in my apartment that night? Why couldn't I just tell you that I still loved you and that the thought of you getting married made me feel physically sick? There had been no choice for me but to run away. Run far away. Run to somewhere I knew you'd never show up and I'd never have to see you again. Maybe if I had told you all those things it would have made a difference. Maybe then you wouldn't have got married. But I got up the next morning and finally I replied.

I'm fine thanks. Hope you're okay. I just decided to get away from the city.

Of course the worst part was that I hoped that you would reply. Say something, anything. But I had always walked a tightrope between my desire to see you and be near you and my fear that you didn't want me. So there were so many misunderstandings and so many times when I hated that you didn't reply. Lisbeth had told me to just be honest with you but there were some things that even she didn't know. I had been honest with you. In the past I had told you how I felt, bared my soul and said I loved you and wanted to be with you. What had I got out of that? Nothing. Why should now be any different? When did it all become so difficult? Screw it, I thought. And I sent another message.

I couldn't face seeing the two of you around town together.

I knew you would never reply to that. It bought me a little more time to decide whether or not to tell you about the baby. And, hopefully, your wife didn't read your messages.

Week Eleven

The rain continued for the next few days but both the new roof and the tarpaulin held firm and the house remained dry. Bjarne stayed home and painted his grandchildren's bedroom but Alexander came to help me decide what to do about the bathrooms. Or so he said. More and more often, I caught him looking at me when he thought I wasn't aware of it. I remembered the songs he had played for me and I couldn't help being annoyed at the irony of fate. Why should it be that the one time in my life I was the one pursued by the attractive male, I was two months pregnant with someone else's child and busy trying to start a new life.

'Coffee?' he asked.

'Please.'

He was at home in my house now. He'd helped me move furniture around, he'd measured the bathrooms for me and given his input and he was so sweet. I found myself humming the tunes he had played and it made him smile to hear it. I thought of you and I could have screamed. You should be the one helping me. You should be the one asking me which foods I was able to eat today. At the back of my mind was the realisation that I had no one to blame but myself. In the end, I was the one who had messed it up. Whatever else had happened over the years, the first time was my fault. If I hadn't ended it that first time, would it ever have ended? On the other hand, a little answering voice inside me said, I probably wouldn't be in this house, pregnant and about to buy a puppy. Besides, given everything that had happened between us since, should that one old mistake really still matter so much? Was I just using that as an excuse? What the hell did I really want?

Alexander went with me to order the bathrooms and then he made me lunch. Fruit and biscuits were all I was ready to face so he did some ingenious things with smoothies. One of the bathrooms was going to have a beautiful, sleek tub with taps in the middle. All were going to have enormous shower cubicles with those rain shower heads that I had always wanted. There would be fluffy towels. Soft and deep enough to drown in. Just the thing to wrap around you for a small moment of happiness when everything else seemed gone. On nights where I felt most alone I wrapped myself in my dressing gown and found the big padded slippers that my mother had given me. I sat in the kitchen, made myself a cup of tea and lit some candles. I tried to breathe deeply and relax. The softness wrapped around me helped keep me warm.

'Are you all right?'

'Yes. Yes, I'm fine.'

'You seemed to be somewhere else.'

'I was just thinking about my plans for the house.'

'I think it's going to be fantastic.'

'I really hope so.'

'But I think you need to practice all your cooking and cake-baking.' He laughed and his eyes were teasing.

'Oh you do, do you?'

'I do. I think you should take advantage of having people around the house to experiment.'

I laughed. 'And I'm sure I will. But first I need to get to a point where I can look food in the eyes without wanting to throw up.'

'Point taken. Come on, let's see what else we need to do.'

I took out my tile brochures and spread them out on the kitchen table. His hand brushed against mine when he reached for his coffee. I looked at him for a moment and he smiled.

It would be so easy. Right now, so easy. The problems would come later. Too big for us to handle. There would be heartbreak and hatred and a fervent wish to never see him again. Right now he just seemed too special to say goodbye to forever. So I looked away.

You never answered my message. Of course you didn't. Anything emotional, anything that came even close to acknowledging feelings and you ran a mile. If I were ever going to be in your life it would always be on your terms. You'd keep me hanging around forever like the gold at the end of the rainbow. The one you could never quite reach yet never live without. The dreams you would chase in your loneliest moments and then ignore when the dawn broke over the horizon. Shouldn't there be more to life and love than this?

Week Twelve

Week Twelve.
    It rose up in front of my eyes in ten foot high letters. I saw it in my dreams carved into an ominous black gate that clanged shut behind me. It chased me down windswept streets filled with happy couples and laughing families who turned away. This was the point of no return. Until now there had been a get-out clause, an opportunity to turn back the clock and take my old life back. From here on in there would be no going back. There would be no chance to change my mind and scream that this wasn't how I wanted it to be. There would be no love affair with the twenty-two-year-old musician. If you came back to me now, I'd always wonder if it was just because of the baby. A baby that maybe provided a quick way out of your marriage and into my arms. But then what would happen the next time you started wondering whether this was really the life for you?
    Sleep became a restless trip to a place from where I'd emerge barely rested and annoyed with the world and everyone in it. In the waning light of the early autumn evenings, I stood by the French doors to the garden and looked out at the great expanse of lawn I had saddled myself with. I smiled as I thought of my gardener who had taken to coming round a couple of times a week 'just to check on things' and have a cup of coffee and a chat. He'd known my grandparents. I think many years ago he'd been a little sweet on my grandmother. It was soothing to talk to an almost stranger, to pass on memories long forgotten, to bring old ghosts back to life.
    My parents called every day from Paris to see how I was doing and how work on the house was progressing. Half the time I found that I didn't really care and I blamed it on pregnancy hormones. But when Alexander knocked on the kitchen window each morning to wave to me before he climbed onto the roof, I always managed to smile. He'd invited me to dinner

in an effort to get me to eat a proper meal and I'd promised to try my best. I'd also given him a list of things which pregnant women were not supposed to eat.

He was so sweet. So kind. And so annoyingly handsome with his dark brown hair and piercing green eyes. But not for me. I was pregnant with another man's child. I had a new life to build. Neither did I want to be one of those women who get laughed at because they're crazy enough to believe that someone that much younger could ever have real feelings for them.

'When does the puppy arrive?'

I looked up in surprise. Alexander was standing in the kitchen doorway with his and Bjarne's empty coffee cups. He always brought them in and washed them up for me.

'He'll be ready to leave home next week.'

'Still certain it's what you want?'

'Right now I'm not certain of anything.' That was when the tears came. Rushed, unbidden, all those tears that had for weeks refused to come when I was ready.. They spilled out between my fingers like little salty diamonds. On and on, they kept coming and I didn't even bother to try and stop them. It was actually a relief to get them all out at last.

Poor Alexander was so startled I could almost feel his uncertainty. He hesitated in the doorway. Then I heard the clatter of coffee cups in the sink, a chair scrape against the floor as he sat down next to me. Without saying anything he put his arms around me and held me close. He smelled of sunshine and fresh air and just the vaguest hint of cologne. While he stroked my hair, I cried out every little frustration. If he hadn't been there I would have screamed. I was so tired of all this. What kind of life was I setting myself up for? How many years of my life had I already wasted on loving you?

I disentangled myself from Alexander, wiped my eyes and tried to smile at him. Up close, I could see the compassion in his eyes and behind them, like a little raw flame, the emotions he was trying to hide.

'I'm sorry,' I said.

'Don't be sorry,' he said and handed me a tissue from the box on the table. 'Are you all right?'

'No,' I said. 'No, I'm not all right. I'm tired and I'm confused and if you say pregnancy hormones I'll kill you.'

He laughed a little and stroked my hand. 'I wouldn't say that. Do you ... do you want to talk about it?'

'Why not?'

So I told him. I told him about you.

When I had finished, I sat looking at him in silence, waiting to see the feelings he had been hiding die in his eyes. But instead he smiled at me and made me tea and found me more tissues.

'You know,' he said to me as he handed me my tea, 'I've never beaten up a guy. But if he shows up, I might just make him the first.'

That evening I lit candles and sat on the sofa with my cashmere throw over my legs. My eyes were still red from crying and my head hurt. Alexander and Bjarne had gone home when it started to get dark. Alexander had given my shoulder a squeeze and asked if I needed anything. I'd shaken my head and sent him home. I owed him that. I owed him time to think about what I'd told him and to let him decide that he never wanted to see me again.

Once you and I had had a chance. Once, during those first magical days when I would find you on my mind during the oddest moments. When I couldn't stop mentioning you simply because I wanted to speak of you all the time. When something finally happened between us, that one amazing night in November, it was my fault that it did not last. I was the one who ran, I was the one who got scared.

You were my first lover. Before you, the men I'd cared for were either in books or far distant from me. I'd never had a boyfriend. Never held hands in the cinema or had someone brush snowflakes off my nose. I'd lived a passionate, romantic life inside my head but I'd never found anyone in the real world to match my dreams. But then there you were. The dream was real at last. It was too much. I wanted your touch, your presence, I was deliriously happy during those few precious weeks we had together. The world was suddenly filled with colour and each new dawn I seemed on the brink of a new adventure. I waltzed through my days with a smile on my face. And then I panicked. So what was more logical than to say goodbye to the person who was bringing such joy to my life?

I'd known instantly it was a mistake. But when I tried to take it back you kept me at a distance. Unwilling to trust me. You didn't want a relationship. Maybe you didn't want to get involved. Or maybe all I meant to you then was quick romp in the sack. Maybe that was all I meant to you now. You told me when I was eighteen that you were afraid of commitment and absolutely nothing had changed since. I was tired of making excuses for you, tired of trying to build a house with no bricks and shifting sand for foundations.

A baby. I was having a baby. Tomorrow I was due to have a scan. Or else tell the nurse that I'd changed my mind and wanted an abortion.

Abortion.

The word seemed very big in my mouth when I tried to say it.

This would be my last chance to choose a future with no lifetime commitment in it.

Week twelve. The legal limit in Denmark. Unless I took a trip to Sweden where I'd be offered a few more weeks leeway.

Either way, you would never know.

I left home early the next day so I didn't have to see anyone. I parked outside the hospital while it was still dark and sat in the empty cafeteria cradling a watery cup of hot chocolate in my hands and fighting the nausea. I wondered who else was awake here at this hour. Doctors, nurses. New mothers who hadn't already been sent home. People in pain. People who were bored. People who were waiting. Waiting to get better. Waiting to die.

The sky was getting light. My appointment was still hours away. I walked through the empty corridors and went outside to get some fresh air. I leaned against my car and yawned. Suddenly I was so tired.

I was never going to have you. If I had this baby I was never going to have anyone else. Who wants a single mother? Who wants to be burdened with raising a child not their own? I never had. The one thing I could never imagine myself being was a stepmother. Maybe that made me a bad person. Maybe you're not supposed to admit it, but I could never envisage myself loving a child not my own. Had I been unable to have children, I would never even have considered IVF or adoption. I'd had no burning need to have children, no passionate desire to be a mother above all else.

I was building a new life for myself. There would be two businesses and a puppy to consider. My house would be filled with people. What about education? Were there good schools on the island? You were never going to want me anyway so what was the use of any of it?

The hospital was slowly waking up. I walked back inside and went in search of the right room. I would find a chair and just sit and wait.

Week twelve.

Last chance.

Suddenly everything seemed so terrifyingly real.

After I left the hospital I drove into town and found a café where I ordered a large latté and a cinnamon pastry. I sat in the darkest corner and breathed deeply. As I waited for them to bring me my order, I wrapped my arms around myself. I still felt sick and slightly shell-shocked. It was done now. There was no going back. My decision was made and, come hell or high water, I was going to stick to it.

I was going to be a mother.

A single mother.

A single mother with a dog the size of a donkey, a lawn the size of a park and a large bill for a new roof. Plus a twenty-two-year-old builder-slash-musician who held me while I cried, carried my furniture, remodelled my kitchen and found me food that I was able to eat.

It wasn't going to be easy at all. None of it was. But there was excitement in the fear. Not panic. Somehow it all seemed more real now. Real in a way that my slightly protruding stomach and all those mornings with my head in the toilet had never managed to make it seem. I wanted to go home and start stripping the utterly hideous wallpaper from the games room and sort out the bathroom tiles. I only had six months to go. Six months to get everything ready.

When I finished my coffee I walked through town. I went into a shop that had a colourful display of baby clothes in the window and although I didn't want to buy anything I enjoyed looking. Little baby shoes. Little cardigans, little dresses. Cloth rattles in bright colours. Soft teddies. Bedtime stories. It was all going to be mine. Mine and my baby's and my dog's.

I would be saying goodbye to a lot of things. But a whole new world was going to open up. Dreams would be so vastly different, but there would still be dreams.

On the way home I stopped at the biggest supermarket I could find and bought real food for what seemed like the first time in ages. While I was wandering up and down the aisles, I remembered how my grandmother used to make the most delicious chocolate cake for me to take to school on my birthday. I was going to make that cake for my child. I'd become one of those hideously annoying mothers who spent more time photographing their food than they did eating it, whose purpose in life seemed to be to make normal people look inadequate because they couldn't master the delicate art of making superheroes out of fondant icing.

That night I dreamed of my baby.

We were sitting in a car by the beach, looking out across the water and the Langeland Bridge. He was probably about four years old by then, a beautiful little boy with your dark blonde hair and my black eyes. It was an uncompromising winter's day, water the colour of slate and skies like lead. Music was playing, one of the songs that Alexander had played for me in his studio. I was gazing out of the window, my mind a million miles away, only half listening to someone singing about droplets in the ocean.

'Mummy,' my son said and I turned to look at him. His little face was so serious and I could almost see the thoughts churning away inside him. 'Why are there chocolates in the ocean?'

'Why are there ...?' Then I realised what he meant and I laughed. I laughed and I laughed until I nearly cried. He laughed too. A wonderful, happy, gurgling little boy's laugh that filled the car and all the world around us. The sun came out to play on the waves and I imagined those chocolates spilling from my fingers and jumping out to dance in the ocean. Bouncing up and down, tossed on the waves like sweet, salty beach balls.

Chocolates in the ocean. What a beautiful dream.

Week Thirteen

When I woke up and realised that the nausea had gone I danced around the bedroom. Then I ran to the kitchen and rummaged frantically for chocolate. No exotic cravings for me. Nothing more than plain, ordinary, old-fashioned chocolate. But God how I wanted it. I had not craved anything as desperately since the last time I saw you. But at that moment you seemed like a distant memory. For once, a happy one. Someone I did not regret. Someone I had loved. Someone who, deep down, I always would love. But everyone has their limits. There are only so many times you can bang your head against a brick wall before you start bleeding. My time had come. I found myself at peace with my situation. Maybe not joyfully ecstatic at how things had turned out, but with a deep sense of contentment that I knew would outlast your fleeting moments of passion.

Bjarne promised me that the roof would be finished this week. Alexander was slowly moving indoors and beginning to map out the bathrooms with the help of Henrik, the latest arrival at my door. In the garden the apple trees were starting to bear fruit and I was experimenting with pies.

I'd taken my box of old letters out from under my bed and relegated it to the storage space in the converted cellar. It was a handy little room, perfect for storing all the things I planned to buy in bulk across the German border. Wine. Soda. Sweets. Coffee. I found myself singing as I tucked it away.

The memories would keep coming back to haunt me. I'd never be able to just let you go. But since that day at the hospital I'd gone over it a million times. It wouldn't matter how many times you came to see me, how close we got, we'd never get there. You would never be able to commit to me. You could say you loved me, you could even mean it, but you would never love me enough. Maybe whatever dream you dreamed was too much for me to live up to. Of all the things that can crush us, nothing hurts more than knowing that we are not wanted by the one we love. That we are not special enough. That we're only there until somebody better comes along. Or for just as long as the orgasm lasts and until they next get an itch they can't scratch on their own.

Too many wasted years. I knew now that was why I had run. Because I would never be able to move on as long as there was chance that I might run into you. A chance that I might open the door one night and you'd be the one outside. I had had to go. It would have hurt too much to stay. One day I'd be able to go back. One day when it was all dead and buried and I could look at you and feel nothing. Then I could go back. Then I could live the life I had loved in the city I adored without secretly hoping to see you around each corner.

I remembered a beautiful summer's evening when we drove out to the country and made love in a field. That was another time we might have made it work. You asked me, when we said goodbye, if I minded us meeting like this. Sex and nothing more. What could I do? I said what I thought you wanted to hear. I lied. I said it didn't bother me. That summer you kept coming back to see me. Unannounced always, you showed up in the evening and were always gone by morning with no word between visits.

Between those visits I met someone else. Someone who made plans to see me, someone who let me into his life. Once you knew I was seeing him you were full of promises. Promises of things that never materialised. You came, you said you loved me, but you were still gone in the morning and you didn't come back. So I stayed with the other man, even though my heart never fully let you go. Of course it didn't last. And by winter you and I started everything over again. Why did we never learn?

Well no more! This time enough was enough. This time it was about someone other than you and me. If there was going to be a man in the lives of me and my baby it sure as hell wasn't going to be one who showed up with no warning and made us seem like a family for a few hours, only to be gone by morning. You'd probably use the baby as an excuse for being 'cautious' and 'not committing.' Damn you, I didn't want to hear it.

I didn't hate you. To hate you I would have to feel. I wasn't sure I'd ever feel anything for you again. My heart wasn't broken, it was frozen. Now the anger was gone, it was easy to be content and at peace without you. When I found myself thinking of you, when I caught myself remembering any of the nights we'd spent together, I'd breathe deeply and count to ten until the feelings went away. It was an effective technique because nausea had been replaced by heartburn and focusing on breathing got rid of that, too.

Alexander, Bjarne, Henrik and Jacobsen the gardener were standing on the terrace admiring the results of Jacobsen's first few weeks on the job. I stuck my head round the door and asked for someone to help me carry the coffee mugs and cake. I wasn't surprised when Alexander was the one who volunteered.

'Thanks,' I said.
'I'm here when you need me.'
I smiled at him.
We carried coffee and cake outside and put it on the table. The others had moved into the garden and were now inspecting the roof. Bjarne was talking about tiles. Jacobsen was asking about the pigeons he had chased away. I smiled at this little community I had created.

'I'm picking up my puppy this weekend,' I told Alexander. 'Would you like to come with me? To be honest I could use someone to drive us back so that I can sit with him.'

He nodded and smiled. 'I'd like that very much. Does he have a name yet?'

'Yes. I'm going to call him Thorin.'
'Thorin? As in *The Hobbit*?'
'Yes. I finished that book just before my thirteenth birthday when I was full of romantic ideals and sensibilities.' I winked at him. 'I had a little crush on Thorin. The only reason I ever read *The Lord of the Rings* was because I had a fervent

hope that *The Return of the King* meant that Thorin would somehow rise from the dead and come back into the story.'

'So you had a crush on a fictional dwarf king?' There was a teasing expression in his eyes.

'I did,' I laughed, 'and a lot of other fictional characters besides. My girl friends liked singers and movie stars, I liked people in books.'

'Unique. And probably much more interesting. So Thorin it is. It should suit him. They're a very regal looking breed.'

'Don't go too far on the regal. I'm also a republican.'

He laughed and picked up a slice of cake. In return for cakes and coffee, Alexander was supplying me with chocolate. I was making sure I walked five times around the garden each morning and afternoon just to attempt to keep in shape. But along with heartburn came sciatica and every so often I had shooting pains down my leg. A puppy in need of moderate exercise and a space beside me on the sofa was exactly what I needed.

Two days later Alexander and I drove to the kennels. He was going to drive back and I was going to hold Thorin.

'It's almost perfect timing,' I said. 'One week more and he could have been my birthday present to myself.'

'It's your birthday?'

'Thursday.'

'I know you shouldn't ask a lady, but how old will you be?'

'Thirty-two,' I told him and nodded to myself, as though I were tasting the word. 'Thirty-two.'

He smiled at me. Fortunately he didn't mention his own age. Those crazy days of long nights dancing till dawn and never caring what tomorrow might bring had long since passed me by. Not that it seemed like he was doing any of those things.

'Are you doing anything for your birthday? Any friends coming to visit you?'

'No. It will just be a quiet day. Maybe I'll treat myself to some more chocolate.'

'Make it the special kind. It is your birthday after all.'

When we arrived at the kennels the autumn sun was dazzling and the golden leaves were piling up under the trees. Alexander had been telling me all about the music business and how incredibly difficult it was to break into. I learned that his passion had begun when he was eight years old and his mother had inherited a piano.

'The first time I sat down and touched the keys, I just knew that it was what I wanted to do. Then it was lessons once a week after school, then twice a week and then I discovered the guitar when I was about twelve. One day I am going to make it. And they say when your work is something you deeply love, you'll never work again.'

'You really are talented,' I told him. 'I wish there was something I could do to help you.'

'Thank you.' He looked at me and smiled. 'If I think of anything, I will let you know.'

'You do that,' I said as I undid my seatbelt and opened the door.

'Hello!' Sisse called as we got out. She was holding Thorin in her arms and by her side was his mother, their prize-winning bitch Now You See Me. I had never understood why show dogs had to have such bizarre names. Sisse had told me that her 'real' around-the-house name was Bubbles. On the other hand, Now You See Me was rather an imaginative name for a dog that looked like it could have you on your back in two seconds flat.

Thorin wagged his tail as we approached. Sisse handed him to me and he licked my face and wagged his tail again. Then he swatted a great big puppy paw at Alexander.

'We've been calling him Thorin for the past week so he's getting used to the name,' Sisse told me. Then she launched into details of his diet and exercise requirements. I took notes while Alexander went to play with the other dogs. I put Thorin down and he and Bubbles followed Alexander.

We stayed for just under an hour. When we left I carried in my arms a puppy and the first idea of what my new life would be like. House-training was a work in progress. But I knew, as surely as I'd ever known anything, that part of what I had always wanted had just clicked into place. I had a dog. I couldn't have been happier.

'Do you mind if I stay for a while when we get back?' Alexander asked me.

'Not at all. I could do with some help to get him settled. Besides, he'll be seeing a lot of you.'

'Do we take him running in the woods every day?'

'Nope. You have to respect his joints and his incredible growth. Moderate exercise is what they need. Which is good because with the baby coming, I wouldn't be able to run around in the woods all the time.'

'You know ...' He stopped. 'Never mind.'

'No, tell me.'

'That's the first time you've mentioned your baby being here.'

'I guess it is. It feels more real now. The scan showed a real person. Tiny of course, but real.'

I strapped Thorin in the back and got in and sat next to him. He climbed onto my lap and looked out the window. Alexander put the car in reverse.

'You're sure you're all right with me driving your car?'

'Quite sure,' I laughed. 'Just don't crash into anything.'

Alexander and I spent the rest of the day introducing Thorin to his new home. We showed him his basket and he climbed onto the sofa.

'If you let him do that,' Alexander said, 'you'll have to get a bigger one when he's fully grown.'

Jacobsen had been through the garden and had mended the few holes he'd found in the fence so there was no chance of Thorin running out onto the road. He ran excitedly through the grass, learning all the new smells and clearly marking his new territory. I'd been saving the local newspapers in preparation for house-training and they were now lined up in front of the garden door.

'My grandmother's dogs never did anything in the garden, we always had to take them for a walk.'

'That would be good. You don't want to run around picking up after him all day. Especially if your guests want to lie on the lawn.'

'Yes. Outdoor yoga would lose its appeal if you stepped in something.'

He laughed. 'Is that what you'll be offering?'

'Not sure yet. It depends what Langeland has to offer.'

'I could teach music.'

Now it was my turn to laugh. 'Yes, because what a woman needs when she's getting over heartbreak is to spend hours alone at a piano with a hot young guy like you.'

'It could work,' his eyes grew serious. 'I could be just the one you need.'

I looked at him and smiled. He really did look like he cared. I couldn't remember when I'd last had a man look at me that way. Despite the baby and the sciatica and the weight gain I suddenly felt desired.

'No,' I said. I continued before he could interrupt. 'It would like a bad romantic film. You'd say you loved me and would be there for me and the baby but just when you made me believe it you'd realise what it meant and you'd take it all back. Oh you'd cry and be sorry and say you still loved me, didn't want to hurt me and couldn't bear to lose me, but you still couldn't really be with me. So you'd relegate me to some hellish limbo where I couldn't use the word "girlfriend" or "relationship" because that would imply that we had a future. And I'd stay because I loved you and I remembered the way you used to make me feel, but deep down inside I'd just feel second-rate and worthless because I wasn't good enough for you anymore. So I'd end up hating you and never wanting to see you again.' I squeezed his hand and I laughed. 'Right now I like you too much for that. Besides, I can already play the piano.'

He looked at me like he didn't know what to say and I knew my pathetic attempt at humour had failed. Then he shook his head and said, 'He really hurt you, didn't he?'

I knew the tears were coming so I dug my nails into my hand and shrugged. 'In my experience, men make promises and spin dreams and then they take them back. Nothing but broken hearts and broken promises. It's just not worth it.'

'Maybe you're just scared. And you're hiding yourself away down here so you don't have to go out and risk getting hurt again. Not all men are bastards.'

I nodded and gave a wry smile. 'Scared? One of my friends was with a guy for two years and then got dumped because she was taking too much time from his online chat with his friends. Another had a boyfriend who wanted her to get breast implants so she'd look more like all those post-op transsexuals he masturbated to on the Internet. And the list goes on. So maybe I am scared. But if you ask me there's a lot to be scared of out there.'

'I'm not like them.'

'Oh sweetie,' I stroked his arm and smiled at him for a moment, 'that's what they all say in the beginning. Besides, when did it become so wrong just to be on your own?'

'I guess that does have its advantages. You can't flirt with your employer if you have a girlfriend.'

I laughed and nodded, relieved that we could move away from awkward personal conversations that could never lead to anything good. We watched Thorin roam around the garden for a little while longer before Alexander started talking about going home. After he had gone, Thorin and I curled up on the sofa and fell asleep.

Week Fourteen

The afternoon before my birthday I took Thorin for a walk down to the beach. He'd been running around the house for less than a week and it already seemed as though he'd been part of my life forever. He slept curled up in a ball at the foot of my bed and in the evenings he lay next to me on the sofa with his head in my lap. I worried about his diet and his exercise routine and tried to faithfully remember everything that Sisse and Lars had told me. I kept notices of his upcoming vet's appointments on the fridge and tried to be a good new dog mother while at the same time making it very clear who was boss. With a dog who would one day be heavier than me it seemed as though that was something we needed to establish as soon as possible.

  It was getting dark earlier now and daylight seemed to move quickly into dusk. The nights were getting colder and when I got up early I had candles burning in the kitchen. I'd taken all the winter clothes out of their boxes and put them in the cupboard. Dresses and shorts had been packed away. Jacobsen helped me cover up the garden furniture. Bjarne had said goodbye after finishing the roof and Henrik and Alexander worked on the bathroom in the basement. I could have been wrong, but it seemed to me that these days Henrik was the one who brought the coffee cups upstairs while Alexander hardly emerged. Alone in the dark evenings I had relived our last conversation in the garden in the hope that it would gradually seem less awkward, but it seemed now as though it had created a barrier between us.

  I skimmed stones across the water while Thorin explored the shore and jumped back each time a wave hit his nose. In my mind I was trying to formulate how I would tell all my friends about my pregnancy. Now that the danger period was over there were lots of people I wanted to call. But there were only a few of them who I knew would understand. In the meantime I was careful not to mention anything to the few mutual friends we had. The last thing I wanted was for someone to mention it to your wife and for her to put two and two together. I wasn't going to show up and ruin your marriage. If that was going to crash and burn it wasn't going to have anything to do with me.

I picked up a large stone and weighed it in my hand. Then I flung my arm back and threw it as hard as I could into the sea. I watched it arch through the air to land pitifully close to the shore.

'You throw like a girl,' I heard Alexander's voice say.

I turned around and smiled at him. 'I know.'

'Look,' he said, coming up to stand next to me, 'I'm sorry if I offended you. It's none of my business. And I shouldn't go making assumptions about your life and accuse you of hiding away.'

'No,' I said, 'you didn't offend me. You were at least partially right. In a way I am hiding. But I'm also learning a lot about what I want from life and I don't think it's what everyone expects me to want. I know leaving the city to come here is strange, but right now it feels right for me. And as far as relationships go …' I shrugged. 'I don't want to live with someone for thirty-five years just to have them come home one day and have them tell me I'm so boring they can't stand the sight of me anymore, like Jacobsen says his wife did. I don't want to have to compromise all my dreams and desires to support someone else, just to have them go off and start a new life when I'm too old to start over. Passion doesn't last. Love doesn't last. It gets replaced by convenience, familiarity. I like my independence. No one ever wanted to take an interest in the things that I liked, but they all expected me to bend over backwards to learn all about their hobbies and passions. No one ever showed up at my door with champagne and strawberries or surprised me at work for no reason. No one ever brought me soup when I wasn't well. All anyone ever did was make a whole bunch of promises just to take them back. So frankly, I could quite happily live the rest of my life and never have another man in it. It's just not worth it.'

'No one ever brought you flowers?'

'No. No, actually someone did once. But then I found out it was just guilt because he was cheating on me. So that doesn't count. All those things we dream of when we're girls, all those things we're lead to believe that love involves … it's all just a lie.' I threw another stone into the sea and heard it fall into the water with a big plop.

'You're very cynical.'

'I know. And yet my parents are so happy in their marriage. So I know it can work. I just don't think I can work for me.'

'Don't you believe you deserve to be loved?'

He looked at me with so much compassion in his eyes, so unaware that with that one question he'd blown up all those walls I'd so carefully built around myself after every rejection, after every broken promise you made. Straight down to the core of the matter, the point to where all the years with you had lead me.

'No,' I shook my head and this time managed to hold back the tears. 'No, I don't. That's what I've learned from the men I've known. I'm not worth it. I'm not what they want. I don't need another lesson.'

The next morning I was awakened at six by a knock on my door. I rubbed my eyes and sat up, surprised to find that Thorin had migrated from the foot of the bed during the night and was now curled up next to me, one big paw resting on my pillow. It was still dark outside and for a moment I wasn't sure whether I was still dreaming. The knocking continued and grew steadily louder and more persistent.

'All right!' I called. 'I'm coming!'

I got up quickly and put on my dressing gown. Thorin jumped off the bed and ran into the hallway, barked at the door and wagged his tail. Grumbling about who on earth it could be at this ungodly hour, I unlocked the door and opened it a tiny crack, ready to slam it shut if the early morning intruders turned out to be Jehovah's Witnesses or timeshare salesmen. But it was neither of those and I slowly opened the door.

There, in the cold dark of the October morning, was Alexander. In a basket next to him were what looked like two dozen red roses, champagne, breakfast rolls and pastries, a small, gift-wrapped box and a rawhide bone for Thorin. I couldn't get a word out. I stood at the door, just looking at him. He didn't move, he just stood there staring back at me. Then I smiled and he moved. He moved so quickly towards me that before I knew it my arms went around him while he framed my face in his hands and kissed me as though it was all he had wanted these past months.

Thorin barked and tugged at the rawhide bone and we broke apart. We smiled at each other and he picked up the basket and handed it to me. 'Happy birthday.'

'Thank you.' I smiled and stepped away from the door. 'Come in.'

I quickly made myself a little more presentable while Alexander took everything out of the basket, made coffee and laid the table. I found three vases for the flowers and spread them throughout the house.

'Thank you for the champagne,' I said, 'but I'm not drinking.'

'I know,' he smiled, 'that's why I got the funny non-alcoholic kind they make for children. And it's strawberry-flavoured so I've killed two birds with one stone.'

I laughed and found some appropriate glasses. When I sat down he kissed me again. Thorin lay under the table and wagged his tail. Alexander picked up the little box and gave it to me. 'I didn't have much time to shop but I hope you like it.'

Inside was a silver locket hanging from a long chain.

'I thought maybe, when the baby is born, you would like to keep a picture of him or her close to you.'

'It's beautiful,' I said. 'Thank you.'

We sat smiling at each other as we ate breakfast, then he went downstairs to continue working on the bathroom while I showered and got dressed. Henrik didn't bring the coffee cups upstairs that day.

That evening we sat on the sofa together and talked while the candles flickered in the windows and the stars came out. It wasn't until I'd kissed him goodbye and watched him drive away that I noticed I'd received a text from you.

Happy Birthday x

Funny, I thought, apart from the one year when you gave me those wine glasses, you'd never remembered my birthday.

Week Fifteen

Ever since my birthday I'd awoken to a world where the colours seemed that much brighter. I got up feeling full of energy and I managed to eat a proper, healthy breakfast before I took Thorin for his morning amble around the garden. Alexander and Henrik usually arrived around eight and while Henrik hurried downstairs Alexander lingered in the kitchen for five minutes and gave me a quick kiss before joining him. We'd spent Saturday driving around the island and had found a beach where we threw sticks for Thorin. Sunday afternoon had been spent baking buns in the kitchen while Alexander perched on the table with his guitar and played me his latest composition. Evenings were spent curled up together on the sofa, talking, touching and kissing.

This morning I had an appointment for another scan. It was time for me to know what I was expecting.

'You're really going to find out?' he asked me.

'Yes, I want to know. I think it's a girl but what if I buy pink and it turns out to be a boy? I just ... I like to know what's coming. I like plans. And to be honest, I really want a boy. If it turns out to be a girl, I will need a little time to adjust and get excited about all the things having a girl will involve.'

'Call me as soon as you know.' We kissed goodbye behind one of the hedges like breathless teenagers before I drove off, leaving him and Henrik to work on the bathroom.

Three hours later I was wandering through the children's section of the Magasin department store, looking at tiny blue onesies, blue booties and funny green hats with pointy ears. It was a boy. I really was having a boy. I'd have a son. Just like I dreamed. I wanted to laugh out loud, run through the aisles singing with joy and grab every blue thing within sight. But part of me was afraid to jinx things by buying clothes too soon, so instead I bought an enormous blue teddy bear, soft and snuggly and perfect for him to cuddle up to once he was older. Then I stopped off at one of my favourite delicatessens and stocked up. Whether it was because of Alexander's attempts at getting me to eat properly or the pregnancy really beginning to show I was having trouble fitting into most of my trousers. In a quaint little boutique in a quiet side street I found three pairs of fairly smart maternity trousers. Looking in a mirror, I also found a reminder that all the things that you're usually tempted to buy when you have a new relationship, like lingerie and slinky back dresses, don't have the same effect when you're four months pregnant.

My pregnancy was something Alexander and I had not discussed. I knew he cared enough to be interested, he had proved that during all those weeks of trying to get me to eat properly and making sure I had enough decaf coffee. But whether he was planning to stick around and see it through or whether he would run away as soon as the bathrooms were finished I didn't know. Not that I could imagine anyone finding me even remotely attractive in my current state. But for the moment, in those first few exciting days when I remembered how it was to see the world like new again, I tried very hard to banish every negative thought and fearful emotion. It was new and special and I was going to let myself enjoy it.

I'd thought long and hard about whether to respond to your text. Eventually I'd decided to just send something quick and easy.

Thanks x

What I'd thought about most was whether to add the kiss at the end. But I remembered all those times when we'd ended up like this. When I'd found someone else and vowed to give up on you and your emotional roller-coaster. Then, when it hadn't worked out, there was so much back pedalling involved. I was carrying your baby. Your son. One day I'd have to talk to you. Alexander and I had barely been together a week. There was time enough to think all these serious thoughts. For now, I just wanted to be happy. And if leaving open a small door in the wall so that I could get back to you turned out to be wrong, Alexander would never know.

The first time we love we do so without fear, without thought. We simply allow ourselves to be swept away and we believe, because there is no evidence to the contrary, that the world will right itself in our favour and everything will work out. We believe in together forever, in beautiful sunsets. We worship a photograph. We smile at the lyrics of songs. To love that way again seems impossible. Because with every broken heart, every disappointment, comes caution and fear and the inability to give all of ourselves in the burning heat of the moment.

But during those first few days with Alexander I allowed myself to be swept away. Despite everything I had said on the beach, I allowed myself to feel. I didn't think about whether it would last or not, I didn't worry about heartbreak. I woke up every morning with a smile and I waltzed through my days singing show tunes. When he came back in the evenings and we talked and kissed the hours away, I felt alive in a way I hadn't for years. I could have sworn I was sixteen again, before the world became complicated, when there was always a new bend in the road and a chance to go back and start over.

On our way back from our walk in the park, Thorin and I stopped at the bakery and bought pastries for afternoon coffee. Henrik had told me how his wife complained that I spoiled him and that he'd better not expect that kind of treatment at home. But I remembered renovating my apartments in the city. Coffee breaks were the best part of the day, a welcome little treat amongst the grout and the Phillips screwdrivers. I had learned a long time ago that builders who were welcomed and valued worked both harder and better. So I baked cakes and asked their advice, picking up lots of useful tips that helped make the next job easier.

'My daughter wants to move back here again,' Henrik told me. 'She's a yoga instructor. Think you could use someone like that?'

'I'd hope so.' I fished out an old business card. 'Here, give her that and tell her to get in touch.'

'Thanks. Lovely pastries today.'

'I've never learned to make those myself,' I admitted, 'so those I'll always have to buy.'

'Good,' he laughed, 'keep the bakery in business. But keep up those bread experiments you've been feeding us with at lunchtime.'

'I'm glad you like them.'

'Very much.'

'Tomorrow will be oregano and sea salt. I'm getting the first part ready now.'

'Sounds fancy.'

I'd never mastered the art of baking bread before but now I was determined to succeed. There was something soothing about kneading dough. In all honesty, the part of my new career that I was looking forward to most was the cooking. Now I would have reasons to try new dishes, to bake three cakes a week. The only thing I sometimes hated about living alone was that cooking seemed so futile. So much effort for something you would eat in under ten minutes while reading a book or watching television. When you cook for people there's a sense of community, of belonging. Cooking is one of the reasons I love Christmas. Biscuits, confectionery, mulled wine – so many things for people to enjoy together.

I turned on some music and went back to my dough. Thorin's basket had been moved into the kitchen. He curled up happily and seemed to get bigger by the minute. When Alexander and Henrik came upstairs later to say goodbye for the day, they found us both curled up asleep on the sofa.

Alexander and I went for a walk in the woods that weekend and watched the leaves change. Autumn has always been my favourite time of year. No summer evening, no summer sun dancing on the Mediterranean waves can compare to the intoxicating scent of an autumn afternoon. When the leaves start to change colour and slowly detach themselves from the branches and fall to the ground, it catches my heart every time. The morning air smells so fresh and the light softens in the hazy mist. It's a time for candles, for throws and scarves, for picking blackberries in the hedgerows and apples in the garden. It is time to sip hot chocolate with whipped cream, time to start thinking about Christmas and snow and carols and treats we will only eat for two months of the year. I get excited about autumn the way other people do when they plan their summer holidays. When autumn comes I relax. I breathe deeply and look forward to each new day. I love the dark mornings where I drink tea by candlelight and get to watch the sun rise. I walk through the parks and breathe in the scent of decaying leaves. I watch ice form on the water in the harbour. I am at peace with myself and the world in the autumn. In the darkness of the dying year, I gather strength and await new beginnings.

Week Sixteen

The first days of November arrived with a cold, clammy rain that chilled Thorin and I to the bone as we ventured out on our morning strolls around town. Alexander and Henrik had moved on to the upstairs bathroom while I looked longingly at the beautiful tub in the basement, always reminding myself that you had to be cautious around things like that while pregnant. So instead I wrapped my hands around endless warm drinks in an attempt to ward off the cold. Most of my time was spent in the basement, finally stripping the ghastly wallpaper from the walls of the games room while Thorin divided his time amongst the three of us.

In my bedroom I tried to sort my clothes out, wondering if I'd ever be able to fit into any of them again. In my experience gaining weight was a lot easier than losing it. I seemed doomed to an endless battle between what I wanted to eat and what I had to do to stay in shape if I chose to eat it. I envied women who could eat anything they wanted and never put on weight. At least I knew, from the one brief encounter I'd had with her, that your wife wasn't one of those.

In truth I'd hardly thought of you since my birthday. Alexander had wiped you from my mind. For the first time in my life I was with someone new and I was happy. It wasn't painful or difficult or complicated. God, it should have been, but it wasn't. Life owed me this one time, I thought. I deserved to know again what it was supposed to be like when you started a relationship that was filled with promise. He made me laugh. He made me smile. When he held me close in his arms I felt cherished, desired and as though there would never be anyone else for him but me. I didn't feel wrong or out of place. I felt like me and it felt good.

But occasionally, when heartburn and my increasing bulk reminded me that part of you would always be with me, I found myself wondering if the last thirteen years had been nothing but a safety net. A convenient, romantic dream that I clung to because that way I never had to be alone. At the back of my mind, you would always be there. There would always be another chance for us, another message, another meeting. There had never been any reason to be upset over someone else because you had always been there to distract me. You were my haven and I had run to you every time. Now I was having your baby. Part of you would be tied to me forever. I'd always have a reason to call you. Knowing that felt good.

With Alexander, as with others before him, I was able to forget about you in the heat of the moment but I knew you'd turn up again. You always did. But as with all the other relationships, I found myself hoping, just for a moment, that this time you'd be out of my mind for good.

Confused, I shut my mind to you and the idea of telling you about the baby, and simply allowed myself the luxury of not thinking. My mother always said my mind would be the death of me. She said someone who thought about things as much as I did could never be happy.

One thing I had learned over the years was that there was no point in struggling against fate. Or life. Or whatever you chose to call it. The more you fight against it, the harder it all becomes. It is easier sometimes to just let go and hope for it all to work out. The strange thing is that the moment I let go is usually the moment that the world rights itself.

I had decided to start on the upstairs next because I wanted to wait as long as possible before I let the men invade my space and chase me out of my living room. The hallway was going to be the most difficult task and I wasn't supposed to breathe paint fumes. So the next crew to arrive would be two painters. Half the enjoyment of renovating the house was being lost to me, so instead I immersed myself in colour samples and the IKEA catalogue. My noticeboard was starting to struggle under the weight and I was forcing myself to sort through my notes, organise all my inspirational photos and establish some kind of order before it simply fell down bringing the wall with it.

Once the bedrooms were complete and ready to be furnished, Alexander and I would be going shopping.

I had ordered the towels online at a clearance sale and each guest would also receive their own dressing gown. In each bedroom there would be books and magazines with a larger selection in one of the rooms downstairs. Fresh flowers on arrival of course, and in each room a beautiful glass bowl filled with Lego. Alexander had laughed at that, but after Emma and Lisbeth went home I'd found a couple of Emma's bricks under the bed while I was cleaning the room. I'd ended up standing in front of the window absentmindedly fitting them together, and before I knew it fifteen minutes had passed and I'd built a sculpture. I'd found it soothing and it had focused my mind on something other than morning sickness.

There would also be scented candles and soft lighting. I wanted to give life to the dream that Lisbeth had given me - create somewhere to run to. A couple I went to university with had started their own web design business a few years ago. She was the photographer, he was the graphic designer and code wiz who put it all together. I'd invited them to stay for a long weekend. Back in Copenhagen they had a one-bedroom apartment where the living room served as a hub for the business. The promise of a weekend amongst old buildings had persuaded her. The chance to take a puppy for walks had decided him.

Alexander refused his cake that afternoon. 'No thanks,' he said with a smile. 'I must cut back. Otherwise you'll end up with a fat boyfriend.'

I looked at him for a moment with my eyebrows raised. 'Boyfriend?'

'Well,' he smiled again, 'I think so.'

Struggling to suppress a ridiculous school-girl giggle, I smiled again and nodded. 'I'd like to think so, too.'

He drew me towards him and kissed me. At that moment Henrik came in.

'I knew it!' he laughed. I found myself blushing. 'You two have been smiling so much lately there had to be a reason.'

'Hello!' a voice called from the hallway. 'Anyone at home?'

'Caroline!' I called and hurried out of the kitchen. Thorin barked and ran after me, then stood behind me while I hugged Caroline and her husband, Martin. 'Come into the kitchen.'

Henrik shook hands on his way out and said he'd be back on Monday. Alexander stayed in the kitchen and Thorin ran up to stand next to him. 'Hi,' he said.

'Caroline, Martin,' I said with a smile, 'this is Alexander. My boyfriend.'

Caroline stayed with me in the kitchen while Alexander showed Martin the work they'd been doing on the roof and in the bathrooms.

'He's gorgeous,' she said and gave my arm a squeeze. 'How did you manage to get your hands on him? And while being nearly four months pregnant.'

'Don't,' I laughed, 'I hardly know myself.'

'He's sweet and obviously crazy about you. How old is he?'

'Twenty-two.'

'Ooh, cougar! Good for you. It's about time it went the other way. So tell me all about the baby. I don't even have to try and guess who the father is, do I?'

We laid the table and I started chopping vegetables. Caroline poured three glasses of wine and I chose fizzy water with a hint of lemon. Since I'd got my appetite back I had spent a lot of time planning the menu. Feeding my chocolate craving, dessert would be three-layered meringue with chocolate sauce. I'd made it for you once for your birthday. We'd ended up rolling around passionately on the kitchen floor with chocolate all over us. Maybe making it in my new home, for my new boyfriend, would erase that memory.

Caroline and Martin were surprised that Alexander didn't stay the night, as Caroline made a point of telling me the next morning. I poured coffee for us both and wrapped my dressing gown around myself with a smile on my face and a dreamy look in my eyes.

'We haven't discussed the future or my pregnancy or what will happen when the baby comes,' I told her, 'but we have decided to take it slowly. The last thing I want is to jump into bed with someone who will leave me two weeks later. Especially since he'll still be here working on my house. He's sweet, he's kind, I don't want to rush things. Besides, it's not like I'm very attractive at the moment.'

'Don't be ridiculous. You look fantastic. I always thought all those stories about the "pregnancy glow" were made up. But look at you!'

I shook my head and smiled. In truth I did feel fantastic. Blooming, just like they tell you you'll feel. Confident, happy, ready to brave anything or anyone to give my baby boy the best life I could. But whether that somehow manifested itself as sexy I couldn't have said. But in Alexander's kisses I felt his passion. In his eyes I read his desire. But we were going to take it slowly and see what happened. I had others besides myself to think about now. As for Alexander, I didn't want him rushing into anything he would regret.

Over the next few days Caroline photographed the house from every angle while Martin and I played with Thorin. Once the sun came out she managed some fantastic autumnal shots of the garden. I took her all around Rudkøbing, pointing out the houses where my family had lived, the streets where I had roamed in the excitement of being a big girl who was allowed out on her own. She adored the picture-postcard side streets, the little courtyards where autumn leaves withered on the branches and the sight of the dark waves racing towards the shore.

'Wasn't that a lonely way to spend your summer holiday, here on your own with no friends?'

I shook my head. 'There were always other children to play with. Some of them lived in my house. I mean the house I'm living in now. I spent hours playing in that garden. If there was no one to play with or the weather was bad I would read. I lost myself in some great adventures. And the after-school club had the most fantastic playground. The only thing I regretted was that I wasn't strong enough to take my grandparents' dogs out on my own.'

'Martin wants a dog more than anything. We just don't have the room. I said we could get a cat but he laughed at me.'

'If you really want a dog, a cat is no substitute.'

'Dog person,' she laughed. 'But it's a lovely town and the house is fantastic. It would almost be worth splitting up just to come here and be pampered.'

'I don't think you need to go that far.'

'We need to keep walking if I'm going to burn off that delicious meringue thing in time for me to have some more tonight. How's your weight coming along?'

'Back on track. Feels so strange being allowed to gain weight after all those years of calorie counting. I lost weight in the beginning because I was so sick and couldn't eat anything at all. My doctor wasn't at all pleased with me. Now of course I have to try to just gain the right amount and not end up with too much.'

'Would be worth being pregnant just to be allowed to eat what you want for once in your life.'

'Forget that,' I told her. 'Half the things I want are on the forbidden list.'

Martin spent most of his time roaming around the garden with Thorin, enjoying having a dog so much that Caroline knew they'd have to move just to get him one. I watched the change in her with interest, wondering in a detached kind of way if it were the same change that had taken place in me. Hour by hour, I could see her relaxing more. I could see the stress disappearing from their relationship. I had often wondered how they managed to stay sane in their small space. I knew that Martin, who had grown up in a large house in the country, felt it more keenly than she did. By Sunday evening they were taking long walks in the woods together and on our way past the estate agent's on Monday morning, I saw her sneak the property listings into her handbag.

I took them for a drive around the island, stopping every so often to allow Caroline to take more photos. The weather was kind to us and permitted the sun to keep shining. She also took lots of photos of me and Thorin and promised to send me the best ones.

'You should have a record of what it was like being pregnant. Something more than selfies.'

'Thanks.'

The evening before they left Martin presented me with a series of sketches for my website. My job was just to come up with all the written content. Caroline promised to come back in a few months when more work had been done to the house itself. We dressed up the kitchen and the downstairs bathroom and managed some beautiful brochure photos. Rustic bread and fresh herbs, bubbles in the tub and candles in the windows. Seeing the photos on her camera, seeing the house through someone else's eyes, gave me a wonderful sense of accomplishment and made the whole project much more real. There was still so much to do, but what fun it was all turning out to be.

Week Seventeen

On Monday morning Alexander called to let me know that he was sick and wouldn't be coming into work that day.

'I don't want you to get sick too so I'll stay home till I'm better.'

'Do you need anything?'

'No, no, I'm okay. I went shopping yesterday so I'll be all right for a while. I'll miss you though.'

'I'll miss you too. Feel better. Call me if you need anything.'

Henrik arrived shortly afterwards to tell me Alexander was sick. 'But you probably already knew that,' he said and winked and me.

'Yes, I did.' I smiled at him. 'Coffee?'

'Please. I'll be upstairs. Grouting tiles this morning.'

After I'd taken Henrik his coffee and he'd told me more about plumbing than I'd ever wished to know, I looked again at the initial designs for the website that Martin had sketched and hung on the fridge. He hoped that by looking at them every day I'd quickly figure out which one I preferred. I'd also sent him the URLs of a few other websites that I liked the design of. I wanted something with lots of pictures, I wanted people to be able to imagine what a beautiful haven the house would be.

'We'll make it beautifully simple and very user-friendly,' Martin had told me. 'If someone's going to come and stay here it's going to be an impulsive decision, this isn't the type of holiday you spend a year planning. You want the process of falling in love to move as quickly as possible to entering credit card details. This place is an escape. Escapes are impulsive.'

According to my pregnancy bible, I was currently in the honeymoon stage of pregnancy when morning sickness was over and all the other ailments had not yet kicked in. My doctor was happy with me, everything was going perfectly. Deep within myself I felt strong, convinced in the knowledge that everything would be all right and that in five months time I would have a healthy son. Even so, sometimes I worried that I would jinx things by being too happy. It was too soon to start buying prams and beds and changing tables. I couldn't bear the thought of something going wrong and having to come home to an empty house filled with things for a baby that would never arrive. The only thing I had was the teddy bear I had bought after my scan. On the one hand five months seemed like all the time in the world, and on the other it seemed terrifyingly short. Only five months until my life changed in ways I could not even begin to imagine. Five months. Five short months.

    My days had taken shape now. I took Thorin for a short walk every morning and then sat at my desk while Henrik and Alexander worked their way through the bathrooms. We had lunch together in the kitchen, which gave me the chance to experiment with more new dishes. Every two or three days I baked a new cake after lunch and then went back my work. I had afternoon coffee and cake with Alexander and Henrik in whichever room they were working and shortly afterwards took Thorin for his afternoon walk. It was normally dark when we came home and sometimes Henrik had already left for the day. I usually lit candles and sat in the kitchen, Thorin lying at my feet. I spent almost every evening with Alexander, either at my home or his. When I went to see him he cooked pasta and played his guitar for me. We curled up on the sofa and often fell asleep there together. Wrapped up tightly in his arms while the autumn rain pattered against the windows, the world seemed like a warm and safe place.

By Wednesday Alexander still wasn't better so I made him chicken soup and garlic bread and took it to his house. His eyes were puffy and his nose red when he opened the door. He looked awful.

    'Oh no,' he said. 'I don't want you to get sick.'

    'You're probably not contagious anymore. And you need food, so I'll risk it.'

'Thank you.' He gave me a hug and led me inside, taking the soup and the bread.

I heated them up in the kitchen while he went back to the sofa and shivered under the covers. 'I feel awful,' he said. 'I'm not even feeling better, every morning I feel worse.'

'Are you drinking plenty of fluids?'

'Yes, yes, I know I have to do that,' he tried to laugh and ended up coughing.

'Tea?'

'I found some green tea with lemon in one of the cupboards but it tastes like medicine. I think I just got worse after drinking it.'

'Warm milk with honey. That's what my mother always made for me when I wasn't well. It's very soothing.'

'Thank you. You're spoiling me.'

'It's no fun being sick when it's painful. You should at least be able to have something nice. I also brought you some Digestives and some more tissues.'

'Keep that up and I might not want to get better.'

'Don't push it.'

After Alexander had eaten as much of the soup and bread as he could he fell asleep on the sofa. I covered him with a throw and found a bin for all the tissues. His forehead was hot and he coughed in his sleep. I kissed the top of his head and headed towards the door to let myself out.

'Wait,' I heard him say, and I turned around. 'Thank you. Will you come back tomorrow?'

'Of course. Get some rest. Call me if you need anything.'

For a moment I found myself wondering how it would be when my baby got sick. Holding him while he cried because it hurt and he didn't know why, wiping his nose, laying damp cloths on his forehead. I wondered what Lisbeth would do now if she got sick. Our arrangement had been that she would call me so I could make sure Emma got to where she needed to be and then come back and stay with me until her mother got better. Lisbeth always said that being sick was the worst part of being a single mother. Because even when you woke up feeling like part of you had died during the night, you still had to get up, make breakfast, pack lunches and take the kids to school. And try to be well enough to pick them up again later. It took all the relaxation out of being sick.

Instead of our usual walk into town that afternoon Thorin and I headed up towards the open-air theatre where I'd pranced around on the deserted stage singing ABBA songs when I was six years old. I'd only ever been there on drowsy summer evenings when we'd gone for walks after dinner. I missed those days. I missed the people I'd shared those evenings with. I missed my grandparents, my great-grandparents. Maybe that was another reason I'd come back to Langeland when I needed somewhere to run to. Here I'd never be lonely. The island was filled with ghosts. I visited their graves, brought them flowers, told them how my pregnancy was going, how work on the house was progressing and what my parents were doing in Paris. I wasn't sure whether what I felt here was a sense of belonging or the relief of escape. But I still felt that I had done the right thing by getting out of the city and coming here.

There were times when I was so tempted to call and tell you about the baby. Tell you that we were going to have a son. But however much I wanted to, I couldn't do it. Couldn't bring myself to blow your world apart and maybe still end up alone. Nor did I want to spend the rest of my life wondering whether it had really been me you had wanted or just the baby. Part of me wanted so desperately to show you the house, discuss baby names, see if Thorin liked you. What if this turned out to be our last chance? And we wasted it? And then there was Alexander.

The prompter's booth had always fascinated me when I'd come here as a child. It seemed like just the kind of secret space where you'd find buried treasure or hidden messages. The stage was overgrown with grass and so were all the tiers of seating. This was where people had brought blankets and picnics to plays and concerts in the years before everything became electrical and digital. I didn't even know if it was still used for anything other than dog walking. But what a beautiful space to waste. I'd bring my son here when he was six and see what he would sing on stage.

The temperature dropped and it started to drizzle so we headed home. I rubbed Thorin down with a towel and he lay down in his basket and chewed on his latest rawhide bone. I made myself some tea, lit some candles in the kitchen window and started rummaging through my cookbooks looking for my next culinary experiment. I'd just decided on chicken with cashew nuts and spring onions in a sweet chili sauce when my phone beeped.

Feeling much better since seeing you but have lost my voice. Had some more soup, it's delicious. Going to try and sleep so I'll feel better tomorrow and be better company. Hope you'll still come over.

Picking up the phone, I realised I was smiling.

I'll be there. Glad you're feeling better.

Thorin looked at me and barked. I nodded and knelt down to scratch him behind the ear. 'You're right,' I said, 'he makes me happy.'

When I arrived at his house the next day, Alexander looked just as bad as he had the day before but the kitchen was spotless.

'You clean when you're sick? No wonder you're still feeling awful.'

'Not usually. But I saw the way you looked at the kitchen yesterday. I don't want to lose you because the state of it makes you think I'm too young for you.'

He offered me tea and I said I'd make it myself. Gratefully, he went back to the sofa and curled up under the covers again.

'You're shivering,' I said.

'I know. I feel hot but I'm so cold all the time. I got my voice back a little but it hurts to speak.'

'I can hear it. You sound awful.'

'Thanks,' he said and started coughing. 'I really was feeling better when I woke up last night. That was when I cleaned.'

'You should take it easy. I promise not to leave you while you're sick because the kitchen is messy.'

I sat down on the sofa and he took my hand.

'Thanks for coming again.'

'You're welcome. Now drink your warm milk with honey.'

'You're right. It is soothing.'

'Well, I have some good news that might make you feel better.'

'Henrik finished all the bathrooms and I don't have to grout?'

'You wish,' I smiled and took a sip of my tea. 'But no. Do you remember me telling you about my friend who has a blog about teenage nutrition and eating disorders?'

'Yes, the one you proofread for every Wednesday.'

Wow, I thought, a man who listens to what you say and remembers it. I should have him stuffed.

'She called me last night for a chat about her next project and told me that her husband, Simon, just got a new job at this little recording studio, I can't quite remember the name. Anyway, part of his job is to take care of the new talent, so I told her about you. Then I talked to him and asked how you get a studio to listen to your demo these days. He said pretty much what you did, you have to know someone.' I looked at him and smiled. 'And now you do. He promised to listen to whatever I send him of yours and, if he likes it, bring you in for a meeting.'

Alexander started coughing again and nearly dropped his mug. 'Are you serious?'

'Absolutely. He knows I have great taste and when I tell him something's good for him he'd better listen.'

'How does he know that?'

'I set him up with his wife.'

Alexander's laugh turned into another coughing fit. 'I know it doesn't sound like it but I'm feeling a lot better now. I ... I don't know what to say. Thank you.'

'I've learned that there's a lot to be said for networking. Half the work I get is because I know someone who knows someone.'

'You really did this for me?'

'Of course. I've heard you play.'

He jumped up from the sofa. 'I have to go and practice, I have to ...'

'You have to rest and get better. You can't sing without a voice.'

'Okay. I promise to rest. I'll write you another song as a thank you.' He squeezed my hand.

'Another song?'

'You'll have to wait to see.'

We curled up together under the covers and started watching a film. Not long afterwards he fell asleep with his head on my shoulder. Sitting quietly so as not to disturb him and wake him up, I looked around the room and smiled at the thought of him cleaning the house because it mattered what I thought. He coughed in his sleep and I stroked the damp hair back from his forehead. I hoped that the door I had managed to open for him would help him become a success. He was far too talented only to play for me.

The next afternoon a van from the florist pulled up outside the house and delivered a lovely bouquet and a big box of chocolates. Alexander might have been too sick to leave the house but he was well enough to go online. I think it was at that moment I realised that I was in love with Alexander. Although it should have complicated my life immensely, it came to me like a gift and the realisation did not make me panic and want to run. I smiled and something tickled deep inside me as my heart leapt and a whole new world opened up before me. This was what falling in love was supposed to be like. This joy, this sense of being able to do anything and that the world was a place full of boundless opportunities. I ran laughing through the rooms to the kitchen to put the flowers in water and call him to say thank you. Then I allowed myself two pieces of chocolate and ran out into the garden, despite the rain, Thorin bounding after me. Everything I was feeling seemed far too large to be contained within the house. Over my head the last leaves fell from the branches, the air was cool but fragrant and I looked up at my new roof which suddenly seemed so much more precious to me because *he* had helped to put it there. I giggled like a schoolgirl, spread my arms out wide and ran through the grass aeroplane-wise, a child again.

Week Eighteen

The next week I didn't see much of Alexander even though he was in my house for most of every day. He and Henrik finished the upstairs bathroom and they moved down to start on mine. The painters arrived to tackle the hallway and the house was suddenly full of people. Alexander spent his evenings perfecting everything he wanted to send to Simon, who had promised he would make it a priority, and would let me know quickly whether they wanted to see Alexander in person. If they did, I was going to go with him and take care of a few things in the city. Amongst other things, I needed to see Hanne and I had a few small matters to discuss with my other tenants. But I also wanted to see the Christmas lights and get some special treats for the holidays.

'Why don't we stay the night if we do go?' Alexander suggested. 'I know Bjarne and his wife would be delighted to look after Thorin. He told me she really misses having a dog around the house.'

'That's a good idea. Bjarne did mention it to me when he came to check the roof for leaks. I'll give him a call and take Thorin to visit if they like the idea. Then we can ... ooh!' I stopped and took hold of my stomach.

'What is it?' Alexander asked, a slight note of panic in his voice as he took in my startled expression. 'Is everything all right?'

'Yes, I'm okay. I think I just felt him move for the first time.'

'Really?'

'Yes. It feels like little bubbles.' I laughed. 'And it tickles.'

Alexander smiled at me. 'That's fantastic. Can I feel?'

I looked up at him and smiled. 'I don't know if there's anything to be felt, but go ahead.'

He gently put a hand on my stomach. 'Can you feel anything?'

'A little,' I said. 'Can you?'

'No. But I guess that comes later. I can wait.'

Bjarne's wife was named Helle and you only had to glance at her once to know that she was a grandmother to her fingertips. When I came in with Thorin there were freshly baked buns on the table, the delicious smell of coffee brewing and a pile of knitting laid neatly to one side. On the large windowsill were photos of children and grandchildren, and in the garden a large swing was fixed firmly to the branches of one of the trees.

'Bjarne's told me so much about you,' she said as she ushered me into a chair and poured coffee for me. 'I think it's wonderful what you're doing. I hope it brings some people and some work to the island. Maybe some of them will fall in love with the place and decide to stay.'

'I'd consider that an enormous success. Then I'd know they had found a refuge and had enjoyed their stay. I've already caught my photographer looking at summer houses while she was here with her husband.'

We chatted for a while about my grandparents and my memories of Langeland. Then she took me through me the pictures of all her grandchildren and I dutifully admired each one. Thorin lay at my feet, hoping for crumbs.

'Now then,' she said after we'd finished our second cup of coffee, 'he's a lovely dog. We never had one as big as this one's going to be. We were Labrador people. I'd love to have another but Bjarne isn't sure I'd be able to hold onto it. I don't have the strength in my hands that I used to.'

Thorin wagged his tail as though he knew we were talking about him. I told her about his exercise routine and his food and how important it was for him to get rest since he was still growing rapidly. 'I'll bring his basket and toys of course. At home he lies on the sofa but just push him off if you don't want him on yours.'

'Oh no,' she said, 'our dogs always lay on the sofa. I like the company. Bjarne is away at work all day and it can get a little lonely. It will be nice to have a dog around the house again, even if it is only for one night.'

'Maybe you could get a smaller dog? If Bjarne thinks a Labrador might be too much to hold onto, you could look for one that weighs less.'

'Do you know,' she said with a smile, 'I'd never even thought of that. They were always the only dogs for me. But you're right. I could. The grandchildren would adore it.'

We talked about different breeds while we finished our coffee and buns and then went for a quick walk around the garden. Thorin sniffed everything and marked his new territory once or twice.

'You do pick up after him, don't you?' Helle asked me.

'Always,' I told her. 'I despise people who don't pick up after their dogs, especially on the street. Especially big dogs.'

'Good. So do we.'

During those rare moments over the last few months when I'd considered going back to the city again, the thought had made me nervous. I'd hated to even think that I might run into the two of you. But now you were the furthest thing from my mind. I was looking forward to showing Alexander where my apartments were, seeing the Christmas lights together and having lunch at my favourite café. The thought of someone writing songs for me was irresistible and romantic, and I spent most of my evenings trying on and rejecting outfits, as though I was going for two weeks not merely two days. We had decided that, even if the record company didn't want to see him, we would go anyway and enjoy our first trip as a couple. The one thing which did make me nervous was the thought of sharing a hotel room. I'd never before waited this long before sleeping with a boyfriend. Sex, usually something I found myself casual and slightly flippant about, suddenly seemed deep and meaningful. I worried in a way I had never done before. Worried about not being good enough. Worried that sex for people his age might mean something completely different to what it did when I was in my twenties. Worried that things I'd never even considered doing were to him par for the course. Worried that he wouldn't want me. Worried that he'd think sex with an older, pregnant woman creepy. Lisbeth's husband never so much as went near her once she started showing. But of course he was also screwing his secretary by then.

I'd chosen a creamy off-white for the hallway to add to the great sense of space and to give me a blank canvas as backdrop for my decoration. The painters arrived on Friday afternoon, not with rollers as expected, but with spray guns.

'Fantastically efficient,' one of them told me. 'Takes bloody ages to mask up and get everything covered but once that's done you can do the room in no time flat. You're the first customer we're trying it on.'

'Great,' I said, unsure of whether or not this would turn out to be a good thing. I wasn't sure I was comfortable being a guinea pig.

'We'll try a small bit first and you can see what you think. It saves a lot of time which of course means we'll be gone sooner and your bill will be cheaper.'

'I like the sound of that,' I laughed. 'Go for it.'

I still planned to have my desk in the hallway. It would be first point of call for new arrivals and would also mean that I wouldn't have to appropriate a bedroom to use as an office. I'd get an extra basket for Thorin so he could lie next to me. He followed me around the house like a shadow and it seemed like he'd been part of my life forever. I was never lonely in the evenings, or scared of being by myself in the enormous house, because he was there with me. I'd taken him out to visit Helle and Bjarne again so he'd be comfortable in their house and I'd tried leaving him there for an hour while I went for a walk. Sisse had suggested it as a good way to let him know I might leave but I'd always come back.

Was that what you thought? That I was a little dog who'd stay home waiting for you because I knew you'd always come back? Well woof you, I thought as the phone rang.

'Anne?' I recognised Simon's voice.

'Hi Simon,' I said as I turned the kettle off so I could hear him better.

'I got what you sent me and pretty much the whole company has heard it by now. I caught the cleaning lady humming one of the songs when she was dusting the conference table this morning. We love it. That is one talented guy that you've discovered and, considering how good the last thing you found for me turned out to be, I definitely want to meet him. How soon can you bring him in?'

'That's fantastic news! Alexander will be absolutely thrilled.' I caught a glimpse of my reflection in the window, a giant grin on my face. 'How about next week?'

'Perfect. I have to run to a meeting but get him to call me tonight and we'll sort out all the details.'

'I will. And, Simon, thanks.'

'I think he's going to be big. But don't tell him I said that. Musicians don't need their egos inflated ahead of time.'

I laughed and told him to give my love to his wife. Then I ran to the bathroom to tell Alexander.

Week Nineteen

It was dark and raining when Alexander and I drove to Copenhagen. We dropped Thorin off at Bjarne and Helle's house, then waited fifteen minutes in case Helle called to tell me he was tearing the place apart.

'Ready?' Alexander asked.

'Ready,' I nodded. 'Let's go.'

He smiled at me and pulled away from the kerb and into the dark morning.

As we drove, I snuggled down into my seat and thought of all those people who consider autumn and winter the darkest, most depressing corners of the human experience. Those people who I will never understand. The changing seasons act on me like a tonic, each turn of the moon bringing a different feel to the world. October is all about falling leaves and that sweet, intoxicating scent of autumn decay in the damp grass and crisp mornings. November is when the darkness comes and the preparations for Christmas slowly begin. The first Christmas biscuits, the first candles in the windows. When winter hits in December it's the most magical month of the year. I love the treats, the carols, the decorations and, more than anything, I love giving gifts. I love spending time picking out just the right thing for someone dear to me and seeing how happy they are when they unwrap it. I was already thinking about what to get Alexander for Christmas.

Driving along in the dark, seeing the houses by the side of the road slowly light up as people head off to work and school, always tugs at my heart. It always seems so cosy, particularly when the trees and bushes outside are strung with white lights. I always thought that people in those houses must be so happy. One day soon that would be me. Getting up early to get my son dressed in his winter coat and gloves and ready for nursery. Maybe it would snow and I could pull him along on his sledge. When I picked him up we'd go home and read stories and have a slice of cake and some hot chocolate with whipped cream. We'd ...

'Are you okay?' Alexander asked me. 'You're frowning.'

'I don't know,' I said. 'I hate to say it, but I keep having doubts about the house. I can't imagine living in a hotel. If I do this, I lose my privacy. I won't be able to pick my son up from nursery and take him home to hot chocolate and stories in the kitchen.'

'Of course you will. It will still be your home. You can't let them chase you into the hall. Even if they are paying for the privilege of being there. Anyway, I'd imagine that your guests will keep to their rooms more than sit in the living room.'

'You think?'

'Yeah, I do. The house is going to look great. And you're looking forward to cooking and decorating and if those cakes you've made are anything to go by, your guests will be so busy working off the food at yoga class they won't even want to sit still. You're always telling me the kitchen is your favourite room. They won't be venturing down there.'

I laughed. 'Thanks. Actually that's a good point. I'll have to set up some boundaries for the guests. What's their space and what's mine.'

'Like, the games room downstairs could be their living room so you can keep yours to yourself. They'll probably all have iPads with Netflix subscriptions anyway and will just watch TV in their rooms at night, if at all. Besides, they'll be too scared to shove Thorin off the sofa once he's fully grown.'

'True.' I nodded. 'And then I can let my baby have his toys in the living room and we can have our own space as well.'

'Exactly. You'll need that. Maybe don't open all year round. Maybe only at certain periods. When's the biggest season for divorce? After Christmas and the summer holidays? I'm sure you'll find a way to make it all hang together. And I hope you'll let me stick around to see how it all works out.'

'I wasn't planning on getting rid of you.'

'Good.' He looked at me as if there was something he desperately wanted to tell me. Then, to my surprise, he pulled the car over by the side of the road and turned off the engine. 'Because I love you.'

I looked back at him and my mouth fell open and my breath caught in my throat. He smiled, but with an expectant, almost fearful look his eyes. Then he took my hand, leaned over and kissed me deeply.

'I love you, too,' I told him as we broke free. 'I'm so in love with you I hardly know what to do with myself.'

We undid our seat belts and held each other close. We laughed and we kissed again as the sun rose and lit up the fields around us. Then we drove on, my hand clasped tightly in his.

We parked in front of the hotel a few hours later. Once we had checked in and found our room, we stood together at the window for a long time with our arms around each other, my head resting on his chest. We kissed goodbye in the lobby and I headed off to my apartment while Alexander went to meet Simon.

It was strange being in my apartment again, strange seeing someone else's photographs on the shelves, someone else's pictures on the walls. My bedroom, the place where my baby had been conceived, did not seem like my space anymore. Hanne was thrilled with her new life and wanted to discuss the possibility of extending her lease or even buying. She and her husband were close to finalising their divorce and she was considering settling permanently in the neighbourhood. Looking around my home and seeing it turned into someone else's, I just wanted to get out as quickly as possible.

Once I had said goodbye to her I met with my other tenants and dealt with their various issues. Then I went to my favourite café to wait for Alexander. I found a table by the window and ordered hot chocolate with whipped cream. When it arrived I wrapped my fingers around the warm glass and smiled as my thoughts drifted back to what had taken place in the car this morning. Alexander had said he loved me and I was walking on air. Tonight was going to be perfect. Hopefully his meeting with Simon had gone well. I was going to take him out for dinner to celebrate. There was a lovely little Italian restaurant that was a particular favourite of mine. Torches burned outside in the winter and the food was always delicious. I was trying to remember the menu and what I was and was not allowed to eat when I looked out the window and saw you walk past.

You!

Arm in arm with your wife, you did not see me.

But she did.

She turned her head and looked right at me. I know she recognised me, I saw the look of panic in her eyes. It was panic. It wasn't triumph or the gloating little smug smile of the one who was wearing your ring. Seeing me, she was afraid. What did she have to be afraid of? Was there already trouble in paradise? What would she have thought if I hadn't been sitting down and she'd had seen that I was now obviously pregnant? Transfixed for a moment, it could have been no more than a few seconds, we stared at each other as you moved on. But I kept watching you from the window, and I saw her look back.

I breathed deeply and felt my hands tighten around the glass. Seeing you was a shock I had been unprepared for. If you hadn't been with her, would I have rushed outside? Would I have called after you? Would you have seen me? Or would I have stayed where I was and simply let you walk by? The worst part was how I felt. Like so many times before, as soon as there was another man in my life you had slid into the background, like an outfit that I packed away in a drawer when it was no longer fashionable. Seeing you today, I almost resented the baby I was carrying. How could I have been so foolish? How could I have let my life be turned so completely around by a man I now felt nothing for?

It was at that moment I realised that I truly did not love you anymore. If I really had loved you with a burning, passionate love that was meant to span the ages, I would not be here with Alexander. I would not have forgotten about you as soon as another man showed up to shower me with the attention I didn't get from you. You simply waited in the back of my mind for those moments when I was the most alone and then you wrapped your memories around me like a soft warm blanket. Then it wouldn't matter what had happened before because here was something beautiful to dream of.

It was time to face the consequences of my choices, bad as they might have been, and move on as best I could. Whether with Alexander or alone, I had to let you go. You would never be part of my life again. You would never have anything to do with my baby. *My* baby. Not yours, not ours. *Mine*.

I ordered another hot chocolate and turned my face from the window. In the wake of the realisation that you were on your way out of my life came a peculiar sense of peace and freedom. It was a relief to know that you were finally gone. It was as though a weight had been lifted and I could breathe for the first time in ages.

When Alexander walked through the door half an hour later I had managed to compose my face and my thoughts. The one thing that was crystal clear to me was that running to Langeland had been the right thing to do. If I'd stayed here, we would have met. And a huge number of awkward questions would then have needed to be answered. Maybe you would even have been able to worm your way back into my thoughts. If I had stayed, I would never have been free of you. Saying goodbye to you, even though it was only in my mind, made me feel as though I had suddenly been given part of my life back.

'So how did it go?' I asked him as he came towards me, beaming from ear to ear.

'Fantastic!' he exclaimed and leaned over to kiss me. 'Couldn't have gone better. They want me to come back tomorrow to go over some more details, but it really looks like I just got a record deal.'

'Oh, Alexander, that's wonderful! Sit down and tell me all about it.'

'I'll just get a coffee. Do you want anything?'

'I'll have one of those raspberry and banana smoothies, thanks. After two hot chocolates I should try and be a little more healthy.'

I listened to Alexander describe his meeting while under the table I dug my nails into my palm to try and not blurt out the happy news that I had seen you and knew I did not love you anymore. It didn't seem like a discussion that had any place in our lives after this morning's declarations. Because here was an enchanting, sweet man who loved me and wanted to spend time with me. He probably did not want to know that I was also happy because I could stop wasting my empty moments dreaming about a guy who didn't even have the decency not to sleep with someone else the night before his wedding. I shivered.

'Are you all right?' Alexander asked.

'Just a little chilly. Must be the cold drink. Or someone walking over my grave.'

'Here,' he said, 'take my sweater.'

'Thanks. Ouch!' I exclaimed.

'What's wrong?'

'Just hurts. Feels like there's a little person inside me kicking me.'

Alexander laughed and laughed while I just stared at him. 'There is! You're pregnant, remember.'

'Oh God,' I laughed and rolled my eyes. 'Of course there is. Those pregnancy hormones must finally have gone to my brain.'

Alexander kept laughing and I smiled at him and pushed you a little further out of my mind. Inside me my baby changed position and gave me another kick. Alexander took my hands in his and told me more about his meeting. He looked incredibly happy so we finished our drinks quickly and headed back to our hotel. When we got to our room, he turned me towards him and kissed me, driving the last thought of you completely out of my mind.

We made love for the first time that afternoon as the snow began to fall. Alexander was gentle and tender and made me feel truly cherished. It was a far cry from the passionate desire that sparked between you and I each time we met, but it was beautiful. In his touch I felt his love and his desperate desire that everything should be perfect for me. He kissed me till

I was dizzy and when we fell asleep in each other's arms afterwards, the whole world seemed quiet and at peace.

Several hours later we left the hotel and walked out into a city white with snow and strung with lights. Torches burned outside restaurants, creating tiny circles of warmth and light on the pavements. Inside, happy couples sat together at candlelit tables, sipping wine and looking forward to what might happen later. Alexander and I walked hand in hand, cold but happy. I'd spoken to Helle earlier and she had assured me that Thorin was behaving impeccably and not pining for me.

'How far is it to the restaurant?' he asked.

'Just around this next corner.'

'It's a little off the beaten track. How did you find it?'

'Lisbeth used to live next to it. She moved after Kristoffer walked out because she couldn't stand the memories.'

'Too many good ones?'

'Too many bad ones. She said the good memories were easy to live with but the memories of how it all had gone wrong, all their fights and all the shouting, were too hard to confront every day. So they sold it and split the money. But we still come to eat here.'

The restaurant was in a converted basement so we had to walk down a flight of stairs from the street. The lighting was soft and there were candles on every table. We were given a space by the window from where we could look up at the boots and coats walking past. Across the street I could see the lights twinkling on one of the lakes and I wondered if the water would freeze this winter.

The waiter brought a small selection of olives and chargrilled cashew nuts along with the menus. I ran through it quickly, eliminating all the delicious dishes that I was not allowed to eat.

'It's so hard being pregnant in a restaurant!' I scowled. 'Half the things I'm not allowed and the other half I don't want.'

Alexander laughed. 'There's always the children's menu.'

I stuck my tongue out at him.

Despite my restrictions, we had a delicious dinner. The owner of the restaurant remembered me from when Lisbeth and I used to come in regularly and made the waiters fuss over us to make sure everything was just right. He congratulated me on my pregnancy and I skilfully avoided questions about the father and where all this was going. Instead I told him about my new house and my plans for it while he poured San Pellegrino and a fruity Chianti. As we tucked into delicious Italian dishes I told Alexander what I remembered about him. His father was Italian and had met his mother when she was a young woman on a package holiday. Their holiday romance had blossomed so strongly that he had followed her back to Denmark with nothing but his grandmother's recipes and passionate ideas about how foreigners should learn what Italian food was supposed to taste like. It took them five years of hard work and a lot of sacrifice, but eventually they managed to open their own restaurant. Now their son ran it while they came in during the busiest times to talk to the regulars and make sure that standards were maintained.

When we left three hours later, after gelato and cappuccinos, the snow was falling hard and the lake was freezing. I was too tired to walk back so we took a taxi instead, holding hands in the backseat and saying very little. I looked out the window as the city flew past. Christmas decorations were slowly appearing in shop windows. Next Christmas there would be a baby in the house. There would be advent calendars and the same Christmas carols that I used to sing when I was a child. It would be the most beautiful time of the year. I turned my head to see Alexander smiling at me.

'Thank you for dinner,' he said, 'it was great.'

'You're welcome. I'm glad there was something to celebrate.'

'Me too.'

I smiled at him. 'Tomorrow will be even better, I'm sure of it.'

'It couldn't be better than today if it tried.'

I smiled at him as he squeezed my hand and winked at me. We didn't get much sleep that night.

Week Twenty

Bjarne and Helle had adored looking after Thorin and he'd greeted me with big, slobbery kisses and a series of barks. Now he was back in his usual place next to me on the sofa while I dozed. Henrik and Alexander were working on my bathroom and the hallway was nearly finished. The spray guns had proven to be just as efficient as promised and I'd asked the painters for a quote for the remaining rooms. My energy levels were unreliable and I knew it would take me four or five weeks to get the job done in my condition. I wasn't sure what effect breathing intensive paint fumes for that time would have on the baby. Once the final bathroom was finished Bjarne would come back to help Alexander take care of the various internal repairs. They would deal with the exterior next year in the spring when there was no chance of snow. I wasn't yet quite sure when I was going to open. My baby was due mid-April and that was the only date that meant anything at the moment.

  Alexander's second meeting had gone incredibly well and he was hard at work every night. I didn't understand half of what he was doing but I was so glad that I had been able to push open a door for him. When I was lying curled up in bed he'd call me and we'd talk till I fell asleep. I wasn't sure what we had or where it was going, but for now I was happy to go along for the ride.

  The feeling that had swooped over me as soon as I had said goodbye to you through the café window, the feeling of peace and of being able to breathe deeply again, had stayed with me. Each morning I awoke and felt as though I could fly. When I let Thorin out in the garden for his morning run I bounded after him, wearing my colourful boots and laughing as the snowflakes landed on my face. It was as though the world had opened up to me once again and revealed itself in all its colourful glory. And all the while Alexander was there.

Loving me, needing me, holding me. Loving him made me happy in a way that loving you had never done. In his love was peace and desire and the sense of a world being reborn each day. There was no heartbreak, no agony, no frightened apprehension. Instead I was, for the first time in longer than I could remember, simply happy and deliciously in love.

The kicks were getting stronger every day but so far I was the only one who could feel them. It was just before my mid-way scan that I started to be nervous about not being nervous. There had been times in my life when I'd felt as though some malign presence was hovering over me, just waiting for the moment when I dared to admit I was happy so it could pounce in and take it all away. Usually around the time I started believing that *this time* it would work out with you. With the baby and the house and Alexander, everything seemed perfect right now. I wasn't afraid for my baby. I knew he was healthy and strong and that I wasn't going to lose him. I *knew*, just as I had always known when I was going to see you.

As to whether I was going to tell you about the baby or not, my mind was now made up. I wanted no part of you in our lives. Never again did I want you to swoop into my dreams, full of promises that would soon be broken, and make me wish for things that could never be. My child would never sit by the window, gazing into the dark night, and wonder why you had not shown up as you had promised. I would spare my baby the heartache that was you. I would spare him the feeling that he was not good enough.

Even so, seeing you with your wife had unsettled me. A small, petty part of me was surprised that I felt no triumph in seeing the two of you together, looking unhappy. I should have been rolling in the aisles at the thought that you were trapped in an unhappy marriage, but I found that I only felt sorry for you. What surprised me even more was that I also felt sorry for her.

The doctor told me that everything looked fine on the scan. I couldn't believe it had been two months since I'd wandered the empty corridors agonising over whether I was doing the right thing and which direction my life was going to take. Just two short months. Two short months since that morning when I stood by my car, plagued by doubts and morning sickness. Everything seemed to be moving forwards so fast. I was free of you, everything I thought I knew had been turned around again. Suddenly I was showing, suddenly I had Alexander. I was only too glad that he hadn't yet tried to have any discussions about the future. For all Alexander's exceptional qualities he was still a man and a young one at that. I was fairly certain I was safe from any discussions about a future I knew in my heart he was not yet ready for.

For the next few days I waited in a fever of excitement for November to be over. I'd always waited until the first of December to put up my Christmas decorations, although the first packet of Christmas biscuits had already found its way into the cupboard, and from there into my stomach. I'd sent my mother her usual assortment by post. When I was still living in Paris I used to bake my own, but it always limited the selection severely. While I waited, I mentally mapped out the decorations. Alexander had fetched the boxes from the basement for me and had strung lights in the bushes in front of the house.

'Where are you spending Christmas?' he asked me one night when we were lying in each other's arms, looking out at the stars.

'Here,' I said. 'My parents are flying in from Paris. I have to have my first Christmas in my new house. What about you?'

'I'm not exactly sure,' he said, 'but it will be with one of my brothers and their family.'

'And your parents?'

'Them too. And my brother's in-laws. Good thing they both have really large dining tables.'

'I'll miss you,' I said and leaned over and kissed him.

'I'll miss you, too. Are your parents going to stay for New Year's Eve as well?'

I shook my head. 'No. A friend of theirs has an apartment overlooking the Champs Elysée. They always go there for New Year's Eve. It's a very glamorous, black-tie affair that has become a tradition.'

'Did you ever go?'

'Once or twice when I was younger. It was quite fun. And a wonderful chance to wear a ballgown. A girl has to grab those chances where she can.'

Alexander chuckled and kissed the top of my head. 'I bet you looked amazing. But you're telling me that you'll be alone?'

'I guess. But that doesn't bother me. New Year's Eve never meant anything to me.'

'How do you mean?'

'I mean we make such a big deal out of it. But it's just an arbitrary point on the calendar that some people believe can magically fix everything that's wrong in their lives. To be honest, if you're single it's worse than Valentine's Day for making you feel weird and unloved because you aren't at some fantastical party being kissed at midnight. In an ideal world I'd go to bed at ten and sleep through it all. Actually at ten o'clock the night before, then I'd be spared all the morning television about the perfect meal and place for the big midnight kiss.' Alexander laughed again and I continued. 'It's just a night that always ends up disappointing you. You're left with such an anti-climactic feeling at midnight because nothing earth shattering happened and life pretty much goes on as it did the day before.'

'Wow, you really feel strongly about this.'

'It's the worst night of the year,' I shrugged, 'I really hate New Year's Eve.'

'Here's a suggestion. How about I come back here and we spend the worst night of the year together? You don't even have to kiss me at midnight if you don't want to.'

I smiled. 'Well, that might make it a little better. But won't you feel like you're missing out if you're not at a big party with your friends?'

'Nah. I'd rather be with you.'

I sighed contentedly and kissed him. He held me close and soon afterwards he was asleep. I lay awake for a while, a little smile on my face. To think that he would rather spend the biggest night of the year in this quiet place with me than at some big party with all his friends.

Week Twenty-One

Snow was falling when I awoke on the first day of December. It was still dark outside so I sat up in bed, gathered the covers around me and looked out the window at the thick flakes falling swiftly to the ground. Thorin lay beside me and woke up briefly to rest his head on my leg, a sure sign that he expected me to stay where I was. I turned on the light and decided to read for a while. Next year I would be unwrapping my baby's first advent calendar present and watching him play with the wrapping paper, not caring about what was inside. For now, I might as well enjoy the quiet moments I could still spend in bed with a book.

I loved that my bedroom looked out over the garden. The snow must have started not long after I went to sleep because by now the lawn was a white blanket. Trees were dotted with white and clouds blocked out the stars. I got up and put on my dressing gown while Thorin rolled over onto his back so I could scratch his belly. He got up and padded after me as I made my way to the kitchen and then curled up in his basket. Alexander called to tell me that his driveway was covered with snow and he wasn't sure he would be able to come today.

'I'll be shovelling snow till lunchtime,' he said. 'Hopefully it won't get any worse.'

'I guess that's a drawback of living so far out in the country,' I told him and he laughed. I made myself a cup of tea and smiled at the thought of him battling the elements. Days when I didn't see him were no fun. I missed him when he wasn't around. Slowly but surely he had tunnelled his way into my life and become part of my day. I was trying not to get too used to it. Despite falling in love, despite the romance and the joy that he brought to me, I was still very aware that he was twenty-two and that I was much older and nearly five months pregnant. I would have been a fool to have forgotten it. Also, I knew from experience that the beautiful in-love stage did not last. So I was enjoying the initial intoxication to the full and closed my eyes to the day when he would leave.

That morning, while the snow continued falling quietly, I lit candles and opened my boxes of Christmas decorations. I brewed coffee and toasted raisin buns for breakfast. While I ate, I read my pregnancy book to find out what my baby was up to this week apart from busily practicing roundhouse kicks. I'd fallen into the habit of resting my hands on my stomach every time I sat down and I found myself wondering how many of the things I was doing were having an influence on him. Would he be born a fan of the music I listened to over and over again? Would he emerge with a voracious appetite for chocolate or would my cravings have put him off it for life? Would I be good enough? Could I provide a loving, secure home for him to grow up in, notwithstanding the confusing circumstances surrounding his conception? How would it be when I picked him up from nursery or from school? Eventually he would bring friends home or go to their houses. We would read stories, I'd help teach him to read. We'd play games, build Lego, make a secret cave out of chairs and blankets and crawl in there with torches and sweets. There would be birthday parties, Christmas dinners, Easter egg hunts in the garden. As Lisbeth had told me, I'd always have to be both good cop and bad cop. The disciplinarian and the fun one. No one else would be there to take him to school when I was sick, I'd have to drag myself out of bed, restraining the urge to throw up until I had made it safely home. There would be no one else to go with me to nursery or school functions, I'd sit by myself like some outcast freak or trail around after him desperate for a sliver of attention. No one to share the highs with, or the lows. No one else to care so deeply about the first trip to the potty, the first tooth lost. No one else to help us decorate the house for Christmas. Instead there would be strangers in and out of our house, pausing for a moment to leave us some memories before they moved on to better lives. We would help people, we would do something worthwhile. It wouldn't be a traditional life, but hopefully it would be a good one.

By lunchtime the house was ready for Christmas; filled with red candles, red and white Christmas hearts and various little *nisser*, Danish Christmas elves, that I had picked up in odd places over the years. When Thorin and I went for our afternoon walk around town we lingered in the square by the old town hall to look at the Christmas lights and I threw snowballs at the trees in the park.

My Christmas tree would go in the living room. There was plenty of room in there for us all to join hands and walk around it singing carols on Christmas Eve while the dining room was filled with the delicious scent of roast duck. This was one of my favourite times of the year. The snow falling outside made it perfect. I put on soft music and sat down to work in the kitchen with a cup of tea. Alexander texted me to say that he was still shovelling snow and hoped to be able to get out by the next day. Otherwise, he wrote, he would walk and be with me that night. I smiled and felt a little twinge of excitement. When it came to relationships, or at least the beginnings of relationships, there was a lot to be said for the digital age and the ease of communication it provided. My phone beeped again.

PS I love you

I smiled and put the phone down. Yes, there was definitely a lot to be said for all these new ways of communicating.

The next day Alexander felt the baby kicking for the first time. He looked awed and happy and, there was no denying it, just a tiny bit terrified. But he still stayed with me and held me in his arms all night while he slept. Whatever we had, it was going somewhere. Maybe not where any of us expected, but somewhere.

Week Twenty-Two

December continued to weave its usual magic around me. The snow stayed on the ground transforming the house and the garden into a winter wonderland of icicles, frosted windowpanes, *nisser* and Christmas biscuits. Every morning I saw tiny footprints of various animals and birds in the snow outside my window and I hung little feeders in the strangest places to help them all make it safely through the winter. Henrik shook his head and muttered something about women fussing too much, from which I gathered that his wife had done much the same. Thorin, growing bigger every day, bounded outside every morning to roll around in the snow and emerged from it white-nosed and sneezing. It seemed to be dark every time we went for a walk, but we enjoyed the Christmas lights in town, the deep red hearts glowing in the morning mist and the garlands of conifer stretched from one side of the street to the other. We listened to Christmas carols and spent the afternoons curled up on the sofa. My energy levels had plummeted and I was content to spend as much time asleep as I could. We spent the occasional night at Alexander's and when I fell asleep on his sofa at eight o'clock, he would kiss me goodnight and go to his studio.

During the early hours of those new December mornings I remembered a time when I'd lain in your arms, warm and content after making love, and I'd told you why I always find Christmas the most magical time of the year. You'd kissed me and laughed and said it was wonderful to find someone who loved Christmas for all the right reasons and not for presents and gain and the freedom to drink alcohol whenever you wanted. I love it because it is family time. Because it is the time you spend with the ones you love the most, when you recharge that love and go forth into another year filled with new challenges. I knew that the year ahead of me would be challenging. I knew I should take the high ground and hope that yours would be happy and trouble-free, but even though I had wished you farewell in my heart, deep down a part of me still wanted you to be miserable and unfulfilled without me.

Sciatica drove me out of bed. A searing pain shot down my right leg and sent me hobbling around the room in frantic search of some kind of relief. Every few steps my leg buckled and it felt as though some malicious little bastard was trying to saw my leg off with a rusty butter knife. Thorin looked at me and thumped his tail on the bed, probably thinking that I was trying out some kind of strange new exercise routine.

I rested my head against the windowpane and gritted my teeth. Then I gave up and just pounded my leg screaming, 'Ouch ouch ouch! Fuck! This hurts!' If labour was going to be anything like this I wouldn't last two minutes without begging for drugs. As if to add insult to injury, the baby also starting kicking me and Thorin jumped off the bed and prodded me with his nose.

'All right!' I half-laughed, half-shouted. 'I'm up! I'm up!'

Quiet mornings have always been my favourite time of the day. Everything is still new and fresh and filled with unexplored potential. This house, which I already thought I knew so well, was revealing itself to me anew every morning. I saw the varying ways the light hit the rooms, how the slanting rays of the morning sun lit up the windows and turned the rooms golden. I saw the winter sun move through the house on its daily tour, each room a new stop along the way. The house was bright and welcoming but what I wanted most of all was for it to feel like a real home.

Over the last few days, I had noticed how my perspective was subtly shifting. My focus had moved from abstract ideas about what fixing the house and running the business would entail to how everything would affect my son. I knew then that I was ready to be a mother. That I was ready to let you and everyone else in the world go to hell to keep my baby safe and warm and happy. That was the morning I finally woke up and said, 'Enough.' I took out my phone and deleted your number. It was the final act of freeing myself from you.

You were never going to want me. Or at least never want me enough to turn it into anything more than an occasional roll in the hay that sent me soaring towards the stars for a week and then plunged me into despair for a month. We should have ended a long time ago. We were a freak accident that ran its course and should have been left to die by the roadside, not kept on life support for thirteen years. Just a safety net. That's what you were. What you always had been. You may have been a mistake, but my son was not going to pay for it. I would love him every bit as fiercely as I had loved you. If I regretted you, he would never know it.

Somehow I had to believe that I was worth more than you. That I deserved better than you. If it meant being all on my own, at least that was better than being with a man I'd never really mean anything to. Anything had to be better than staying on this emotional see-saw for the rest of my life.

Alexander found me curled up with the IKEA catalogue and a notebook when he arrived an hour later. He kissed me good morning and I showed him my final plans for the rooms.

'I'm mapping out the furniture,' I told him.

'I'll get the van ready for another trip,' he said.

'Please. I want to start getting things ready now. Once the bathroom is finished there won't be much left to do.'

'Nope,' Alexander nodded. 'The upstairs bedrooms are all done, your bedroom is finished, the kitchen and hallway are complete. We need to finish the downstairs bedrooms and get them painted, then there's the the living room and dining room. Most of the window frames need work, but that can wait till spring.'

'We can get the things for upstairs first and take care of the rest later. I couldn't manage it all in one trip anyway.'

'Shall we go this weekend?'

'If it's all right with you, I'd like to.'

'Of course.'

I smiled at him. Why would I waste time thinking about you when I had someone like Alexander?

I slept all the way to IKEA and could happily have lain down on one of the beds and gone back to sleep. I had a long list of furniture to buy and as we walked through the 'rooms' things got taken off and new pieces were added. The budget bounced up and, before we were even halfway through, I had to stop for a rest and a snack. Bjarne had promised to round up some people to help us unload when we got back and Helle had jumped at the chance to look after Thorin again. In addition to the furniture I also bought a few bits for Christmas. Caroline had suggested decorating one of the rooms so that she could come down and take some Christmas photos.

'How much more do we need?' Alexander asked.

I looked at my list. For each bedroom I had chosen a double bed, a wardrobe, a small table and a large comfortable chair, perfect for curling up in to read a good book, or to play with an iPad or to just cry and curse the bastard who had led you to my haven of a hotel.

'I still need curtains, pillows, duvets and all those things. Some cushions for the beds and chairs. And notebooks.'

'Notebooks?'

'Yes. I am in charge of the healing-your-life-hotel. I find notebooks are a good way to go about that.'

'Okay. Notebooks it is. But you do know that no one writes anything down anymore. Anything else?'

I frowned. 'I can't think of anything right now - oh no, I'll need some paintings or prints for the rooms.'

He nodded. 'And then we're done?'

'Yes. Maybe a mirror too. I think that was on my list.'

'Or at least it is now,' he laughed.

I had in my mind's eye the perfect picture of what my guests would experience. There would be a comfortable bed for my guests to rest on and awake in each morning, hungry and hopeful. For those long rainy days there would be a snuggly chair with a soft throw to curl up in. There would be pots of tea or coffee and an endless supply of home-made snacks. There would be paints and yoga and music and anything else I could think of. My haven was not going to be somewhere you put your life back together while working out how to go off and blaze a trail in the creative world of digital start-ups. My haven was was going to be the place you would go before you were ready to go and do all those other things. Somewhere you rested, gathered strength, came back to yourself. Somewhere to breathe again after the world had collapsed. For some it would probably be too feminine, too indulgent and I'd be criticised for conforming too much to gender stereotypes.

'Penny for your thoughts,' Alexander said and squeezed my hand.

'What? Oh, nothing. I was just thinking about how the rooms will look.'

'I'm sure they will look great.'

'Once I have them ready I think it will be time to call the papers.'

'What will you tell them? Do you think you can generate some national publicity?'

'I'm certainly going to try. But let's get Christmas over with first. Anyway,' I shook my head, 'that's prime season for divorces. And everyone wants to start over in January.'

'So that would seem like the perfect time to starting shouting about it.'

I nodded. 'Come on, let's get the last few things and go home and have cake.'

It took over an hour to unload all the furniture. Alexander, Bjarne and Henrik went up and down the stairs while Helle and I directed operations and the neighbours watched from across the street. Snow started falling as the afternoon sky began to darken. When they were almost finished, I made coffee and served up the chocolate coffee cake I had baked earlier that morning. Thorin sat next to Alexander and thumped his tail on the ground. Alexander shook his head and scratched Thorin behind the ear.

'I'm not feeding you at the table. Soon you'll be big enough to eat off it on your own.'

'That's not going to happen,' I said firmly and Thorin barked.

Bjarne and Henrik laughed and Helle smiled. I looked around my beautiful kitchen and out to the garden. I could see little animal prints in the new snow and the scent of fresh coffee made inside seem like a warm, homely place. I looked over at Alexander and he was smiling at me. I realised that I was completely at home here. At that moment I had no desire to ever return to the city. My baby gave a series of small kicks and I rested my hands on my little bump. There was peace here. I had found what I wanted to give others. It was as simple as good company, good food and a safe place to rest at night.

Week Twenty-Three

The week before Christmas was filled with last minute preparations, baking and assembling furniture. Henrik finished work on my bathroom, the hallway was done and we were ready to tackle the converted basement first thing in the new year. My parents were arriving on Saturday afternoon and Alexander was leaving to spend Christmas with his eldest brother and his family. I hadn't quite realised just how much I was going to miss him. The thought of spending nearly two weeks without him was actually quite painful. I would miss his smile, his touch, the way he laughed at my jokes, the little everyday gestures that showed his feelings more clearly than words ever could. More than anything, I'd miss lying in his arms on the sofa at night when all the remnants of the day's activities had been cleared away and it was just the two of us. The gentle sound of his breathing as he slowly drifted off to sleep. The warmth of his body pressed against mine. Seeing his face on the pillow next to me when I woke up in the morning. His kiss on the back of my neck when he came into the kitchen. The way he chased Thorin around the garden. The songs he played for me. And that look of naked emotion in his eyes when he held me close.

I was writing my final Christmas cards when he came into the kitchen with Henrik.

'We're all set now,' Henrik said. 'After Christmas Bjarne will come back and see about the last few things that need doing. And you'll be having the painters round again, no?'

I nodded. 'Yes, I can't stand the smell and I'm so tired all the time.'

'You shouldn't be around all those paint fumes anyway,' Alexander pointed out. 'It could be bad for the baby.'

I smiled and felt another kick.

'I'll be off then,' Henrik said.

I got up to follow him out to the door. 'Thank you for all your help.'

'I'll miss those cakes of yours.'

I laughed. 'I'll make sure there's one ready next time you come.'

He waved as he headed down the steps and over to his van. When I went back to the kitchen Alexander was teaching Thorin how to sit. I yawned and sat down.

'Tired?'

'Again. All I want to do is lie down on the sofa and snooze. And I'm actually sleeping really deeply at night.'

'Still in pain?'

'God, yes. The sciatica is making me want to get a big stick and hit something. But the heartburn has left me alone so far this week.'

'Mood swings? I've been expecting those, I hear they're big amongst pregnant women.'

'I keep them well hidden.'

'Really?'

I nodded and smiled. 'Really. Once the first one hit me I figured out what it was pretty quickly.'

'You can control them?'

'No, not really. But when I started wanting to sing and dance one moment and then beat everyone with a shovel the next, I figured hormones had something to do with it.'

He laughed and Thorin thumped his tail on the floor. 'Well, I'm glad you didn't come for me with the shovel.'

'Nah,' I answered, 'I like having you around too much.'

'Good.'

When I woke the next morning Alexander had gone and it was late enough for the sun to be up. But when I rolled over to get out of bed I found a note and lovely bouquet of winter flowers.

Didn't want to wake you. Merry Christmas. I love you.

I sighed and stretched and then burrowed down under the warm covers and went back to sleep.

Week Twenty-Four

Monday was *lille juleaften*, the day before Christmas Eve. My parents were still sleeping soundly in one of the guest rooms upstairs when Thorin and I emerged from my room and crept into the kitchen. I yawned and stretched, trying to reach the ceiling. Thorin ran to the garden door and I let him outside quickly, before he barked. As I waited for the kettle to boil I watched him running around the lawn sniffing all the morning's new scents. The baby kicked me and I rubbed my lower back.

'Good morning,' my mother said as she came into the kitchen.

'Good morning. You're up early.'

'I know. It must be the healthy country air. How's the baby?'

'Kicking away happily. Do you want some coffee?'

'Yes please.' She came over and put her hand on my stomach. She smiled as she was rewarded by a kick from a tiny foot. 'Can't quite believe I'm going to be a grandmother. And you still haven't told him?'

I shook my head. 'No. And I'm not going to.'

She looked up at me, her eyes questioning, but not shocked, as I had expected.

'I'm through with him. I don't want him in my life anymore. He's married and he can work that out on his own. If he wants to get out of it he can find another escape route. I don't want to give my son a life where he's shunted back and forth between me and him. We've had our chance, actually we've had several, and we can't make it work. Why go through all that again and have it hurt other people as well? I'm done. It's my baby, my decision.' I sighed. 'It's just better this way.'

'It's not for me to say,' she said as I got the cups out of the cupboard, 'but I think you're right. I just wonder what it will be like if he does find out. One day he probably will. You don't seem able to avoid him.'

I laughed. 'No, I guess I don't. But right now he's out of my life and I have a baby to focus on.'

'His baby.'

'My baby.'

She smiled and shrugged. 'Don't you think maybe he would want to know? Then it would be up to him to decide whether he wants it to turn his life around. What about child support?'

'I can support my child,' I said and my eyes flashed. 'Keeping this baby was my decision and I accept the consequences. I'm not going to go and ask him for money. And what about *my* life being turned upside down? It's not just about him. Why should he get the luxury of deciding if he wants to be part of our lives? If he really wanted me he wouldn't have married her. I don't need him coming here with another load of empty promises. I can manage perfectly well on my own without a man to keep the wolf from the door.'

She smiled. 'That's my girl.'

For us, little Christmas Eve is a day filled with traditions that have been built up gradually over the years. Since it's usually the first day we all manage to get together, it's the day we decorate the Christmas tree. Then, in the afternoon, we drink mulled wine with raisins and almonds and eat *æbleskiver*, sweet dumplings with icing sugar and strawberry jam. I'd bought some last week and they were now waiting in the freezer. My mother flatly refused to make her own.

'Absolutely not!' she said. 'I have to make my own every year in Paris and get told by know-it-alls who've never tried to make them that they're not fluffy enough or round enough or golden enough. If we can buy them, we're doing it that way. If you want to cook them from scratch in your five-star hotel, that's your decision. But in my opinion sometimes it's all right to use frozen.' She winked at me. 'And sometimes it's all right to get the men to do the work,' she whispered as my father came into the room carrying the last of the Christmas tree decorations.

We'd put the lights on the tree over the weekend and now it was starting to look festive. My father and I opened boxes of decorations and my mother disappeared upstairs. She came back down with a small box in her hands.

'An early Christmas present for you from us both,' she said.

I saw down on the sofa and unwrapped the box. Inside was a collection of Christmas tree ornaments. The star that used to crown the top of my grandparents' tree. A *nisse* made of felt and cotton wool that I'd made when I was little. Woven paper hearts that I'd made with my mother one Christmas when I was university. Baubles that been my great-grandmother's. Small pieces of family history that made here my home.

'And this,' my father said, handing me another little box. 'It's this year's Georg Jensen ornament. Then you'll always remember your first year here.'

'Thank you,' I said and hugged them both. Thorin wagged his tail and sniffed around the tree. Ever since we'd brought it home he'd been circling it, wondering why there was suddenly a tree inside and why this one was not to be marked like every other.

We hung the ornaments and my father brought a tray in from the kitchen with the mulled wine and the *æbleskiver* and a smoothie for me. My mother followed with the icing sugar and the strawberry jam. The lights on the Christmas tree lit up the living room as the windows grew dark.

We spent the next hour putting presents under the tree. I wondered what it would be like next year when there would be toys under it. There would be soft teddies and musical rattles. Maybe there would be stacking blocks that he could pick up and knock over. I had no idea what babies were supposed to be able to do at eight months. But I would know when the time came.

When I went to bed that night I lay in the dark talking to Alexander on the phone for over an hour and watching the stars through the window. The space beside me was empty without him.

I was woken on Christmas Eve by my baby kicking me. I lay quietly under the covers for a while, feeling the little tickling movements. Thorin sensed I was awake and licked my nose, planting an enormous paw on the pillow. He was growing bigger every day and was the gentlest dog I'd ever known. Every so often he'd come up to me and sniff my stomach and sometimes he'd bark. When he did, I'd always feel a kick. I was looking forward to seeing what he thought of the baby when he arrived. He'd taken a real shine to my parents, especially my father who had taken over his morning walk.

I did wonder for a moment what you were doing and where the two of you would be spending Christmas. Would there be songs and laughter and presents under the tree? Next year would be your son's first Christmas. And you wouldn't even know. Maybe by then you'd have another child of your own. Maybe that was what had made up my mind. The thought of finding out that knowing made no difference. That you didn't want our baby any more than you wanted me. I knew I could not bear for that to be true. Of all the things that scared me when I thought of telling you, none were more frightening than that. Not because I wanted you, but because it would have made a lie out of so much of my past.

When I came into the kitchen, my parents were pouring coffee and Thorin was lying contentedly in his basket with the little squeaky carrot that Alexander had given him.

'Good morning. Merry Christmas.'

'Merry Christmas,' my parents answered, and each of them gave me a hug.

I sat down at the table and helped myself to coffee and a bun. I'd never been in a home where you didn't automatically gravitate towards the kitchen. No matter how many comfortable chairs, sofas or soft cushions you had, everyone always found their way to the kitchen to sit on hard chairs and wait for food and drink to be served.

'Are we going to church today?' my mother asked.

'I think I'd like to,' I answered.

Faith was something I'd grown up with as a little girl and gradually lost as the world in all its glory and despair revealed itself to me. Then, like any teenager, I'd gone in search of beliefs and reference points of my own. I didn't know what I believed in now except that it didn't have a name or a structure. Like so many other people all over the world, at Christmas I found a sweet comfort in the traditions of childhood. The familiar carols, the remembered stories, opened up a host of forgotten memories that slumbered throughout the year only to be re-awakened for one day in the cool calm of a church filled with pinecones and candles.

'We just have to decide which service we're going to go to. Dinner will take a while.'

'If we go at two o'clock,' my father said, 'will that give us enough time?'

My mother did a quick calculation in her head and nodded.

'And give us time to take Thorin for his walk this afternoon.'

Snow started falling as we walked to church. As we sat inside singing I could see the falling flakes through the window. The temperature dropped and the wind picked up. As I sat on the hard wooden pew and listened to the priest speak of this time for family and loved ones, it seemed as though the church was suddenly filled with ghosts. I saw my grandparents so clearly beneath the window, my great-grandparents beside them. They were all smiling at me and I found I had tears in my eyes. Unrelated to the sermon, the place, the day, was a tremendous sense of love and continuity. The ones we love never leave us as long as we carry them in our hearts. My baby kicked away inside me and I smiled. I didn't need you. I had everything I needed right here.

When we came outside again the snow was already piled high against the walls of the church. The last time I had been in this church was for my grandfather's funeral. I had sat in one of the front pews and felt like I would never be able to live in a world that did not have him in it. That I would have given anything for five more minutes to hold him close. I remembered how, later that day, I had stood by his grave and waited for tears that would not come because I could not imagine ever feeling anything ever again. My grandfather loved peonies. He hated to admit it because he thought liking flowers was effeminate, but they were his favourite. That was why I wanted them in my garden. I knew that whenever I cut them from the bushes and brought them inside, I would be bringing a part of him back into my life.

But now it was Christmas Eve and my mother tucked her arm in mine and the three of us walked home together through the snow. It was still light but as we moved through town we could see lights coming on in people's houses as Christmas trees were lit. When we got back to the house my mother and I took off our boots and coats and headed for the kitchen while my father took Thorin out for his afternoon walk.

'Right,' she said, 'I need to warm up first. I'm freezing. You put the kettle on while I go and find the recipe.'

'Don't you know it by heart yet? You've been cooking it for years.'

'Yes, Little Miss Chef,' she said and laughed, 'more years than you've been making chocolate chip cookies, and I've seen you still check the recipe every time.'

'That's different!' I quickly protested. 'All you have to do is remember temperature and oven time. Nothing like a cookie recipe with specific amounts of flour, butter and all that. Maybe you're just getting old.'

'Very funny. I can still remove those presents from under the tree, you know.'

'Oh no, no, I'll be good.'

She laughed and went upstairs.

Dinner was the traditional roast duck and my new oven cooked the old recipe to perfection. Thorin lay under the table, his head on my foot. We talked about my plans. With four months to go everything still seemed like a lifetime away. There was time enough to decide between natural birth and drugs, to wonder how long to breastfeed for and all of those things. Caroline and Martin were coming down on Boxing Day to take Christmas pictures of the house. I hoped the snow wouldn't melt. I was certain that pictures of the snow-covered lawn and bedrooms with soft pillows and Christmas candles would be a good addition to the website come next Christmas.

We talked of Christmases long ago, laughed at old stories and remembered old friends.

'Do you remember that summer we spent here when ants kept getting into the kitchen?' my father laughed as he helped himself to more duck.

'Oh yes,' my mother nodded. 'There were coffee grinds everywhere to try to keep them out. And then they just vanished.'

'I loved the fresh peas and strawberries from the garden. I'm hoping the ones I'm growing will be as good.'

'What else have you got growing in the garden?'

I frowned, trying to remember everything Jacobsen had told me. 'Potatoes. Strawberries. Peas. Apples. And I'm sure there were a few other things. Blackberries and tomatoes.'

'What about flowers?' my mother asked.

'I've insisted on peonies. And I want roses and tulips.'

'Lovely.'

'I'm also getting to get lots of loungers and blankets so people can relax in the garden. Even if they just want to lie on the grass with a book.' I found I was looking forward to that too. Rolling on the grass with my baby, holding out a rattle for him to grab and watching him wiggle around.

Once everything had been eaten and cleared away we went into the living room and Thorin went for a quick run in the garden. Every year when we joined hands to walk around the tree I found myself remembering how there had been a time when there had been enough of us to reach all the way around it. Then, slowly over the years, the circle had become smaller and smaller. But next year there would be another little body to help us form a full circle. Thorin came inside and watched in amazement as we walked around the tree singing. Halfway into the second verse he tried to join in, running between all our legs and tripping up my mother, nearly sending her head first into the tree.

My father handed out the presents one by one. We'd always taken our time when it came to unwrapping gifts rather than ripping off the wrapping paper like ferocious animals and moving on without a moment's hesitation. Since my favourite part of Christmas was giving gifts, I wanted to see the reaction of whoever I gave them to. For my mother I had bought a pair of antique earrings I had seen in one of the shops in Rudkøbing. She gave me a big hug and said they would go perfectly with her dress for this year's New Year's Eve party. Recently she had been complaining that there was never anything good on television to keep her entertained while she did the ironing. With that in mind, I had bought her a Netflix subscription.

'I've got three friends I've barely seen this they got this,' she laughed. 'I hope I don't turn out quite as bad.'

'Don't worry,' my father said with a smile, 'the January sales are coming up. Television won't be able to compete with them.'

'Let's see if they can also lure you outside,' I said and handed him a parcel.

'You know how I love my walks. It will take something really special to keep me inside. Although this,' he said with a big smile as he finished unwrapping his present, 'might just do the trick. Thank you.' It was recently published book on the architectural history of Paris. He'd mention it several times over the last few months.

'Until you've finished it,' my mother said. 'Then you'll be dragging me out to see all the buildings it mentions.'

They smiled at each other and I could picture them quite clearly in the wintry Paris afternoon, walking arm in arm and looking at buildings.

'Who is this for?' my father asked, holding up a soft parcel. 'It seems to have lost its label.'

'It's for you,' I replied. 'From me.'

It was a new leather cover for his laptop. 'It's perfect,' he said as he gave me a hug. 'I guess you noticed last time that the old one is looking a little worse for wear.'

'I did. And I knew you would keep meaning to replace it and keep forgetting.'

'Oh thank you very much!' He laughed and my mother joined in. 'But point taken. And thank you.'

Thorin lay in his basket munching on a new rawhide bone while we unwrapped the rest of the present. My parents gave me a lovely selection of baby clothes, the softest little baby blanket, a beautiful maternity dress and a large hamper of various creams and lotions for both me and my baby. There was no present under the tree from Alexander, we had decided to wait and exchange gifts once he got back. I'd bought him a soft, cashmere polo neck for the cold winter evenings in his studio and a leather-bound notebook and fountain pen for his lyrics. He'd told me that too often he ended up writing them on Post-its that he would subsequently lose. I had left his presents in my room. Seeing them under the tree for the next few days would only make me miss him more. I also wasn't sure Thorin could be trusted to keep away from them.

When all the presents had been unwrapped we made coffee and I brought out a selection of chocolates, home-made biscuits and confectionery. The snow on the grass made the garden glow in the light of a full moon and a sky full of stars. It was going to be a cold night. Even though I loathed New Year's Eve, I did love the way the year wrapped itself up at Christmas. The week between Christmas and New Year always seemed inconsequential, a final holiday before it all began once more. My parents would go home, Alexander would come back and in the spring my baby would be born. When Alexander and I talked on the phone as I lay curled under the covers in bed that night, it reminded me of the happiness I'd known as a child when I would take my new Christmas books to bed. I knew it would be a wonderful, eventful year.

I woke up in the middle of the night with a cramp in my leg that almost made me scream. I stuffed a pillow into my mouth and writhed around on the bed, trying to stop myself from crying out and scaring the life out of my parents. I managed to hobble out of bed and tried to straighten out my leg while I bit down hard on my knuckles and whimpered. It was ten minutes before I was able to crawl back into bed and lie curled up, quietly moaning. Thorin licked my nose. I rested my head on his back and must have drifted off to sleep again. When I awoke the wind was buffeting snow against my windows and I could see little frost flowers forming on the glass.

I remembered a time when Christmas Day and Boxing Day had meant family lunches with distant relatives that you only saw once or twice a year. They would go on for hours and involve enough food and drink to provide sustenance for a small army. Like so many things that seemed part of a long-forgotten era, those lunches had ended with my grandparents' generation. Most of the relatives we had enjoyed those lunches with were no longer with us. But I had decided to resurrect the spirit of the tradition tomorrow when Caroline and Martin arrived.

I had enough food in the fridge to withstand a siege. Today I needed to bake bread and make meatballs, meringues and ice cream. Tomorrow I would need to peel prawns, roast pork and make sure the crackling came out nice and crunchy, arrange smoked salmon and herrings in attractive displays, fry bacon and mushrooms for paté. As a concession to the changing times, there would also be at least one salad on the table. While my guests were served beer and akvavit, I would enjoy my San Pellegrino and possibly splurge on another smoothie. After dinner there would be coffee and home-made liqueur chocolates. The last time you vanished without a trace after promising me the moon I wanted to do nothing more than curl up in bed and stuff myself with chocolates. Instead I took a course at a confectioner's and learned how to make them. Diving into the sensual pleasures of food had made me forget about the pleasures I had lost when you'd gone. Whatever the reasons that would bring my guests to my haven, they would certainly be treated to something delicious once they arrived.

'What will you have in the bedrooms besides Lego?' my mother asked.

'Furniture,' I said with a wry smile. 'But yes, there will be chocolates on arrival. And flowers.' I showed her the notebooks I had bought and she suggested supplying drawing pencils.

Caroline and Martin arrived next day shortly before lunch. The table was beautifully decorated and the house smelled of freshly baked bread, roast pork and just a faint hint of chocolate. Thorin barked as their car pulled up in the driveway and my mother opened the door and waved to them.

'Close the door!' my father shouted from the kitchen. 'You're letting all the heat out.'

My mother shook her head and then went outside and closed the door. Five minutes later she came back with Caroline, Martin, various suitcases and photography equipment.

'Welcome,' I said as I took off my apron and ran forward to greet them. 'I hope you're hungry.'

'Starving!' Martin said and gave me a hug. 'Where shall I put all our things? Same room as last time?'

I nodded. 'If you can recognise it. It looks a little different now than it did the last time you were here.'

'I look forward to seeing it. And I'll be sure to shout if I get lost.' He winked at me.

'I'll give you a hand with all that equipment,' my father said as he came out from the kitchen to shake hands. 'Good to see you again, Martin.'

'And you. What's it like to be back on Langeland again after all these years.'

'Feels like coming home again. Especially when I walk past my parents' house.'

'I can imagine.'

'All right, you two,' my mother said. 'Go and put those things away and then come and have a drink before lunch.'

It was a long time since I'd laughed so hard for so long. And every time I laughed my baby kicked me in protest. Martin told stories about his latest clients and made them all sound like those in 'clients from hell' stories that get circulated on Facebook. Caroline took lots of photos and promised to send them to us. Left to her own devices while we cleared the table and Martin helped make coffee, she took her camera and her coat and took Thorin for a run in the garden. Tomorrow we would get lots of pictures of the inside of the house.

When she came back inside, she looked at Martin and said, 'All right, we can get a dog.' You could tell by the look on his face it was the best Christmas present she could have given him.

If only Alexander could have been there, the day would have been completely perfect.

Week Twenty-Five

On the last morning of the year I woke up next to Alexander with a voracious appetite and a craving for cinnamon pastries. When I rolled over and told him he thought it sounded like a great idea, so he threw on some clothes and went off to the bakery with Thorin. He was gone twenty minutes and came back with fresh orange juice, rolls, pastries, assorted jams, cheeses and cold meats. And some newspapers.

'Mmm,' I said and stretched, 'I could get used to this.'

'I'm not going anywhere,' he said and kissed me. 'But you can make coffee. I'm not quite comfortable with your weird new machine.'

'Deal.'

So Alexander laid the table while I made coffee and we spent our New Year's Eve morning lounging in the kitchen, eating and reading and talking. There was an article about Paris in one of the papers he brought back and I pointed out the errors while he poured more coffee. He suggested I write an angry letter to the editor.

'If I weren't so tired these days I might do. Now I'll just feel sorry for the poor people who go on this honeymoon trip they're describing.' I put the paper down with an exasperated sigh. 'But that was one thing I was always a little bit sorry about, growing up in Paris. That I could never have my honeymoon there, 'cause what would be the point.'

'You mean our honeymoon.'

'I ... excuse me?' I stared at him.

He winked at me.

'Uhm ... was that a proposal?'

'An informal one.' He smiled at me.

I looked at him, unsure whether he was joking or not. 'So I guess I should give an informal answer?'

'Something like that.'

'Well,' I shrugged, 'all right then.'

'Maybe not that informal.'

'Then ... in that case ... in an informal way, yes.'

He smiled at me again and offered me pastries. I stared out the window, examining the patterns the frost had left on the glass. I got up and stood looking out across the garden. Thorin was sniffing around outside, his nose covered in snow. Alexander got up and came to join me. He put his arms around me and rested his head against my back. I held onto him and we watched the last part of the sunrise together.

'He's kicking,' Alexander said. 'And I can see it.'

'I know.'

'How does it feel?'

'Painful. Like there is a little pro footballer inside me practicing his kicks. But aside from that it's incredible. There,' I took his hand and placed it on my stomach, 'feel that?'

He grinned and nodded. 'That's amazing. There's a real, live person inside you who's going to come out and live a whole life of their own. Wow. And I'll be able to say I knew him way before that.'

We stood like that for a long time.

It was a windy, blustery afternoon with grey clouds scurrying past under leaden skies. We wrapped ourselves in coats and scarves and took Thorin for a run along the beach. For an hour we walked along the sand, holding hands and sometimes throwing sticks. We found a sausage vendor who was still open and ate hot dogs for lunch, smothered in ketchup, mustard and remoulade with onions and pickled cucumbers. I was so hungry I ate two.

'I like a woman with a healthy appetite,' Alexander said and wiped mustard off my nose. 'I'll never forget how much you ate the first time I took you to McDonalds.'

'Just not too healthy an appetite,' I warned him, 'I have to lose it again once he's born.'

'You haven't been really hungry for months, no matter how hard you've tried. It's good to see you eating.'

'It's good to be hungry again. What's for dinner?'

Thorin barked and dropped a big stick at my feet.

'I thought you were cooking!' Alexander said with fake horror.

We went back to the house as it began to get dark. Alexander went downstairs for a long relaxing bath and I stayed in the kitchen, yearning for the day when I was allowed back in the tub. But in the meantime there was cooking. I had always found it very relaxing, as long as I was left alone to do it. I love company in the kitchen but chopping and grating, weighing and beating, stirring and seasoning, are things I always prefer to do alone. Some people hate backseat drivers. I hate backseat chefs.

I turned on soft music and got my apron out of the cupboard. Thinking of Alexander lying downstairs in the bathtub made me smile. This morning's conversation replayed itself in my head and I could hardly believe it had been real. It seemed so soon in our relationship to be talking about a real future. And yet... And yet the thought of him dreaming of a future for us was intoxicating. Right now I could not imagine my world without him.

'That was fantastic!' Alexander stood in the doorway wrapped in a towel and looking extremely delicious. 'And I was glad to find that the bath didn't leak, so I'm sure Henrik and I did the job properly.'

'Absolutely. I'm glad you enjoyed it. Anything else you'd like to test?'

'The shower in the bedroom? Maybe later?'

I laughed and tilted my head. 'Maybe. I'll just finish up here and then I need to get changed.'

'Can I help you with anything?'

'No, thanks. I don't think you're really dressed for the kitchen.'

'Then I'll be in the bedroom.' He winked at me and headed down the hallway.

We lay in bed for an hour. When I got up to finish cooking, Alexander stretched and burrowed deeper under the covers.

'Maybe we should forget the whole New Year's Eve palaver and just stay in bed.'

'That's a tempting thought,' I said. 'We might manage to wake up just in time to see a few fireworks.'

'We can make our own fireworks.' He drew me to himself again and tickled me till I squealed. 'That's the problem with sleeping during the afternoon. I just don't want to get up and finish the day. No matter how delicious the food.'

'I know what you mean,' I said and yawned. 'It's very tempting to just stay here. But then the oven would probably burn the house down.'

'We can't have that!' he cried in mock horror. 'After all the work I've done on the roof and the bathrooms!'

I wrapped myself in the dressing gown that seemed to be getting tighter each day and went off to the kitchen. I mixed olive oil, garlic, salt and pepper to make a marinade for the steaks. I opened a bottle of wine for the sauce and dusted the earth off the mushrooms.

'Can I help with anything?' Alexander asked.

'You can pour yourself a glass of wine if you like,' I answered. 'And there are some crisps in a bag in one of the cupboards. You could get them out and put them in a bowl. I can't be bothered to do something elaborate with potatoes so we'll just have those.'

'Okay. And I'll lay the table while you go and get changed.'

'Thanks. Just let me get the cake out of the oven.'

'I'll do that. You go get ready.'

I kissed him and headed back to the bedroom to get dressed. I was going to wear the dress my mother had given me for Christmas.

Just before midnight we stood on the front steps and watched as my neighbours treated us to an impressive firework display. Alexander had his arm around me and Thorin stood next to us, barking at the more colourful fireworks and wagging his tail. I felt the baby kick in protest and put a hand on my stomach to see if that might quieten him down. Alexander looked at me and smiled and put his hand over mine. He kissed me while we dimly heard the church clock ringing in the new year.

'Happy New Year,' he said.

'Happy New Year.'

I closed my eyes for a moment as I rested my head against his shoulder and couldn't suppress a smile at how the last year had turned out. It seemed impossible that only twelve months ago I had been living a completely different life, a stranger to the man now standing next to me. I looked down at the distorted shape of my body in my stylish maternity dress. Last year I had been wearing a shimmering grey gown that I could not imagine ever being able to fit into again. I had been at a big party in an apartment overlooking the harbour with vintage champagne and black-tie waiters. Now I had a large dog, an even larger house and a baby just four short months away from being born. There was no champagne for me and the company consisted solely of the man who, earlier that morning, had informally proposed. If I could go back to last New Year's Eve and tell myself about the year I was about to have, I think I would have laughed in my face for telling such impossible lies.

When we got back inside, just before I called my parents to wish them Happy New Year, I noticed a message from a number I recognised as yours.

Happy New Year x

I smiled and shook my head. Then I deleted it. This time it was definitely going to be over. Even if I had to push you kicking and screaming out of my life. I had said 'Happy New Year' to Alexander and I had meant it. I wanted no part of you in the year to come.

Week Twenty-Six

As usual, once the celebrations over, I roared into the new year with all the energy of a greyhound on speed. The first time I woke up and realised that my baby was going to be born *this year* I had leapt out of bed in a panic just have my legs buckle under me in cramp. I practically screamed and Alexander had to help me back into bed and rub my back. Now it was almost a week later and I had nearly got my panic under control. I was hungrier than I had been been for months and all of a sudden there were not enough hours in the day to do all the things I wanted to do and feel all the things I was feeling.

It was on a beautiful crisp winter's day when the skies were blue and there wasn't a cloud to be seen that I fretted away an hour in the hospital waiting to find out if I had gestational diabetes. After they had made me drink the most disgustingly sweet drink I had ever tasted, I had to sit still for an hour before submitting to yet another blood test. I had been so certain that I would be allowed to leave immediately afterwards that I hadn't even brought a book with me. I had planned to look around Odense for a while and then drive back for my first appointment with the florist in Rudkøbing. After a hopeless five minutes I gave up trying to feign some kind of interest in the celebrity scandals that were all over the magazines in the waiting room. Instead I started reading a novel on my phone with one hand while I rummaged in my handbag for my headphones with the other.

Lately Alexander and I had taken to spending the evenings in his studio. While he played and perfected and recorded everything, I curled up in the armchair, Thorin and a stack of notebooks beside me. Every so often I would look up, twirl my pen between my fingers and see him looking at me and smiling. His music surrounded us and I was getting adept at recognising my favourite pieces. When I began to sing along he would always stop for a moment and smile at me before continuing.

During the autumn he had, every so often, casually asked me about the songs that I liked. He had secretly compiled a list of my all-time favourites and recorded his own unique musical interpretation of them for my Christmas present.

'Everyone knows that when a boy loves a girl he makes her a mixtape,' he had said with a smile as he gave it to me. 'I figured I could do a little better than that.'

I found my headphones at the very bottom of my bag, hiding under my keys, and lost myself again in Alexander's music while looking at my watch every few minutes and secretly dying for a pastry. I resented the wasted hour because of all the things I had to do. The painters were finishing the downstairs bedrooms and I had another round of furniture to buy. What I was most looking forward to was putting the finishing touches in all the rooms. The flowers. The Lego bricks in their glass bowls. The little boxes of chocolates. The notebooks, pens and pencils. Suddenly my phone beeped, interrupting my music. I stared at in disbelief. It was you.

Are you coming back home? Is that other woman is still living in your apartment?

I stared at my phone, unsure what to think. When did you suddenly decide to care about where I was? Since when did you write to me before I had replied? Now that I had reconciled myself to the idea of hearing no more from you, now that I was all right with my life without you, now, of course, you wanted to know where I was. You were just a spoiled child who only wanted a toy because someone had told him that he couldn't have it. It seemed so unfair that I, who just a few shorts months ago would have been ecstatic to know that you were reaching out to me, should now read your message and not want it. I shook my head. The last thing I needed was to get stressed out and ruin my test results, I couldn't bear the thought of ever having to taste that drink again. So instead I texted Lisbeth the latest news.

So? It's not like he's leaving his wife. He's pretended an interest before. You get nervous and make plans and nothing happens. Until he shows up with divorce papers, ignore him.

Lisbeth made me laugh. Now I had decided that I was saying goodbye to you, she seemed determined to support my decision and break the drum she had previously beaten about the two of us being destined for each other. Besides, I thought, if you're that desperate to talk to me then don't write, call.

After the doctor had taken a blood sample and told me I could come back in a week's time to pick up the results, I drove back to Rudkøbing. The florist's shop was large and beautifully filled with amazing creations and fragrant blossoms that I had no hope of identifying. The owner, Ruth, came out from the back room with an armful of branches and smiled at me. She was a tiny woman with a mass of red curls who wore long flowing dresses and chunky necklaces.

'Welcome,' she said. 'You're right on time.'
'I was afraid I'd be late. I was in the hospital having another test.'
'Test? No problems I hope?'
'No, no, just the standard one-hour glucose test.'
'Oh no, not that disgusting drink. I'll make you some coffee.'
'Thanks.'
We discovered that our grandparents had known each other and we dug up vague memories of playing in someone's garden together when we were children. One thing I'd loved about coming to Langeland as a child was that every holiday I had made new friends. Three weeks later we'd usually forgotten all about each other, but it had always added to the summer magic of the long softly lit evenings on the playground or by the beach.

'I'm so glad you're doing something with the house,' she said. 'Thanks to Bjarne I already knew all about it. His wife plays golf with my mother.'

'I know. They've asked me to join them once the baby is born. Right now I wouldn't even last three holes. But I really hope the hotel will be a success. Right now it seems like I have too much to do and not enough time to do it.'

'I felt that way before my first baby was born. It will work out, I promise. Otherwise just cross your legs tightly towards the end.'

We laughed and she poured the coffee and popped the lid of an elaborate biscuit tin decorated with angels and clouds.

'So you plan to have flowers in all the bedrooms as well as the living and dining room and activity room, is that right?'

I nodded. 'The bedrooms will just get them when new guests arrive. And the other rooms once or twice a week.'

'We can definitely work something out. How do like lilies?'

'I loathe lilies,' I confessed. 'I associate them with funerals and dead French royals.'

'Fair enough.' She dipped a biscuit in her coffee. 'What flowers do you like?'

'Peonies. And roses and tulips and daisies.'

'Carnations?'

'God no. Even my grandmother wouldn't have had those in the house.'

'Okay. I think I've got a pretty good idea about where to start. Come with me to the back and I'll make up a bouquet for you and we'll see if we're on the right track.'

'I know it will be ages before I need flowers,' I told her, 'but if I wait I'll end up putting it off and then I'll have to navigate your displays with a pram and I know that will end in disaster.'

Ruth nodded and guided me to the back room. 'I understand completely. I'm very big on forward planning myself.'

The skies were still the same brilliant blue when I walked home, and my ears were quickly numb with cold. Ruth had bound a lovely bouquet of brilliant winter-white flowers whose names I had already forgotten. Thorin greeted me with a bark and a wagging tail when I walked through the door. The painters were just finishing off the second bedroom.

'It looks great,' I told them. 'Coffee?'

'Thanks. We'd love some.'

While it brewed I trimmed the flowers and found a glass vase that had been my grandmother's. I filled it with water and stood staring at it for a while. These things that I had brought with me to this island showed me how great was my desire to make this place my home. All these things were part of me, part of my life and my history. In Copenhagen I had kept most of them in my little storage room in the basement, here they were on display. I took the vase into the living room and put it on a table high enough to be out of reach of Thorin's tail. I took the coffee down to the painters and started rummaging through boxes in the utility room, ready to decide which picture frames, throws and candlesticks would go in which bedrooms. Tomorrow I would buy a pram and a cot and all the other baby things. Today I would dress the upstairs bedrooms. But first I would tell you goodbye.

I'm not coming back. You don't need me hanging around in your new life.

Week Twenty-Seven

I was sitting in my usual café in Odense with Alexander after an intense morning of shopping for baby things and with an hour to go before my appointment at the hospital. Not caring about my imminent meeting with the scales, I attacked a steaming glass of hot chocolate with whipped cream and chocolate sprinkles. I was exhausted and my feet hurt but I was happy. I had found a pram that would eventually transform into a pushchair, once the baby was old enough and I had earned the degree in advanced engineering it would take to figure out how to do it.

'The girl in the shop made it look easy,' Alexander pointed out.

'Of course she did, she's probably done it a million times. After completing an obligatory three-week course.'

'Fair point.'

I stirred my hot chocolate and yawned. 'But I've got it now. And the crib and the bath.'

'How do you plan to wash him in that bucket?'

'It's not a bucket, it's a Tummy Tub.' I smiled and took a long sip. 'Lisbeth had one. Emma screamed and screamed for a week with colic, but the moment Lisbeth put her in that tub she had the most ecstatic look of pure bliss on her face.'

'Do you think he will be a screamer?' he asked with an anxious look on his face.

'I don't know. But I hope not.'

'Do you have a name for him yet?'

I nodded. At first I had thought that I was going to name him after you. But the more time passed the less comfortable I was with that, and once I had said my final goodbyes it seemed like a ludicrous idea. 'Yes. I'm going to call him Émile. I always liked that name. And he has to have something to show that his mother grew up in Paris.'

'Émile. I like that. But we should be going if you're going to make it to your appointment.'

'Oh, is it that late? I'll go and pay.'

'Already taken care of.'

'Thank you.'

Alexander picked up the bags of baby clothes that I had bought and held the door open for me as we left.

My usual chair in the hospital waiting room was ready for me when we arrived. It seemed a regular part of my pregnancy by now. I had barely managed to lower myself into it before my obstetrician opened her door and beckoned to me. She ushered us in and looked surprised to see Alexander but refrained from asking questions.

'How are you feeling?' she asked as we sat down.

'A little up and down this week. Last week wasn't great but my energy levels are being nice to me this week.'

'It's to be expected. Any pains?'

'Occasional leg cramps.'

'Can't do much about those I'm afraid. Now, I have your test results here. You don't have gestational diabetes which I'm sure you'll be pleased to hear, but I'm a little worried about your liver.'

I stared at her. 'My what?'

'Your liver. Some of these results are a little strange. Now, I'm sure it's nothing that you need to worry about. It's probably just suffering because your baby is kicking it.'

'Kicking my liver?' I stared at her uncomprehendingly, my mind forming a picture of my baby in boxing gloves with a towel around his neck while some hard-drinking coach yelled at him to jab with his right.

'In a manner of speaking. But what we have to do I'm afraid is test you for hepatitis C, just to be completely sure. It's probably nothing and I don't won't to worry you, but let's be safe.'

'Hepatitis C?' I kept staring at her until something clicked in my mind and all the wrong buttons went off. 'But that's what junkies get when they share needles and sleep in stairwells! I've never done drugs in my life!'

She gave me a sympathetic smile and stroked my arm. 'Don't think of it in those terms. You'll be fine. It's just to be sure. It's just a test to be absolutely sure that there is nothing wrong with your liver and it is just your baby kicking it. I have seen this happen before, although only once or twice, and all those women turned out just fine.'

'How could I suddenly have got that? Don't you test for that with all the other things?'

'Actually we don't.' She tried another smile. It can occasionally be sexually transmitted but we only test for the most common STDs.'

'Oh God.' I rubbed my temples and tried to breathe deeply.

Alexander took my hand and smiled at me. 'You'll be fine.'

'How do you know that?' I snapped at him.

'I just do.'

'And I'm sure you will, too,' my doctor said again. 'But let's be sure.'

I nodded and we spoke for a few more minutes, pointless small talk that went in one ear and out the other. She took another blood test which she told me would be ready in a week.

'Try not to worry,' she said as we left. 'Even if the test is positive there's lots that we can do. But I'm quite sure it won't be.'

I wanted to scream, 'Then why even do it?' But I didn't. Instead I merely nodded, not trusting myself to speak.

In the car on the way home I just stared out of the window. I still didn't trust myself to say anything, I was afraid that the first volatile words out of my mouth would reduce me to tears. Instead I sat trying to remember if I had ever had unprotected sex with someone who could have given me this. I couldn't think, couldn't see anyone's face clearly in my mind. I had always been so careful. I'd never ever taken any risks, I'd always ...

You!

You were the only one I had ever left myself that open with. Oh my God, I would kill you if you had given me this! If you were the one who was going to cut short the time I had with my child I was going to hunt you down in all your marital bliss and beat you to death with a spoon.

'Are you okay?' Alexander asked.

'No. Not really.' I tried to smile at him. 'I'm sure I'm fine. But I will worry about this and feel awful all week. I knew things were going too well. At some point there had to be a bump in the road. I know I always imagine the worst, but this is just ridiculous.'

'We all do that. But you are going to be fine. And I'll be right here with you, no matter what happens. And stay away from the Internet. Don't spend a week looking this up and worrying yourself into an early grave.'

I smiled at him and he took my hand. I stared out of the window again and tried to remember what I knew about the illness my doctor was testing me for. I vaguely remembered something about liver failure, cirrhosis, liver cancer and ultimately death. Great. I'd turned my whole life around to have a baby and now I wouldn't even get to be there as it grew up. I closed my eyes and tried to sleep so I wouldn't cry.

When we got home Alexander went out to get us some food while I curled up on the sofa and Thorin put his head on my lap and whined.

'I know what you mean,' I said and stroked his head. Then I leaned back on the sofa and closed my eyes as I felt a kick on the right side of my stomach. Maybe the doctor was right and my bizarre test results were purely the result of being used as a punch bag. Of course, that was it. I sat up and shook my head. Thinking dark thoughts about death and disease was the last thing I needed. I got up and went to look out across the lawn. But what if this beautiful house that I had made, the lovely garden where my baby would play, my wonderful dog, would all be lost to me? I'd be stuck in a hospital bed pumped full of medication, would probably need a liver transplant before I finally collapsed and died. What would happen to my baby then? All the plans I had made, all the dreams I had for our life together, the magical childhood I would give him and now it was over before it had even begun. Thorin nuzzled my hand and whined again and I smiled at him.

I lived through the week like a zombie, worried at every unfamiliar kick and strange sensation. I cried into my pillow when I woke up afraid, and each time Alexander was right beside me, rubbing my back, holding me close till I fell asleep again. My energy levels were up and down six times a day. I wanted desperately to get the house ready and yet half the time all I wanted to do was sleep. I spent hours walking through the garden with Thorin at my side, throwing sticks and watching him gambol through the snow. I tried to think positive and believe everything was going to turn out all right, but deep down I was so scared. What was going to happen to me?

 I was more frightened than I dared to admit, even to myself. I feared for the world I had built, I feared for the future I had begun to dream of. I feared for my child, for what would happen to him if I were no longer here. I worried about provisions I had not made, I worried about his life without me. In my mind I pictured my son, my little Émile, and I knew that nothing was more important to me than him. My fears were all for him and none for myself. The little life was not even truly in the world yet, but the thought of it filled my entire being. I *had* to be all right for his sake. I had above all things to stay healthy to ensure a good life for him. If it turned out I did have this disease then I would have failed as a mother before I had even truly begun. That was the fear which kept me awake at night. It was the first cloud in my sky, the first glimpse into the true terrors of parenthood. The life I had previously known was now gone forever. In my dreams, my new life was going to be so perfect. The thought of it being ruined before it had even begun was heartbreaking.

I knew I was being wildly irrational. I knew there was no possible way that I could ever have contracted the disease whose name I couldn't even bring myself to speak, but I desperately hoped that by worrying enough I could somehow make everything all right. I wondered if other women had suffered similar scares but I knew that Alexander was right about staying away from the Internet.

To banish the phantoms of disease I tried to keep busy and threw myself into the task of dressing up the guest rooms. I washed the baby clothes I had bought and marvelled at how tiny they seemed. The kitchen was where I spent most of my time. When the house was quiet I curled up on the wooden bench with a cup of tea and lost myself in my favourite novels. When I was with Alexander I tried to laugh and smile and worked very hard at not pushing him away, although the temptation to shut him out and withdraw into myself was sometimes almost too great. I had no intention of telling my parents anything until I absolutely had to. Why worry them before I knew for sure that there was something to worry about? So I waited. And each morning, I marked off another day with a big mental X as I counted down the hours until I could get my test results.

Week Twenty-Eight

The hospital corridor seemed unusually loud and empty as Alexander and I waited to be called in. He was distractedly leafing through a magazine while I stood staring out of the window. The morning sun was slowly creeping up over the horizon, revealing frost on the on some of the cars. I imagined they belonged to the doctors and nurses on the night shift. They had probably got more sleep than I had the last few nights.

'She's late,' I said, looking at my watch. 'On the bright side, if I were dying I'd think she'd have been here on time to tell me."

'You're not dying. You're going to be fine.' I thought I detected a slight edge to his voice.

I sighed. I knew he was probably right and I had spent a week worrying over nothing, but the thought of not getting to spend my life with my baby seemed so terrifying. I'd spent most evenings hugging my stomach and trying not to panic. I knew I had been shutting him out despite all efforts to the contrary. I also knew it wasn't fair.

'I'm sorry,' I said and sat down next to him. 'I'm sorry I've shut you out this past week. I didn't mean to. I'm just not very good at sharing my problems. And I didn't want to bore you with endless repetitions of doom and gloom.'

'Yes,' he said, 'you did shut me out. But you wouldn't have bored me. I wanted to help. But it seemed as though you didn't really want me around.'

'No!' I took his hand and tried to smile. 'I guess I'm just not used to having a man in my life who doesn't run away at the first sign of trouble. Maybe I thought that if you really knew how worried I was, you wouldn't be able to deal with it.'

'Anne, I love you. That means that if you're upset so am I. If you're worried about the baby I worry too.'

'I should know that, I suppose.'

'Yes,' he smiled at me, 'you should.'

'I love you, too.'

'Good morning,' my obstetrician came hurrying down the corridor with an armful of files. 'I'm so sorry I'm late.'

'That's okay,' I lied and smiled politely at her. We followed her into her office and I burned holes in her back with my eyes and cursed her under my breath for not even bothering to be punctual when I'd just lived through a week in hell. We sat down in silence.

'Well, the good news is that you're fine.' She shuffled her papers and smiled at me and stole a quick glance at Alexander.

'Oh thank goodness!' I let out an explosive breath and Alexander squeezed my hand. 'I was so worried.'

'I'm sure. And I'm sorry you had to go through that. Unfortunately we couldn't hurry the test along. I think I told you, it's only the second time that I've seen test results like yours so we don't really have a procedure for dealing with it. We don't even have a pamphlet or a webpage for you to read.'

'I tried to stay away from things to read,' I told her. 'I wasn't quite sure what I would end up believing or worrying about.' I smiled at Alexander. 'But I think your punchbag theory might have been right. Most of the jabs I feel are on that side.'

'So that's the good news.'

'There's bad news?' Alexander asked, speaking for the first time.

'No, no,' she shook her head and passed me some of the papers she had been shuffling.. 'Not bad news. But you are a little anaemic so I want you to start taking some iron tablets. It happens to a lot of women during their pregnancies. At least this is something we can give you information about.' She then wrote an illegible scribble on a piece of paper. 'You can pick these up at any pharmacy.' I reached for the papers automatically, hardly hearing her. I glanced quickly at it, her doctor's scrawl a bad cliché. Hopefully the pharmacy would be able to decipher it.

Alexander took me out for smoothies and muffins to celebrate. Walking through town he didn't once let go of my hand. I wondered if he could feel me trembling.

'Feeling better?' he asked.

'Much. Now I feel silly having spent a week worrying. I should have known it would all come to nothing.'

'Of course you worried. I'd have been surprised if you hadn't.'

'I'm amazed that you stayed with me all this time,' I squeezed his hand and smiled at him. 'I must have driven you crazy this past week.'

He shook his head. 'You didn't. I could see how upset you were. I could understand that you were worried. All I could do was tell you that you would be okay and that really didn't seem like enough. I didn't want you to have to go through all that by yourself. But I did sometimes think you were pushing me away.'

I nodded. 'I tried so hard not to. I've never been good at asking for help, never been good at reaching out to people when I'm in sad situations. When people ask me if I want to talk about it I always shrug and tell them I'm fine.'

'Why?'

'I honestly don't know. I guess it's partly because I'm embarrassed, partly because I have to prove that I can do everything by myself and partly because I'm secretly worried they wouldn't want to help me anyway.'

'Why on earth would you worry about that? Who wouldn't want to help you? You're sweet, you're kind and you're so good at helping others. Just look at what you've done for me already and how Henrik and Bjarne are fighting over who gets to finish off the work on your house.'

'They are?' I couldn't help laughing at the thought of it.

'Of course they are. And their wives are in despair because every man who comes near your house immediately puts on five kilos.'

'Okay, I can take a hint, no more cakes.'

'Let's not be hasty.'

'Right now I'm just glad this week is over.'

'Me too,' he said. 'On the bright side,' he squeezed my hand, 'it will have been good practice if we have to go through the same thing next time.'

'Next time?' I stared at him.

'Next time,' he repeated and looked straight at me. 'When we have a baby.'

'When we …'

'One day.' He smiled and squeezed my hand again.

I laughed nervously. 'One step at a time. You are only twenty-two.'

He made a face at me and held open the café door. 'There's plenty of time. You'll believe I'm staying one day.'

I tried to keep my mind on other things as I headed towards a table and sat down. There would be time later to think of all that, time to wonder about whether he meant it or whether he had just gone temporarily insane. For now, I could breathe again. I could keep making plans and enjoy the rest of my pregnancy. Now I knew what people meant when they said that a weight had been lifted. I didn't want to think about the future or what tomorrow might bring. Right now all I really wanted was to have something nice to eat and then go to sleep.

'You seem hungry again,' Alexander said as I devoured the menu with my eyes.

'I am. But I'm not eating more than one muffin. However much I might want to. And I need to find a pharmacy that can decipher the doctor's bizarre squiggles. Can't believe I … ouch! Oh damn this hurts!'

'Sciatica again?'

'Yes.' I gritted my teeth and tried not to scream. 'Whatever nerve he is bouncing on like a trampoline it's probably one that terrorists aim for when they torture their victims.'

Alexander laughed and shook his head.

'Oh God,' I hissed. 'Whatever labour is like it can't be worse than this.'

'That bad?'

'Like someone is trying to saw off my leg with a rusty blunt knife.' I took a deep breath and tried to remember some crap I'd once read about pain being a mental state and how it could be mastered. I breathed again, slowly and deeply, willing the pain to go away and digging my nails into the palm of my hand.

'Muffin?'

'Please. And a hammer to bash it with.'

When we got home I fell asleep on the sofa and Alexander took Thorin for a walk. Half-asleep, I heard the sound of the front door opening as they came back but burrowed deeper under my throw and went back to sleep. In my dream I saw Alexander bouncing on a trampoline with twenty-two babies while terrorists came swarming into the garden with baskets of rusty knives.

About an hour later I woke up and noticed that candles had been lit and delicious cooking smells were wafting through the house. I yawned and stretched and walked into the kitchen. Alexander was covered in flour, wearing my apron and kneading dough on the worktop.

'What are you doing?' I asked, sitting down on the bench and tucking my feet up under me. Thorin sat next to me and wagged his tail. I patted his head.

'Trying your recipe for rosemary and garlic bread. I figured it was time for me to branch out.'

'Okay. Although I think the flour is meant to go in the dough and not all over you.'

'We had a little accident.'

'We?'

'I took it out of the cupboard with one hand and then Thorin wagged his tail. I tripped and fell backwards.'

'That explains those strange white patches on his fur,' I laughed.

'I got most of it out. I was planning to brush him.'

'I'll do that. I'm just sorry I missed the show. And whatever else you're cooking looks interesting.'

'Chicken breasts in white wine sauce.'

'I'm really very impressed.'

'I have my moments.' He winked at me.

I looked at him and allowed my thoughts to return to what he had said earlier. Could his mind really be going down those paths, mapping out a future for the two of us that not only involved my baby, but more babies later down the line? He was so young. Wasn't this just a dream that he was chasing, based on the belief we have when we're young that every relationship is going to lead to the altar because surely we've found the one? Before we get older and wiser and find out that love doesn't always last forever and we stop expecting a crock of gold at the end of every rainbow. Part of me wanted nothing more than to believe in the promises he wanted to make, but at the same time I was all too clearly aware of the dangers of letting myself do it. What he believed himself ready for and what he was truly ready for could be worlds apart. If that was the case he would realise it one day. And then he would leave.

'Penny for your thoughts,' he said and I came abruptly out of my reverie.

'What? Oh, nothing worth a penny.'

I walked over to the worktop and put my arms around him, resting my head on his back. Why would he leave? He wasn't you. I realised then that I was letting my memories of you poison my relationship with him. You had always left, so he would, too. You could never handle any situation fraught with emotion, so of course neither could he. I'd focused so much on the age difference between us, picturing him as more immature than he actually was. But when I thought of his life, the choices he had made, the dedication he brought to his music and his work, I knew that this was no ordinary twenty-two-year-old. He really did love me. He really did want to be part of my life and my baby's. When he looked into the future he saw a life that we would live together. As I stood there with my arms around him, I began to see it, too.

Two days later Henrik's daughter Tina came for lunch. She was, as he had said, a yoga instructor. She was also tired and stressed after holding down three teaching jobs in Copenhagen to pay rent on a minuscule apartment she never found the time to really live in. She kept running her hands through her short curly hair that was so blonde it was almost white, and all her nails were chewed to the quick. She cradled a cup of green tea in her hands while I finished laying the table and we talked about our favourite cafés and shops in Copenhagen. Her apartment was only a few streets away from mine and we knew a lot of the same places. She talked a lot about food and how much she believed in organic produce, so naturally she got very excited when I told her about my plans for the garden. For lunch I had decided to treat her to the culinary experience I pictured my guests enjoying. Three hours and three courses later I took her outside to show her the garden.

'You know,' she said as we trudged through the snow, 'it's amazing, but every time I've come back here lately I don't want to leave. As soon as I cross over the bridge I'm full of energy. I even manage to stop biting my nails.'

'I know just what you mean. I've found that since I've been back here. It's a wonderful place of respite. Like a cocoon.'

'The perfect place to come to when you need to unwind.'

'The perfect place to run to when something has happened that leaves you needing to unwind.'

She nodded. 'So how do you see all this working? Tell me how people are going to unwind here.'

I knelt down and scooped up some snow while I started telling her about everything I had planned. Thorin barked and I threw the cold snow to him. He sneezed as it hit him on the nose.

'This garden would be a fabulous place to practice yoga when the weather gets warmer. Particularly that spot over there under the trees,' Tina said and pointed to the apple trees. 'I can just imagine it. The green leaves rustling in the breeze. Sunlight dappling through the branches. And the fresh air. Oh the fresh air.' She took lots of deep breaths as though she were trying to store up enough clean air to last till her next visit.

'Could you see yourself living here again?' I asked. 'Langeland is lovely but it is small and far away from lots of things we take for granted in the city.'

'I know that,' she nodded and smiled, 'I grew up here, remember? Ironically, I couldn't wait to leave and now I can't wait to come back. Maybe that's just because I don't like my life back there right now. After a few years here I may be dying to get out again.'

'I never would have guessed that I was going to end up here. After the year I've had I'm ready to take things as they come.'

We went back inside and Thorin ran after us. I made coffee and put an assortment of home-made chocolates on the table. Tina's eyes widened.

'Wow. This really is going to be a VIP place.'

I nodded. 'One thing I've learned is that it's during those times when we feel at our worst that we most need the comfort of little things. Soft sheets, good quality food, rest. Unfortunately it's during those times that we forget to take care of ourselves and the little things are the first to go. You know, we end up in our dressing gowns eating biscuits straight out of the packet.'

'I'd never thought of it like that. But you're right.' Tina selected a chocolate. 'Coconut ones are my favourites.'

I poured coffee for us both. 'So if we're going to make plans for you to give lessons, I'd like to get some photos of you and some information for the website. The more we can push all the different things we have to offer the better.'

'So I got the job?'

'If you're moving back here, you got the job. Such as it is. 'Cause you have to know that I don't know when I'm going to open and right now I really can't promise anything permanent. It'll be a freelance gig. I'll offer my guests the option but what they want to do or pay for will be up to them. Maybe most of them would rather just walk in the garden. You never know.'

'I understand that.' I could see her making preliminary plans in her head. 'Actually, I have to admit I was kind of hoping for an immediate solution that would just whisk me away from all my current jobs, but this is probably better. I'm not sure exactly when I'm coming back here and I also need to look at the other things available to me. Like you said, this would be a freelance gig. Roughly when do you see it all starting?'

'My baby is due in April,' I told her. 'We have a few more things to do on the house that have to wait until the weather gets better. I don't want the first guests to be disturbed by workmen swarming all over the place, so it'll probably be autumn before we're completely ready for business.'

'Can I ask you a personal question?'

'You can ask,' I laughed, 'I may not answer.'

'How are you going to manage all this and a new baby? What if your baby just wants to feed all day or cries all night?'

'My mother is taking time off to come and help me,' I told her, 'and I'll find a way to make it all work.' Last week I'd been worrying that I'd barely get to enjoy my baby's life. I wasn't going to worry about the minor details right now.

Week Twenty-Nine

As the year crept into its second month I was ready to start generating a little publicity for my project. An initial talk with the local newspaper led to me being awake and cleaning the house at five o'clock on the morning the journalist and photographer were due to arrive. I threw together a batch of buns and dug out some home-made jam I'd bought at a roadside stall when Alexander and I drove through the countryside last autumn. Once the buns were rising in a warm spot out of the reach of Thorin, I attacked the dust with a vengeance. He ran outside and I worried about him coming back inside and trekking all over my floors with his muddy paws. When the sun began to come up I knew it was going to be one of those dazzling winter days where the world really seems like it is starting anew. The sky was clear, and when I opened up all the windows a brisk winter breeze blew through the house and left crisp, fresh air in its wake.

  I dusted, polished, hoovered and washed. I plumped up pillows and cushions and lit scented candles. I made all the beds, thankful that the last great shopping trip had been completed two days before and all the last pieces of furniture put together yesterday. By the time they arrived, just before ten, the house was as clean and fragrant as it had ever been. If the estate agent who had sold it to me could see it now, he would have clapped his hands with glee.

They stayed for three hours and took photos of everything from every angle. I managed to avoid answering when the journalist asked me exactly why I had returned to Langeland and what had inspired me to buy the house. I closed my eyes for a second and saw so clearly, for some reason, the cup of coffee I had left behind in the kitchen on that April morning last year when I had run from my apartment. But I didn't tell him about the coffee, your wedding, or that all of this had just been an insane impulse. Instead I told him about the night Lisbeth and I had sat in the garden and how her remark about having somewhere to run had started the wheels turning in my mind. I went through the work that had already been done and outlined my plans for the future. He loved hearing that a yoga instructor had already signed on and that one more person would be returning to the island.

'It's fantastic,' he said, spreading jam on his third bun. 'We have to ensure that the island doesn't turn into nothing more than a tourist park and a summer festival.'

'It's not that bad,' I told him and laughed.

'It's bad enough,' he said. 'The population is dropping. We don't really have any industry left. There's no thriving job market. Actually there is no job market, thriving or otherwise.'

'But even my guests will leave, so they will almost be like tourists.'

'How many people have you given work to since you've been here?'

'Uh ...' I did a quick calculation. 'Six. Plus the yoga instructor. And my photographer and web designer.'

'Nine people who have had work because of what you're doing. And I imagine at some point you'll be wanting a cleaner or two. Your guests will come and go, but you're bringing a business here. You're doing something. You're not just buying a holiday home and renting it out through an agency.'

'Then I hope you'll write a good article.'

'Oh I will. Actually, I'd like to try and get three articles out of this.'

'Three?'

'Two now and then we could come back and talk to you again when you're ready to open.'

'That would be perfect.'

'For the first instalment, I think I'd rather focus on you than the hotel.'

'On me?'

'Yes,' he nodded. 'It's a wonderful story. Prodigal granddaughter returns. Your memories, your love of the island. Why you came back here ... So I'd like to get some photos of you around Rudkøbing. Maybe a shot down by the beach with the bridge in the background.'

'Okay,' I nodded, seeing it take shape in my mind. 'Okay.'

'For the second article we can focus on the project so we can use all the photos we've taken today. But I think you are the way to get people interested and make sure they read the second article and spread the word. Then they'll be ready for the big spread when you open.'

'That's far more than I could have hoped for.'

'I think people will like your story. Can we come back next week and hear more about that?'

I nodded and showed them out. Thorin followed them to the door and wagged his tail. I went back to the kitchen to clear up. They'd eaten every last bun and all of the jam.

That evening I toured in my beautiful house. Alexander let me in as though he was the owner and I was the guest. My imaginary suitcase in hand, I climbed the stairs and went into one of the bedrooms. I opened the cupboards, I sat in the comfortable chair, I got up to admire the view from the window. In the bathroom I enjoyed the cool, clean space and fondled the soft towels. Walking down to the kitchen, I stopped in the living room and opened the doors to the garden. Even though the evening was cold I stood in the doorway and tried to count the stars. In the city I had tended to forget them. I had rarely given it a second thought when I looked up at the skies and didn't see them. There were so many things about life here that seemed far removed from everything I remembered from the city. The longer I stayed here, the more I found that I enjoyed it. It surprised me in countless ways, but I got more enjoyment out of taking Thorin for his walks along the beach than I used to get from endless window shopping or whiling away the hours in cafés. Looking up at the stars gave me an enviable sense of peace. If someone had told me a year ago that I would be content spending my days poring over cookbooks and experimenting with cakes and interior design I would have been disbelieving and envious all at the same time. To think that I could so happily turn my back on all those things I used to believe I would be desolate without. One of the things I most enjoyed here was going to sleep at night in silence, so different from being awakened by the neighbours arguing or people coming home from the night shift.

Alexander came and stood next to me and put his arms around my waist. There was no denying that he was one of the things that made Langeland so special. I could not imagine being here without him. He had helped me create this beautiful refuge and made me certain that I would never need anything like it for myself again.

But even the successful day could not chase away my nightly cramps. Waking up wanting to scream, I knew in theory it would help if I were to get out of bed and try to press my foot into the floor to straighten my leg out, but even the thought of doing that was too painful. I lay whimpering in bed, biting my pillow and just hoping the pain would go away soon. If all these pregnancy aches were meant to be preparation for labour I had no idea how I would ever get through it. But even through the painful haze that seemed to make the walls liquid, I could not suppress a bubbling sense of happiness inside me. After the cramps had subsided and I had got comfortable again, I lay there with a smile on my face. Whoever would have thought that getting bigger and being filled with aches and pains would make me so happy? All the things that had mattered so much before seemed insignificant beside the miracle happening inside me. As another cramp hit I found myself grateful for my enormous house which afforded me the privacy to scream the walls down without worrying about what the neighbours might think. Alexander awoke with a jump, convinced I'd gone into labour.

Week Thirty

Alexander surprised me early one morning with breakfast in bed. I had been vaguely aware of him and Thorin getting up, but I must have gone back to sleep. He came into the bedroom carrying a tray laden with coffee, carrot buns, pastries and freshly squeezed apple and carrot juice with a hint of ginger. I'd put so many miles on my juicer during the early weeks of my pregnancy that it had burned out. I'd decided to invest in a new industrial-strength one now I could write it off as a business expense and be absolutely sure that it wouldn't be some useless piece of kitchen paraphernalia that would just gather dust in a cupboard. Alexander had bought me a recipe book and I was diligently making my way through it.

'Mmm, that's delicious,' I said as I took the first sip.

'I know,' he said, 'I've got my own glass of it in the kitchen. I'm still not quite on a first name basis with the new coffee machine, but the juicer and I are getting along fine. And when you've finished, I've got a surprise for you. Oh, and I've taken Thorin for his walk.'

'This is a surprise. Thank you. Breakfast and dog walking. What's the occasion?'

'I'll tell you about that when you're finished. But for now just believe I really wanted to spoil you.'

I laughed and he waved at me from the door on his way back to the kitchen.

I reached for my book from the bedside table and sipped my coffee and juice. I buttered my carrot bun and told myself it was healthy because it had vegetables in it. I was meeting the journalist and photographer later that morning and I wanted to look relaxed and radiant for my photos. My heartburn had returned with a vengeance but, for the moment at least, the cramps were leaving me alone. Good thing too, or there would have been juice and buns all over the bed.

When I came into the kitchen there was a big bouquet of colourful flowers on the table. Alexander took my hands in his, kissed me and led me to one of the chairs. Thorin lay at my feet and wagged his tail, looking as though he was in on whatever Alexander had planned. I scratched his ears and he licked my hand. Alexander had made more juice and he poured me another glass.

'I heard from Simon again,' he said. 'He liked what I sent him. Really liked it. And so did everyone else. Apparently they liked it so much that they want me to come in for an initial recording session. I think I got myself a record deal!'

'Oh Alexander, that's fantastic!' I clapped my hands and threw my arms around him to give him a big hug and a kiss.

'It would never have happened without you. So breakfast was about spoiling you because I wanted to, but this is to say thank you.' He handed me an envelope.

I took it from him with a puzzled look. When I opened it I found reservations to a hotel for a long weekend, but the name of the hotel and its location had been blacked out. Accompanying it was a photo of what looked like part of a wall, artistically lit up in the moonlight.

'What's this?' I asked. 'Are we going away?'

'Yes. I'm taking you away for the weekend.'

'Really?'

'Yes. We leave on Friday and stay till Monday. I've already spoken to Bjarne and Helle and they'll take care of Thorin. You should have some time away to relax before the baby comes.'

'That's a wonderful surprise. Thank you so much. I'm looking forward to it already. But you won't tell me where we're going? Please?'

'No. It's going to be a surprise. But you don't need a passport. I know you can't fly right now.'

I kissed him again and finished my juice with an excited little smile on my face.

I met Aksel the journalist and Torsten the photographer as planned on the beach later that morning. A brisk breeze was blowing and there were little white tops on the waves. The sea was a dark slash of grey under slightly brighter skies. All the time I had spent on my hair was wasted, blown away by the wind, but Torsten was kind enough to pretend I had a beautiful pregnancy glow. In reality I was simply red-cheeked from the cold. Thorin ran beside me and Torsten kept taking photos. I told Aksel stories of my grandparents, my great-grandparents, my parents' life in Paris. When we left the beach we walked all the way through Rudkøbing, stopping outside houses where I had known the owners and could remember stories about them. Finally we came to my grandparents' house and to my surprise Aksel knocked on the door.

'I told them we were coming,' he said. 'Look, they even weeded the front garden for you.'

I laughed. 'Really? We're going in here? I get to see it again?'

Aksel nodded and I beamed at him. 'Even if they had refused, it would have been worth nagging them just to put that smile on your face.'

I laughed and gazed up at the house, enveloped by memories. 'And they're okay with having photos taken?'

'Yes. They quite liked the idea of being in the paper.'

'Most people would.'

It was a young couple who opened the door, looking nothing like the people I had been secretly scowling at for the last seven months. They introduced themselves as Sara and Nikolaj and stepped aside to let us come in. I stopped dead as I walked into the hallway. There on the walls was the curry-coloured wallpaper that my grandparents had put up in the fifties. So retro it was almost hip again. On the floor was the same brown carpet. I half expected my grandmother to poke her head out from the kitchen and tell me to shut the door because I was letting all the heat out.

'Anne?' Aksel asked. 'Are you okay? You look a little pale.'

'No, no. I'm fine. It's just ... nothing's changed. I haven't been in this house for ten years and it's like I was here only yesterday. It's the same wallpaper, the same carpet. Even the same smell in the hallway. Do you know how many hours I spent reading on those stairs?'

Aksel looked at me and his eyes narrowed. I could tell he was framing sentences for his article in his head.

'You used to read on the stairs?'

I nodded and ran my hand over the banister. Even the long scratch I made in the wood the day I slid down it in my jeans was still there. 'I never found the sofas very comfortable and during the day there were always so many people in the living room. When I couldn't read in the garden this was a nice place to sit. Close to the kitchen for snacks and I could still hear if anyone called me.' In my mind's eye I could see a much younger me sitting on the stairs, devouring a book with two more ready on the next step.

Sara cleared her throat and I came out of my reverie. She took us along to the kitchen while Nikolaj brought up the rear.

'Even this has hardly changed!' I exclaimed. The same red linoleum was on the floor, I even thought I could still detect a whiff of the countless welcoming buns and coconut biscuits that had been baked in here. The larder was still there and I was nearly certain it was the same old fridge. I found I had tears in my eyes. Opening the door to the garden, I walked outside to see if they had also left everything there as it was.

Sara followed me out. 'Is this also the same?' she asked.

I shook my head. 'The vegetable garden is gone,' I said. 'When I was little there was a tiny patch of grass here by the apple tree. The rest of the garden stretched out in rows of strawberries, peas and cabbages.'

'We're not big gardeners. The front garden was quite a project,' Nikolaj said as he came out to join us. 'But when Aksel told us your grandmother would have turned in her grave to see it, we had to tidy it up. My own grandmother would never have forgiven me if I'd left it after that.'

We all laughed and I looked across the garden at the long stretch of lawn, perfect for playing badminton, football and everything else you could think of on long summer days. The small garden shed had been torn down and replaced. I was glad to see it gone, I had been scared of that shed since a wasp had followed me in there one summer while I was looking for my ball. At the very end of the garden a hammock was strung between two trees.

'Sara can show you the rest of the house while I make coffee.'

I followed Sara upstairs. There was just one bedroom and a bathroom up there and it all seemed much smaller than I remembered it.

'The owner is letting us rent it cheaply while he figures out what to do with it on condition that we paint and maintain it ourselves. We've only just moved in. But I couldn't stand looking at all the dead weeds in the front garden. *I* would never have forgiven us if we'd let it stay like that, never mind Nikolaj's grandmother. But the back garden was easy, there was only the grass to cut and a hedge to trim.'

'I'm glad. When I first moved here and got my hands on a pair of secateurs I was so tempted to creep over here during the night and do some violence to them. The weeds. Not the owners. I guess you weren't the ones who dug up the vegetable garden?'

Sara shook her head. 'No, that was already gone.' She pointed to the windows. 'So far all I've done up here is taken down the curtains. They were so old and dirty.'

'I know. I saw them from across the street. Would you believe my mother bought those curtains in Paris? She gave them to my grandparents the first time she came here to visit them with my father. Right around the time they found out she was pregnant.'

'Then maybe you would like to have them? I just put them in a bag. I thought maybe I'd wash them, cut up the fabric and use it for scraps. I like sewing.'

'Thank you. I think I would. My mother would certainly get a kick out of knowing that they lived on as something else. Don't know what though. Sewing and I don't exactly get on.'

She handed me a plastic bag and I peeked inside. 'Maybe cushion covers. That's what I was planning on. Let me know what you decide and I can help you.'

I nodded and thanked her again. I asked her what had brought them to Langeland.

'Nikolaj got a job managing one of the holiday-rental agencies. Compared to where we used to live this is almost like a big city.' She laughed. 'I'm still looking for work. If I can't find anything when the tourist season starts I'll get something cleaning the summer houses that people rent out. Nikolaj's company are always looking for cleaners then. I love cleaning, making things look nice. You really dream while you clean, do you notice that?'

'No, can't say that I've really thought about it that way. But I guess you could be right. Actually ...' an idea was forming in my head. 'I need some help with the cleaning. I did the whole house last week and it was exhausting. I'm getting too big and have too many aches and pains to manage that big place. It wouldn't be much at first, but when we open up and the guests start coming I will need someone full time.'

'Really? Your house? The one across the street?'

I nodded and told her what I was turning it into. She looked more and more excited with each word. 'I'd love to take the job,' she said. 'I've been looking over at the house every morning, wondering who lives there.'

'Well, now you know. Only do you mind my dog?' I asked.

'I love dogs. Let's go back downstairs, coffee must be ready by now.'

I picked up my bag of old curtains from the bed and walked downstairs, remembering again how I used to slide down the banister. Too big for that now, I thought as I stopped on the bottom step to catch my breath. I looked at the familiar walls and breathed in the familiar smell of the tiny cupboard under the stairs and remembered so clearly the day I said goodbye to this house, thinking I would never set foot in it again. It was ridiculous and irrational, but at that moment the very walls of the house called out to me, welcomed me home, told me everything was going to be all right. I thought about the man who was renting it to Sara and Nikolaj, I wondered whether he had ever washed the curtains and whether it really was the same old fridge in the kitchen. Sara had mentioned that he was trying to figure out what to do with it. I didn't know why, but somehow I didn't like the sound of that.

When we came down and told Aksel that now one more person had a job thanks to my project he was thrilled and immediately wanted to add that to his story. We sat at the table by the window, eating buns and drinking coffee, and it was as though the clock had rolled back twenty-five years and I was a child again. Even though the furniture was different and the people had changed, it was still just like coming home. It made me think about memories. How they lie dormant in our minds, just waiting for the right moment to spring to life again and take us back to times we'd almost forgotten. People we've lost live again. Fleeting acquaintances return to us. I wondered whether I ever lived in anyone's memory that way. Did memories of me ever return to children I had played with, people I had worked with, lovers I had briefly cherished?

'More coffee?' Nikolaj asked?

I shook my head. 'No thanks. I have to limit my caffeine intake these days. Another little drawback of pregnancy.'

'You seem to be coping well so far,' Aksel laughed. 'Starting a new business and creating jobs.'

'I try my best,' I smiled. In truth I had such terrible heartburn I just wanted to go home and lie down, but it was another hour before I said goodbye to the others and closed the door behind me.

When I eventually got in I spent an hour on the phone to my parents telling them how the house we remembered was just as we had last seen it. My mother loved the idea of making cushion covers out of her old curtains. She'd be shopping for the extra material we'd need first thing tomorrow. I called Alexander and he said he hoped he'd also get to see inside it one day.

After I put the phone down I sat with Thorin in the kitchen and thought about how I had spent my afternoon. To be in such a familiar place again after so many years was at once melancholy and uplifting. So many happy memories and such a desperate longing for the people time had taken from me. An insane desire to have the house back in the family began to take possession of me. I knew it was ridiculous given everything I had already taken on, but if a chance came to get that house back I would move heaven and earth to get it. I needed to look out of my window each morning and know that it was being well cared for. I wanted my grandparents to know that I was looking after the things they had left behind. I wanted to one day be able to give that house to my son, and tell him how his great-grandparents had lived there nearly all their adult lives.

On Friday morning I finished proofreading three articles, packed a small suitcase and took Thorin to Helle and Bjarne's. Getting his basket in and out of the car was proving increasingly difficult. Helle had told me that he didn't like it when I said goodbye so I slipped quietly out of the house while he was sniffing around the garden.

Alexander picked me up just before noon and hinted that I was free to go to sleep once we got on the motorway so I didn't see which way we were going. I laughed at him. By now he knew that I usually fell asleep in the car anyway so I lay back and closed my eyes. Sleep these days was like a drug I couldn't get enough of. I hungered for the moment when I could close my eyes and vanish into the world of relaxing dreams. I'd never been very good at staying awake all night and I worried that once my baby came I'd fall asleep and not hear him crying. I squirmed in my seat trying to get comfortable while Alexander put some music on. I didn't recognise the song and wondered if it was his own but before I could ask him I was fast asleep.

When I woke up there was a slight drizzle and we were parked next to a wall I recognised from the picture in the envelope. I could smell the sea and, as I got out and looked around, I thought I recognised the area.

'Are we in Copenhagen?'

'We are. Don't be disappointed,' he said quickly. 'I know it's not the most novel destination but it's a trip with a twist.

We're going to be tourists. You always talk about how much you love it here but I bet you've lived here so long you've got used to going to all the same places. So you're forbidden from going anywhere familiar or sorting out any little details about your apartments. I thought you could do with a chance to go to the theatre, visit museums and shop before the baby shows up. Places you don't usually go. No favourite cafés, restaurants or shops. Deal?'

  I nodded. 'Deal. Sounds like this is going to be fun.'
  'It will. Come on, let's go and get checked in.'

It was the perfect weekend and, just as Alexander had promised, we became tourists and I saw new sides to the city I thought I knew so well. We studiously avoided every place that I normally went to and instead discovered out-of-the-way cafés where they were very good at administering to all my strange dietary requirements. Tucked away down side streets and in cobbled courtyards we found funny little museums and start-up art galleries. Alexander bought me a framed black-and-white photograph series of the old bridges of Copenhagen in the snow. I decided to hang them on the wall behind my little office space in the hallway. The temperature rose and it almost felt like spring was on its way. We walked for hours, stopping for hot chocolate whenever I needed to sit down. On Saturday evening he told me to get dressed up because we were going to the opera. We took the water taxi and as I looked out across the harbour on that cold February night, my head resting on Alexander's shoulder, I was very happy and very much in love.

Week Thirty-One

The following week found me back at the obstetrician's office and once again she was shaking her head at me.

'I'm not quite happy with your liver,' she told me.

'Again?' I stared at her in disbelief. 'Haven't we just been through all the liver problems? Can't we ring the changes a little?'

'Yes. I know it's annoying. It's probably still just caused by your baby kicking it so this time we don't need any more tests and I won't worry you with any weird diseases. I just want you to rest a lot, sit up straight and sleep on your left side from now on.'

I stared at her. Why couldn't I just be one of those people who had problems with too much energy and worried because they felt too perky during pregnancy? Instead I had a future kickboxing instructor inside of me. Sit up straight indeed. She sounded like my grandmother. 'I think he's turned,' I told her.

'Let's have a look. Aside from that, how are you feeling?'

I told her about my cramps and my heartburn and she nodded sagely. 'All perfectly normal. Just don't ask me for a magic cure.'

'And I think I'm getting a cold.'

She prescribed rest and lots of fluids.

'I can't help you with the cold I'm afraid. You've also lost 600g.'

'That's weird. I thought I'd gained 1.5kg.'

She smiled and then she dimmed the lights, hooked me up to the monitor and I had a wonderful few moments of seeing my baby again.

'Do you have a name yet?' she asked me.

'Yes, I think so.' I nodded and smiled, tasting the name again in my mind. Émile.

'Is it one that you keep coming back to?'

I nodded.

'Then that's probably the one.'

By the time I got home again my cold had finished breaching the last defences of my immune system and I had succumbed to fever, sore throat and a runny nose. I hardly noticed where in front of the house I parked the car, I just unlocked the door and practically crawled into bed. Thorin gave me a puzzled look and then climbed up next to me. I patted him on the head, closed my eyes and hoped I'd go to sleep quickly. On my left side.

Being ill is usually something I enjoy, as long as there's not too much pain and discomfort involved. Rather than focussing on the lying in bed and feeling miserable, I consider it a time for relaxation, a chance to recharge my batteries when there's no reason to turn on the computer or do any work because I know that my mind is too woolly to produce anything worthwhile. Instead I sleep, I read all the books I haven't had time for, I drink endless cups of tea and bury myself under a throw on the sofa. Invariably, at some point during my illness, I turn a corner and emerge bursting full of energy for the next project, the next mountain I intend to climb. By the time I'm fully recovered, I have a whole new direction mapped out and a dozen other projects to launch.

Right now I knew I was sick because my body was telling me that I needed to rest. If everything continued as scheduled I had barely two months left until my life would change forever. Of course I knew that was a big 'if.' Very few babies stuck to their expected schedules, or so people kept telling me. In my bedroom, the crib I had bought was ready to go and the pram was waiting in the hallway. There was a drawer full of baby clothes and an assortment of toys that I had hidden away from Thorin's inquisitive nose. Practically, I was as prepared as I would be. Emotionally, I was a mess. I was ready for the baby. I just wasn't sure that the rest of my life was.

Alexander was so sweet and I loved him more with each passing day, but he was still so very young. No matter what he said about marriage and children and the future he dreamed of for us, I couldn't let myself get carried away. I wouldn't. The thought of giving in to his dreams, just to have them snatched away, was too much. It reminded me too much of you. I didn't miss you, I didn't imagine you, I didn't even think of you. Alexander had loved and cherished me more in these past four months than you had done in the past few years. He cared for me in ways you never had. In his eyes, my needs and my pleasure were just as important as his. Maybe even more so. I did want to believe the things he told me, but part of me was scared. Part of me was terrified. I could cope with a new house, new career and new life as a mother. But throw in a broken heart and I wasn't quite sure how I would manage. So part of me was holding back.

    My side and my throat hurt but I didn't want to move. Instead I pulled the covers up to my neck and burrowed deeper into the warmth. I was cold and I shivered but my forehead was hot. Alexander was at home getting everything ready for his next meeting with the recording studio and I didn't want to disturb him. Eventually, I drifted off to sleep.

When I woke up I was still shivering. I wondered what had woken me and then I noticed the phone was ringing. It was Alexander. I picked it up and then realised that I had lost my voice. When I tried to say hello, all that came out was a croak.

    'Anne?' Alexander said. 'Are you okay?'

    'Sick,' I managed to whisper. 'Lost my voice.'

    'Oh. Don't talk anymore. Text me what you need and I'll come by with it later.'

    I put down the phone gratefully and reached for the tissues. Thorin was still curled up by my feet. I closed my eyes and went straight back to sleep.

    Alexander came by later that evening with milk and honey, soup and tissues. I managed to croak the latest news from the doctor even though my throat felt raw. Every time I swallowed it was as though someone was pushing rusty razor blades down my throat. He made up a little bed for me on the sofa and I sat there with him and tried to eat. I was exhausted and at some point I must have drifted off to sleep again. When I woke up he was sprawled out on the sofa, also fast asleep. He keeled over the moment I got up so I covered him with the throw and waddled off to bed with Thorin padding after me. At some point during the night I woke up to find Alexander lying next to me, his arm around me. I lay awake for a long time that night, just feeling him there, wondering how much I dared to dream.

It was still the distant future that he talked of, not the present. We didn't talk about moving in together, we didn't talk about forgetting the hotel and turning the games room into a studio. In my heart I was glad that he was not trying to rush into anything, no matter how many dreams he spun. I just wished I could have known whether he was truly aware that there would soon be a much more immediate future to deal with, and a much more real baby than the phantom ones he talked of.

Week Thirty-Two

My cold lingered long into the following week. Alexander had gone to Copenhagen for his recording sessions and every morning when I woke up I felt as though I was getting worse rather than better. I was so grateful for Sara. She was kind enough to take Thorin for his walks and do some shopping for me, which mostly involved buying more milk and soup. I had hardly any appetite and what little I was able to eat I puréed and practically forced down my throat for the baby's sake. Every day I remembered to sit up straight and sleep on my left side. I found I had trouble catching my breath and I imagined that Émile was rolling over when it looked as though little ripples were passing along my stomach.

  Midway through the week, I was well enough to get dressed. A long shower refreshed me and I went into the kitchen, smoothing back my wet hair. I let Thorin out into the garden where the last of the snow had now melted. It was getting light earlier every day. All winter I'd been accustomed to seeing the sun rise but now it was sometimes up before I was. The changing of the seasons is one of the things which always makes me so glad that I'm not stuck in an office all day. I was looking forward to the time when Alexander and I could pick Émile up from nursery and then spend the afternoon together. He had already sent me three pictures of the recording studio and had kept his promise to call every night. I smiled to myself as I pictured him in Copenhagen with Simon, singing the songs I had come to cherish. The days seemed much longer without him beside me.

As the light started fading on Friday afternoon I finally felt normal so I went into the kitchen, got my pasta maker out and started beating flour and eggs together in a bowl. Alexander had decided to stay in Copenhagen and spend the weekend catching up with some friends. He rarely mentioned his friends to me. I knew their names and some basic facts about their lives and relationships, but sometimes their absence worried me a little. I wondered whether this omission meant a reluctance to allow his life on Langeland to become his real life. If he did become a success, as I fervently hoped he would, would there come a time when coming back to a wife and children on a small island would seem more like a chore than a respite? There were times when I came close to asking him about it, but I wasn't sure I wanted to hear the answer.

Week Thirty-Three

The local paper, *Ø-Boen*, came out on Tuesday and I had the novel sensation of finding myself on the front page. Just as promised, Aksel had chosen one of the photos from the beach with the bridge in the background. The wind was in my hair and somehow my bulky winter coat and Thorin standing in front of me almost managed to disguise the fact that I was seven months pregnant. But seeing the first real photograph of myself in months came as quite a shock. To my eyes it seemed as though half the weight I'd gained had gone to my face and I shuddered.

Sleeping on my left side all the time was making me sore and I was pretty sure that something new and uncomfortable was happening to me. My pregnancy book suggested so many disgusting-sounding scenarios that I couldn't even bear to imagine which one was now plaguing me. For the first time I found myself utterly miserable and fed up with being pregnant. All I wanted to do was to lie on the sofa and stuff myself with chocolate biscuits. Once again the very thought of real food made me sick. When I pulled my chair towards the table, my baby kicked me away from it. When I ate, I got heartburn. When I walked, sciatica hit me like a hammer. For the first time in ages, I thought of you and I cried. At least Alexander was busy pursuing his dream in Copenhagen and didn't have to see me like this.

I tried to focus on the article but the letters swam before my eyes when I tried to read it. All I could see was a cartoon image of myself as a beached whale. It took an effort to remember my manners and how important it was to network, but I did manage to pull myself together enough to call Aksel and tell him how much I loved the article. Even though I still hadn't read it properly.

On Thursday morning I was trying to get warm under the shower and there wasn't a single part of my body that wasn't aching. I was, however, determined to stop being sorry for myself, read the article properly and start feeling hopeful about the future again. To look forward to my new life as a mother and my new career as an alternative hotel owner. When I emerged from the shower, I sat in the kitchen in my dressing gown and watched the wind whip through the branches outside the window.

Earlier in the week Martin and I had spent an hour on the phone talking about the final designs for the website. Some of his remarks had got me thinking a lot about which parts of the business I was passionate about and the parts I wasn't. Sara was now in charge of the cleaning, Jacobsen was taking care of the garden and had promised to teach me the basics when I decided I was ready for it. Martin had suggested that I find an accountant to take care of the books. He knew I hated numbers. Somewhere in my vast network I was sure to know someone who knew someone who could help me.

To take my mind off the pain and the nausea I tried to think about why I was going through all of this and of the little baby boy who was making it all worthwhile. The weather would be warmer when he arrived. I could have his pram just outside on the terrace when he was taking his nap and then, as he grew older, a little playpen for him by the side of my desk. I'd chase him through the whole house once he learned how to walk, and Alexander would put baby gates on the stairs. I sighed as another kick pushed me away from the table. So I put my books away and took Thorin for a drive and a walk and added Braxton Hicks contractions to the day's list of aches and pains.

Week Thirty-Four

The day before Alexander was due to come back I was lying on my bed crying. I was sick of the house, sick of being pregnant, sick of the fact that I had let you and your damn fiancée run me out of town. I felt useless, worthless and utterly mean for saddling Alexander with a pregnant girlfriend nearly ten years older than him. When I looked in the mirror all I saw looking back at me was a fat, ugly woman with far too many ailments. It hurt every time my baby kicked me. Even my breasts were sore and now they were leaking. I didn't feel like a beautiful, maternal creature who was about to do something miraculous. Even my translations wouldn't come right for me. I left the house when Sara was due to come over because I couldn't bear to just lie around weeping while she polished and scrubbed. For the first time I missed my old apartment and nearly found myself wishing that none of this had ever happened. If I were back in my old life I would probably be with a client or networking over lunch at some delectable little café. I would not be sitting here, miles from any decent shops, overweight and ugly. This was all your fault. Your fault I'd run away, your fault I was pregnant, your fault I was fat. Your fault I'd met Alexander. That thought made me smile. But if at that moment I could somehow have miraculously transported myself back to my old life and away from the misery of being pregnant I almost think I would have.

I drove to Odense and waddled around the shopping centre, looking at baby clothes and toys. I sat down at a café, had a smoothie, and read a book for an hour. Walking was increasingly painful and I had difficulty catching my breath. I wanted to be done with being pregnant. I was ready for the next stage. More than anything I couldn't wait to meet my baby. But everything about the wait depressed me. Looking at my reflection in the shop windows made me shudder. Alexander was due home tomorrow and I wanted to do something to celebrate his success. It wasn't his fault that I was miserable and in pain. Last week we had only managed a few hurried conversations and scattered messages. I imagined that Simon and the others in the studio were keeping him really busy.

After looking around hopefully for a crane to help lift me out of my chair I went to the supermarket and bought my very first packet of nappies. Then I gathered a big bag of fruit and vegetables so that I could at least make believe I was being healthy while I was cursing my existence. The last place I wanted to be was the kitchen, but now that I had spent so many months spoiling Alexander with dinners and cakes I thought he would be crushed if he came home in triumph to find that I had prepared no celebration. On the way out I picked up a pastry. At least I could make the most of this being the one time in my life when it was permissible to gain weight. Even if it meant I would never want to look at myself in the mirror again.

By the time Alexander arrived the next evening I'd had a long shower, done my hair and my makeup and was more relaxed and presentable than I'd been for days. Every part of me still ached but a glass of refreshing juice and five minutes with my feet up had made me feel slightly better. Tonight I just wanted to be happy for him and let him tell me all about his time in the recording studio. Then, once he had left, I could crawl back under the duvet with a bar of chocolate and a book.

He came with flowers, chocolates and a bottle of champagne. Seeing him standing there in the doorway reminded me of the morning of my birthday. 'I know you won't be able to drink it for quite some time,' he said as he handed me the bottle, 'but I wanted to get it anyway. They assured me that it would keep. So we can drink it in a year's time and it will be even better.'

'Thank you. And chocolates too! Those we can eat now.'

He laughed. 'I missed you. I know I haven't been very good at staying in touch but so much stuff has been happening. It's been like another life in another world. But I knew that no matter how bad you were feeling, you would be able to eat chocolates. And chocolates are always good. There should always be chocolates in the house.'

'Oh goodness,' I shook my head and laughed. 'Our kids are going to be fat, aren't they?'

He looked at me and smiled for a long time. 'So you finally believe me?'

'Yes.' I nodded and he kissed me deeply. 'I do.' I didn't know what it was that had suddenly made the difference, or what had clicked in my mind, but I knew now that I believed him completely. Maybe it was because he hadn't run away screaming when the whale had opened the door, maybe it was because he had brought something that we would have to wait a long time to enjoy together. Or maybe it was just because I loved him and wanted to be near him and not be afraid anymore. He had gone away but, unlike you, he had come back again. 'So now tell me everything that happened,' I said. 'Leave nothing out. I want to hear it all, right down to the restaurants Simon took you to.'

He took my hands, led me to the sofa and spent the next hour telling me every single detail of the last few weeks. I just let him talk and enjoyed the intense look of rapture in his eyes. Whatever else happened, I hoped that he would always remember me as someone who had tried to help him live his dream. The candles in the windows had long since burned down by the time we went to bed. As I lay in his arms I felt warm and safe and kicking him out to eat chocolate was the last thing on my mind.

When we woke up the next morning I heard birds singing in the garden for the first time that year. Smiling, I managed to roll myself over and slide out of bed so I could waddle to the window. Opening it up, I leaned out and I could see the first of the winter flowers poking through the grass. I identified snowdrops and eranthis. Alexander stood behind me and put his arms around me. He pretended that he couldn't make his hands meet in the middle and I laughed. The calendar said

March and to me that meant spring. The air even seemed a little warmer.

'What a beautiful morning,' I said. 'I love spring.'

'What's your favourite season?' Alexander asked.

'Autumn,' I answered with a smile. 'When the leaves change colour it's the most magical time. There's that special, hazy mist in the air and that wonderful scent of decaying leaves. Another year is drawing to a close and soon it will be time for Christmas, for snow, for family.'

I put on my dressing gown and headed to the kitchen. I still didn't want any food but I was determined to try to eat something.

'You look a little pale,' Alexander said when we were sitting at the kitchen table. 'Are you all right?'

'I think morning sickness has come back to haunt me.'

'Oh no! Is that why you're not sitting properly at the table?'

'No. I'm not sitting properly at the table because the baby kicks me away every time I get too close to it. A little more power behind those kicks and he could tip me right off the chair. Look. I'll show you.' I looked so pitiful that he couldn't help but laugh.

'Let's go out for the day,' he said. 'Anywhere you want. We can have lunch somewhere. Maybe that will tempt you into eating something.'

I nodded and smiled. 'I'd like that. And a walk.'

He handed me the map and told me to pick a town. I was willing to brave aches and pains rather than gain too much weight and still be struggling to get rid of it in two years' time.

We headed off an hour later, Thorin lying on the backseat and a few digestives and a bottle of water tucked away in my bag. I'd struggled through the first round of morning sickness unsure of what to do. This time, I was prepared.

'You know something?' Alexander said to me as we drove off. 'We're going to need a bigger car soon. He's getting too big for this one and soon we'll have a baby seat.'

Thorin gave a little bark.

'Apparently he agrees with you. Let's do that today.'
'Okay. I'm a man, I'm always up for looking at cars.'
'But still lunch and the walk.'
'Anything you want. You just relax and try not to feel sick.'

Week Thirty-Five

The next week I was so uncomfortable that I could barely sit down and I found myself longing for the time when my baby had pushed me away from the table. That had been a minor annoyance compared to this pain.

'For God's sake, Émile,' I eased myself onto the edge of a chair and steadied myself with my hands, 'can't you do something to me that doesn't hurt!'

The snow had returned the previous afternoon and hadn't stopped since. Thorin was once again bounding through the garden, sending snowflakes flying everywhere he went. I was annoyed. I had thought spring was on its way. Alexander was to spend more time in the recording studio the following week and he was at home getting everything ready.

'I'm sorry to leave you when there's so little time left before the baby is born,' he said when he called me later. 'I wondered if I should ask them to change the date.'

'Don't you dare!' I said. 'It's okay. There's still a month to go and everything is ready. There's not much else I can do except wait.'

'I love you.'

'I love you, too.'

I put the phone down and tried to stretch, failing miserably. I was really going to miss him. I no longer resisted the future he painted for me. When he told me he would love my baby like it was his own, I believed him. When he talked about the children we would have together, I believed him. When he held me in his arms and made me feel so incredibly cherished, I believed with all my heart that he truly loved me. Part of me was still scared, but scared like someone who was about to embark on a thrilling new adventure. Right now it was the excitement and anticipation that was foremost in my mind. I trusted Alexander and I trusted what we had together.

Later that morning Martin sent me the final design for the website. I just stared at the screen for a few minutes, utterly mesmerised. It was simply beautiful. He had captured the essence of what I was trying to create. It was peaceful, creative and made me want to pack my bags immediately and head out to the place on the screen. I made myself some lunch, then went back to the computer and looked at it again. It was still perfect. Caroline's photos were wonderful. Looking at the house I had created and how I was going to present it made me smile. A deep-down-inside smile. How on earth could I possibly have felt useless? I had so many irons in the fire and so many plans. Not to mention all the people who cared about me. Beginning with my baby. It was just pregnancy hormones conspiring to make me feel useless.

Sara had invited me for coffee so when the snow stopped later that afternoon, I waddled across the street. She had told me that she had something to show me and I was looking forward to seeing what it was. I had a feeling that she had done something new to the house. I rang the doorbell but no one answered even though I was sure I could hear movements in the corridor.

'Hello!' I called through the letterbox. 'Sara? Are you there?'

'Coming!' a muffled voice answered, and moments later I heard the key turn in the lock. Sara stood in the doorway and I couldn't help noticing that her eyes were red and puffy.

'Are you all right?' I asked. 'Shall I come back another time?'

'No no, please come in. It's just …' She sighed and ushered me in, closing the door behind me. 'Well,' she said, hanging up my coat, 'what do you think?'

The curry-coloured wallpaper remained on the wall heading up the stairs, but everywhere else it was gone, as was the brown carpet. The floorboards had been sanded and the remaining walls painted off-white. Even the banister was no longer the dark stained wood I remembered.

'What do you think?' she asked again. I could sense the nervousness in her voice. Letting someone into a home they had cherished from childhood to see what you'd done to the place would have been a nerve-wracking experience for anybody.

'It's great,' I said, meaning it, and smiled, squeezing her hand. 'I love it.'

'Oh good. I was so worried about what you'd think. You remember this house so well.'

'It's your house now.'

'No,' she said, 'that's the problem.'

'What do you mean?'

Sara went through to the kitchen. She poured two cups of coffee and put them on a tray together with milk and sugar. I took it through to the living room while she cut two generous slices of cake for us. She rubbed her eyes and smiled at me as we sat down. 'I'm sorry,' she said, 'I'm being really silly. It's just been a difficult day.'

'What's wrong?'

She sighed again and ran a hand through her hair. 'Remember how I told you that the guy we're renting from was trying to figure out what to do with this place?'

I nodded.

'He told us it would take at least a year so, in exchange for a low rent, we would have to repair and decorate it. He promised us first refusal if he decided to sell. And that was fine. We had so much fun doing the hallway.'

I poured milk and sugar into her coffee and handed her the cup. 'So what's happened to change that?'

'He called this morning to say that he needs money. Apparently some business deal he was doing went wrong. He's already sold his share of the rental business and he's moving away.'

'And he wants you out of the house now?'

'He said we could buy it from him at a good price. He needs a quick sale. Otherwise he knows a developer who might be interested, but he'd want to tear it down.'

'Tear it down!' I nearly chocked on my cake. 'He can't!'

'Apparently he can.'

'Yes, legally he probably can,' I said, waving an arm in the air, 'but really he just can't. He can't tear down this house. This was my grandparents' house, they lived here almost all their lives. I can't come out of my house every morning and not see this place across the street. I couldn't bear it.' I stopped myself, feeling suddenly selfish. 'And this is your home. You've spent so much time and effort making it look nice. You had such big plans.'

'I know. I am upset. We have spent so much time on it. And effort, and money. But worse is we'd have to move again. And if this partner is having problems, then what about the other ones? Could Nikolaj's job be in danger? It took him so long to find and he's really enjoying it.'

'Have you thought about buying the house?' I asked, taking my first sip of coffee.

Sara shook her head. 'He's not asking a lot for it but we know there's a lot of work that needs doing. So even though the price is very reasonable, we'd need a lot more to really fix it up. And if there is a chance that Nikolaj's job could be at risk we can't commit ourselves to a life here. Buying a house would do that. Suppose we couldn't sell it again or find someone who wanted to rent it?'

'I see.' I looked around the room where I had spent so many happy hours and felt sick at the thought of a bulldozer tearing through my past. 'If you don't mind my asking, how much is he willing to sell it to you for?'

She told me and I nodded slowly. It wasn't a vast amount, but for a young couple just starting out in a strange place with only one full-time income and that one suddenly uncertain, I could see why things seemed bleak.

'When does he want to know your decision?'

'Sunday.'

'That's still a few days away.' I smiled at her. 'Something will come up. Something always does. I'll have a think about it. Maybe I can think of something.'

'I hope so.' She tried to smile. 'But this is a depressing topic. Cake?'

'Please.'

We made small talk and ate cake and Sara told me about the other plans she had made for the house. We looked at colour samples but I knew both of us were thinking of what more could be done. To me, it was still my grandparents' house. I remembered how sad we'd all been when we had to let it go, how pleased I was to now see people taking care of it again. I remembered the passionate desire that had flamed in me the first time I saw it again, the desire to make it mine. I looked around the room and smiled, the thought of actually doing that sweeping through me. But it was as much a dream for me as it was for Sara and Nikolaj. Right now, with everything else I had committed myself to, I couldn't afford it. So someone else would buy it. Someone who would bulldoze my memories, eradicate my past and put up some hideous new construction in its place. Somewhere with no musty cupboard under the stairs, no mislabelled taps in the bathroom, no curry-coloured wallpaper in the hallway. My head hurt and I began to feel sick. If this house was no longer here, Langeland would be ruined for me. My own house and everything I had built would become strange, alien, and I would no longer feel at home in it.

It was dark when I took Thorin for his last walk of the day. When we got back I stood for a long time on the front steps, remembering how Alexander and I had stood there together on New Year's Eve. I remembered the day I first pulled up outside my grandparents' house and saw the big 'For Sale' sign on mine. How could the house just vanish so I would never be able to visit it again or show it to my son?

I went over my accounts and juggled numbers and made copious notes, but there was no way that I could afford it. I wanted to talk to Alexander about it but, busy in his studio, he wasn't answering his phone. Somewhere there had to be a solution. That night I didn't sleep. I tossed and turned waiting for Alexander to call me back but he never did. Whenever I closed my eyes I saw wrecking balls tearing through the street, missing my grandparents' house but hitting mine instead. I felt sick, apprehensive and anxious, as though the storm clouds were gathering and I hadn't brought my umbrella.

The next day was cold and wet and I spend most of the morning curled up in bed with Thorin. I called my bank manager when a need for coffee drove me into the kitchen and he was polite but firm in his refusal to lend me any more money.

'Anne,' he said, 'I appreciate your emotional attachment. But there is no rental market for properties like that. Yes, you may potentially have tenants but you tell me they might be out of work soon. I'm sorry, Anne, I just can't.'

My parents said much the same when I called them with the news. They were also devastated at the thought of the house being torn down, but they were not going to be the ones who had to look at the ruins every day. I put the phone down and signed so loudly that Thorin nearly jumped out of his basket.

By lunchtime I was valiantly trying to look on the bright side. Sara and Nikolaj would find somewhere else to live in Rudkøbing. Nikolaj's job was probably safer now that the partner with financial problems was out of the business. Yes, they had spent money unnecessarily on a few tins of paint and on hiring the machine to sand the floorboards, but they would get over it. It was only me who saw this as the end of the world. I couldn't explain why, but it seemed as though the cloud I had seen in the sky a few weeks ago, when I worried about never getting to see my baby grow up, had now been magnified and drawn even closer. The memory of that house was what had drawn me to Langeland on that day in April when I had fled Copenhagen. Langeland would never be Langeland without that house across the street. It would never be home.

I heard my phone ring and exclaimed, 'At last!' but it wasn't Alexander. It was Hanne, the woman who was renting my apartment in Copenhagen.

'Hello, Anne,' she said and we made small talk for a few minutes while I wondered why she had called.

'Nothing's happened to the apartment, I hope. The storage room isn't flooded, is it?'

She laughed. 'It wasn't last time I checked. No, everything is fine. Better than fine. Actually that's why I'm calling. I've got a new job right around the corner and my ex and I have finally sold our old house.'

'Congratulations! So now you're calling to tell me you're moving on because you're going to buy something in the neighbourhood?'

'Not exactly.' She paused and I could almost hear a smile in her voice. 'I was going to ask if I could buy yours.'

For a moment I wasn't sure whether I had heard her correctly and just sat staring at the phone.

'Hello? Anne? Are you there?'

'Oh yes, sorry,' I said, 'you just really surprised me. You want to buy my apartment?'

'Yes. It's so lovely here,' she said. 'I know people in the neighbourhood. That's a first for me and I'm really enjoying it. I know we extended the lease but I just can't bear the thought of leaving. We did talk about the possibility of me buying it, remember? It has become home to me and I don't want to have to move again. But I also want to invest the money that I got. I want my own place, do you know what I mean? Somewhere that's really mine.'

I nodded, then remembered that she couldn't see me. 'Yes. I know what you mean.'

She told me what she would be willing to offer and I mechanically wrote it down in the notebook lying beside me.

'Okay,' I said slowly, 'I need some time to think about this. Can I let you know by the end of the week?'

'Of course. Thank you. Please do think about it. I know it's sudden. It is for me, too.'

I put the phone down in a daze and just sat staring out of the window. Sell my apartment? How ridiculous. I knew we had talked about it, but for me it had never really be a serious option. Surely there were other apartments in the area? I laughed out loud and tried to think. It was, undoubtedly, the solution to the problem of my grandparents' house. If I sold my apartment I could buy the house and have money to spare. So why didn't I just leap at the chance? What was I afraid of? What would it mean if I sold? That I wouldn't be able to go back to the place where I had spent the last few years of my life. The place from where I had built up my business, where we had last been together, where you knew how to find me. The place where you had tried to find me. Was it really time to give all that up? I knew I'd still have a base in the city if I really wanted it, all I had to do was get rid of my medical students. But that wasn't the point. It would be as though I'd be irrevocably shutting the door on my old life forever. Was I truly ready to say goodbye?

I sought relief in movement but couldn't think of anywhere to go, so I just wandered aimlessly through the rooms, running my hands through my hair.

When Sara came over to clean later that afternoon I had gathered my thoughts enough to tell her that I might have a solution to the house situation, but that I still needed some time to think it all through.

'Really?' Her whole face lit up. 'So we could stay?'

'Maybe.' I told her about Hanne's offer to buy my apartment. 'I'm still working out all the details. But if I sold then I would have the money to buy the house. And then you could stay. With the same agreement as you have the current owner. Provided of course that he would sell it to me.'

'That would be wonderful. Then you'll be employer and landlord.' She smiled at me.

'Hopefully friend as well.'

'Absolutely.'

I smiled at her and my baby kicked me. It was the right thing to do. There was nothing for me to cling to in Copenhagen and my old flat was utterly impractical now. Alexander and I could never live there with Émile and Thorin. If Hanne decided to buy somewhere else I would need to spend time and effort looking for another tenant. I should sell. I needed the money, not only for my grandparents' house but also as something to fall back on in case the hotel didn't work out as I had planned. Even so, something was holding me back. I wondered again if it was the thought of saying an irrevocable goodbye to you that I couldn't come to terms with. But if that were truly the reason, then I should sell. I owed it to myself, to Alexander, to the new life that we were building together.

Alexander came by just before dinner with many apologies for not having answered his phone.

'It ran out of juice yesterday and I was so wrapped up in my music I didn't even notice.'

'It's okay,' I said with a brief smile, and told him about Hanne's offer. 'I'm not sure what I should do. On the one hand it will solve the problem of the house, but I'm just not sure. What do you think?'

'It's your apartment,' he said, 'and your decision. Buying another house is a big thing. You're like a woman with her own Monopoly board.' He smiled at me and I laughed.

'Yes, I know it's my apartment,' I said. 'But if we're supposed to be facing the future together I'd like your opinion. The place would never be big enough for all of us to live in anyway, but it might work as a base in the city.'

'Maybe. But is that really practical? It will just be an empty property that costs you money but brings in no income. That won't be good. I'm not a millionaire musician yet. I think you should do what you think is right. It's not really anything to do with me.'

'Okay ...' I looked at him with a puzzled expression on my face.

'I mean,' he said, 'I just think it's your decision. It's your apartment and your money. I don't want you to think that I'll try to influence you. I don't have anything financial to contribute, so I don't think I have the right to decide.'

I smiled. 'Okay. I understand.' But really I wanted to roll my eyes and mutter, 'Men!' under my breath.

Sunday morning found me in the kitchen on the phone to Hanne. When Alexander took Thorin for his walk, I went over to see Sara and Nikolaj and had a long talk about the house, its owner and where we could all go from here.

Week Thirty-Six

Early Monday morning the doorbell rang. Alexander opened the door as I came out from the kitchen, wiping my hands on a tea towel.

'Good morning,' Sara said. 'We brought breakfast.' She and Nikolaj were standing there with rolls, pastries, juice and flowers.

'Thanks,' I smiled. 'Please come through to the kitchen. What's the occasion?'

'It's a "thank you for agreeing to be our new landlord" breakfast,' Nikolaj said and smiled at me.

'Well, thank you,' I said and gave a small bow. 'It looks delicious. Although I still can't believe that I'm doing this. Selling my old apartment is an enormous step. I guess I'm really committed to Langeland now.'

'From what you've told me,' Alexander said, taking the bakery bags and putting plates on the table, 'it seems like a good move. I understand that profit is a good thing.'

I smiled at him. 'Well you were no help, Mr. It's-Your-Life-And-Nothing-To-Do-With-Me. But I've actually given this more thought than I did when I bought this place. I must be learning something. But the difference in property prices between Langeland and Copenhagen also played a part. A large one.'

'Okay, I get it. And I'm sorry. But now there's no apartment in Copenhagen I guess I'm in love with a wealthy woman?'

'You always were, darling,' I winked at him and he laughed. 'But wait till you have your first number one hit and rush off to New York. You'll be the wealthy one, then.'

'So you could be my intelligent, charming trophy wife of independent means. Who can also tell me where there's a vase for these flowers.'

We all laughed as we sat down to breakfast. I found myself getting more excited about the way everything had suddenly turned out right. There was really nothing to worry about. Of course Alexander would soon feel like it had something to do with him as well, he was just being macho and proud. As though he agreed with me, my baby rolled over and the tickling sensation made me laugh some more.

Later that day I invited the owner of my grandparents' house to come and go over the details. We'd spent a long time on the phone together the day before, but since the deal was either 'buy it or I'll sell it to someone who will tear it down' I wasn't really in a position to quibble about anything. Ideally I would have liked a survey but with so little time it wasn't an option. Instead Bjarne and Alexander spent an hour going through the house and inspecting the roof and the outside walls for me. The report they came back with was anything but glowing. Bjarne winked at me and said he suddenly saw a lot more cake in his future. Alexander squeezed my hand and said he was looking forward to working on another roof for me. Especially considering all the great things that had happened since he had come to work on the last one.

I had been pleased to discover that the owner was not the one we had sold the house to after my grandfather died. That couple had retired and gone to live with their son in Jutland five years later. I hadn't wanted to think that we had sold off our memories to someone who just wanted to raze them to the ground.

I drove to Copenhagen with Alexander the next day, leaving Thorin with Helle. She had started talking about getting a puppy and I told her it could come and play with Thorin any time.

'Remember he's still a puppy himself. Even if he really doesn't look like one.'

Helle nodded. 'I do love having him to stay. He's very good at walking on the lead, he doesn't pull at all. But I think a smaller dog is the way to go for us.'

I nodded. 'I'd be happy to help you look for one. I love looking at puppies.'

'Haven't you got enough on your plate already?'

'True.' I smiled and patted Thorin. He rested his head on my lap and went to sleep. 'This will make getting out of here a little difficult.' I edged myself gently off the sofa but he woke up and whined.

'I'll let him out,' Helle said. 'You get going. Then I'll take him for a walk and he'll forget all about being sad.'

I opened the front door and snuck out while Thorin was in the garden. I was a little apprehensive about whether seeing my old apartment again would make me change my mind about selling. Besides the administrative details of the sale, I had to arrange for the last of my things to be taken to Langeland and say a mental goodbye to my old neighbourhood.

'It would be hard to live there with a baby anyway,' I told Alexander in the car. 'It's on the third floor and the front door doesn't lock, so anyone could just walk in and steal his pram. After the space I've got used to having in Langeland I'm not sure I could go back to living in an apartment again. At least not for a while. Besides, it's too small for all of us and I could never drag Thorin up and down those stairs three or four times a day.'

He nodded as we turned onto the motorway to cross the Great Belt Bridge. 'I like living on Langeland,' he said. 'I guess ... well, I hope, that I will be travelling a lot because that will mean things are going well with my music, but I like having a base to come back to. Do you think the children will mind that their father is a rock star?'

I laughed. 'I don't think they'll mind that a bit.'

'You're sure you'll be all right taking the train and the bus back home?'

'I'll be fine. You have to work and I have to get back to sort the other papers out.'

'So you've got used to the idea now?'

I nodded and it was only slightly untrue. 'It will be strange but I think I started saying goodbye to the place the day I ran away and let someone else move into my space. It's time for a new start. If I need to find another tenant I could end up having to go back and forth all the time, at least in the beginning. That would be so impractical with the baby. It's not my home anymore. This just makes it official.'

'Sure?'

'Selling it did come as a surprise. But I've had a lot of time to think about it and it feels like this is the right decision. It will be nice to have a day to walk around and say goodbye to the place, visit my favourite shops and cafés. But no more than that. If he will leave me in peace for five minutes!' I shifted in my seat.

'Does it hurt?'

'A little. Feels like I've been pregnant forever.'

'I don't even know you when you're not pregnant,' he laughed. 'Pregnancy hormones could be changing your personality. You could be a psycho loony for all I know.'

I laughed and then grabbed my leg and winced.

'Sciatica again?'

'Oh yes. Bad.'

He took my other hand while I bit down on my knuckle and tried to breathe deeply. The pregnancy book was right. After the honeymoon of the second trimester, the third one was a real bitch.

When I walked into my old apartment a few hours later it was nothing like I remembered it. It seemed small and cramped and I wondered how I could ever have endured such a tiny kitchen. The few pieces of furniture I had thought I might still have wanted no longer appealed to me. I couldn't mentally place them in my new home. They were Hanne's now. Someone else's pictures were on my walls, someone else's bedspread was on my bed. In the windowsill were photographs of someone else's friends and family. It wasn't my home anymore. The few personal things that I had left behind were downstairs in the storage room. The plates and glasses that I had left in the cupboard for her to use were all old stuff that I had bought from IKEA when I had first moved in. I looked around the place where I had spent so many years of my life and realised that there was hardly anything of me left to take away. When I had first gone to Langeland I had been convinced that I had only taken the bare essentials, now I found there was hardly anything left. If I had managed without all these things for eight months, I suppose I had either forgotten I had them or could manage without them forever. I almost felt sad.

Hanne and I sat down at the dining table together and sorted the last details. There were new cushions on my chairs. Looking around, it really did seem as though she had managed to make a home here. She certainly looked both happier and healthier than when I had first met her. My lawyer had drawn up the sales agreement, all we had to do was sign and send. Once we had signed our names I leaned back in the chair and sighed. She suggested going for a celebratory latté.

'I'd like that,' I said. 'I want to take one last walk around the neighbourhood.'

'What do you mean one last walk? You'll come back.'

'Nah.' I shook my head. 'A neighbourhood is something you come to if you live there or go to meet friends. I've loved living here and I know that I might say I'll come back, but I doubt I will. Even my though my favourite delicatessen is here, I can find the same brands in Odense. I'm okay with saying goodbye to this place.'

'Starting a new life?'

I nodded and patted my stomach. 'And how!' I laughed.

'When does the hotel open?'

'Not entirely sure yet. I need my baby to arrive first. The windows need fixing and repainting and there are some cracks in the outside walls. But we have to wait until we're certain the cold weather is gone. Then we'll paint the house. Then we'll open.'

We found a seat outside my favourite café and I planted myself next to the heat lamp and wrapped a blanket around my legs. The last time I'd been here I'd seen you and your wife through the window.

'Are you okay?' Hanne asked as our drinks arrived.

'Fine,' I nodded and took a sip of my latte. It was every bit as good as I remembered. That was the only thing I missed when I was in Rudkøbing: a lovely café to go to on a regular basis for a wide variety of coffees, smoothies and pastries. Much as I loved the bakery, I craved my coffee to go in its little cardboard cup.

Hanne cradled her glass in her hands. 'I can't believe I've actually got my own apartment,' she smiled. 'This is the first time I've bought somewhere rather than renting. On my own, I mean. My ex-husband and I had a house together.' She sounded as nervous as I had been before I had walked in through the door.

'I'm glad you ended up liking it so much. I guess in the beginning having someone to rent to it was quicker than selling and it meant I would have somewhere to go back to in case things didn't work out in Langeland. At least I imagine that's what was in my mind at the time.'

'I'm glad I could help,' Hanne laughed. 'By the way, remember that guy I texted you about? The one who showed up that night looking for you?'

I nodded.

'I've seen him in the supermarket a couple of times. I guess he lives around here.'

I took another sip and looked around. The street was busy with people walking from shop to shop, probably all as fed up with winter as I was. I didn't want another snowstorm. I wanted spring and green leaves and my baby to sleep in the sunshine. I wondered if I could see the building you lived in from here. I wondered if you and she ever came here and sat in this café together. If you ever looked out onto this street and wondered if you would see me pass by. I'd seen you walk past here. Hanne saw you in the supermarket. You were married in the church around the corner from my building. You had moved into my neighbourhood. You selfish little shit. It wasn't just about me, but your wife. You'd told me that every time my name was mentioned it turned into a screaming row. So why live where there would always, as far as you knew, be the chance of running into me?

I finished my coffee and said goodbye to Hanne. I'd thought about arranging for a removal company to pick up the last of my things and bring them to Langeland, but what I had decided to take could fit in a single box. I'd called Alexander earlier and he had agreed to pick it up on his way home. Watching Hanne run across the street and back up to the apartment wasn't the painful wrench I had expected. Instead it was as though I had rid myself of a large chunk of excess baggage, although the large sum of money that would soon be resting comfortably in my bank account might have helped. Smiling, I put on my gloves and turned up the collar on my coat. Eight months pregnant and I looked like an inflatable toy for a swimming pool.

There was the bus stop. A short ride would take me straight to our hotel in the city centre. That way I wouldn't need to risk running in to you. I stood there for a moment, checking the time table. Then I stopped. I'd already let you run me out of my apartment, out of my city. No matter how many good things had happened to me since, it had still been a flight. So I'd be damned if I was going to let you ruin my last moments here. Head in the air, I walked down the street to finish my goodbyes. There were a few things I could pick up from my favourite delicatessen and take back home with me.

Home.

Langeland was home now.

Alexander found me asleep in our hotel room a few hours later. He woke me up with a kiss and rubbed my shoulders while he told me all about his day at the studio. I warmed to the excitement in his voice and asked what I hoped were intelligent questions. Then I went for a shower to try and wake up properly and wash away the impressions of the day. Saying goodbye to my old life was still a big step for me. Copenhagen was the last place I'd seen you.

'Where do you want to go for dinner?' Alexander called through the door.

'I have an urge for Chinese,' I shouted back. 'I know a great place.'

'Okay. Chinese it is.'

Five minutes later I turned off the water, wrapped myself in a towel and went back out into the bedroom. Alexander was asleep on the bed.

The next day I said goodbye to Alexander in the morning and went to meet Lisbeth for coffee. The only condition I had stipulated for our morning together was that it did not involve too much walking. I was sick of the cold weather and fed up with not being able to move without wincing.

'Don't worry,' she'd told me with a laugh, 'I'll find us a rickshaw if you need one.'

I walked into our usual café just after ten o'clock. Lisbeth was already perched at the bar, a tall latte in front of her.

'I hope you're not expecting me to crawl up there,' I laughed as she jumped down and gave me a hug.

'Don't worry, our table is available.'

We sat by the window as we had so many times before. The café was in a small side street off the main pedestrian street, conveniently close to Lisbeth's favourite shoe shop. I ordered a small latte and Lisbeth decided that we needed pastries.

'So what have you got planned for us this morning?' I asked.

'We'll get to that. First I want to hear how it's going with Alexander.' She winked at me. 'You certainly look happy. It's good to see.'

'It's going really well. I really ... I really can't imagine my life without him anymore.' I smiled. 'Way to jinx it, I know. But if you want to keep me looking happy, we need to stay away from anywhere with mirrors.'

'Ah. You've hit the "I'm fat and miserable" stage. I figured we'd go shopping, but if you're feeling like that maybe it's not the best day for it.'

'Nah, not really.'

'Oh come on, you need new clothes for when you're done being pregnant. You know, something that says "new mum, new life" and all those things.'

'Right now the only clothes I'd fit into would say "fat" and all those things.'

'That depressed?'

I sighed. 'A little. Everything hurts. I just want to get this over with so I can meet my baby.'

'I remember that feeling. But you have a whole new life about to start. You should do something to mark the occasion. And say goodbye to the old one.'

'New clothes isn't it. I've bought a new handbag. That can be enough newness for now.'

'Okay. How about something for the house?'

'There's nothing more I need.'

'How about the kitchen?'

'Yeah. A meat mallet. Then whenever I think about the bastard who made me fat I can beat the hell out of something. I'm sorry. I'm just not in a very good mood today.'

'Actually I think a meat mallet is a great idea. You must have put the sledgehammer away by now. And, no offence, but right now you really sound like you just need to beat something to death.'

I laughed and nodded. Maybe there was something to be said for a meat mallet. We finished our coffees, paid the bill and went shopping. I did buy a meat mallet. With summer coming up and that enormous garden, I figured there were a lot of barbecued steaks in my future. Alexander had told me he was good at those.

By mid-afternoon Lisbeth must have tried in vain to interest me in every clothing store in the city centre. I tried to play along for her sake but I simply could not feign enough interest in clothes I knew wouldn't fit. In the end she gave up on her experiment and found somewhere we could sit down and relax. I breathed deeply and tried to imagine away the pain.

'It won't be long now,' she said.

'I know. I can't wait. I wish it were now. I want to meet him. I want this to be over. I want the next phase of my life to start now. With my baby and my new business and Alexander.'

'I remember that feeling. I kept thinking, come on, get on with it!'

'I know. How much more development is going on in there anyway?'

'How's Alexander taking all this?'

I smiled. 'Better than I expected. We haven't talked about him moving in or what's going to happen when the baby's born, we're just taking things slowly. But we are moving towards something substantial in the future. Which to hear him talk, involves a wedding and lots more babies.'

'I'm sure everything will fall into place. Once the baby comes you can start getting everything together.'

I nodded. 'He's practically living with me as it is.'

'True. Has he figured out the new coffee machine yet?'

'Almost.'

'When he does that he's done.'

We laughed at that for a long time.

It was in the train on the way home that I at last managed to say my last goodbyes to my old life. I watched the landscape fly past as people chatted and laughed beside me. Names of towns were a hazy blur as we whizzed past small stations without stopping, snow still piled up by the sides of the tracks. The wind whipped the trees and the skies were a steely grey. As the train pulled me further and further away from you, away from places we had been together, I felt my thoughts flying free, fragmenting in the breeze. The life I had led in the city was over. The place I had lived, where we had made love, where you had always come back to me, was gone. At the end of my journey was a new home, a new life. Another man would hold me at night. Another man would watch my baby as he learned to crawl, walk, feed himself. When I returned to the city it would be as a guest. My home was in Rudkøbing now, in the house I had brought back to life, opposite my grandparents' old home that would now also be mine. You and I, whatever we had shared, was finally over.

Week Thirty-Seven

The next week I was utterly miserable. Everything I had been going through during the previous weeks was apparently no more than a warm up for this one. My hands and feet swelled up and it hurt when I moved them. I wondered whether this would be how I'd feel when I was old and arthritic. Each time I took Thorin for his walk I had another series of Braxton Hicks contractions with a side of sciatica. Whatever I ate gave me heartburn. On top of everything else, my sex drive had gone through the roof and Alexander was still in Copenhagen. The sexy little photos he kept sending me did not help but they certainly cheered me up. In my bloated, unhappy state it was very gratifying to know that he still wanted me. Apart from that I wanted to snap at anyone who so much as looked at me and wanted to be like one of those cartoon characters who threw anvils off cliffs to squish their enemies.

To pass the time I decided to pack my hospital bag. I picked out the first clothes that my baby would wear, I packed nappies and wet wipes and some things for myself in case there were complications and I ended up staying for a few days. In my mind I loathed the idea of being sent home on the same day. I actually found that thought more frightening than that of giving birth. If they sent me home too quickly, I'd feel as though I'd showed up at a DHL facility to collect a parcel they hadn't been able to deliver.

I worried as I walked around the house. I worried about my baby, about not making it to the hospital in time. In my mind I pictured myself getting stuck in the midst of roadworks, giving birth on a bridge while someone who was retouching the white lines on the road helped me with my breathing. I worried about gaining too much weight or not having gained enough. I worried about being a good mother, about the pain of giving birth, about my new business, about my houses and the sale of my apartment. I worried about whether Thorin would take to the baby. What if he growled at him all the time or was too jealous? I worried that Alexander would panic once we took a real step towards the future he talked of. Maybe that was why he didn't call as often when he was working in Copenhagen?

In front of the mirror in my bedroom, I looked at my body and tried to convince myself that my baby had dropped. Surely it couldn't be long now. Then I took a good look at myself and was horrified by my lank hair and un-made-up face. I'd make an appointment at the hairdresser's first thing tomorrow. Émile deserved a pretty mother. Maybe pampering myself a little would cheer me up. God knows something needed to.

Two days later I met with the owner of my grandparents' house and we signed the necessary papers. The money from the sale of my apartment had arrived and I had paid off the remainder of my mortgage. He would have the quick sale he wanted and the house would be saved. Sara and Nikolaj could stay in their new home and take good care of it for me. Looking up at it as I went home, I couldn't believe what I had just done. The light was mellow, the air was warm and I could have sworn my grandparents were on the front steps, smiling at me and waving.

Week Thirty-Eight

April dawned with clear blue skies, warm breezes and the first real hint of sunshine. It seemed as though this winter had lasted forever. The snow melted away and Jacobsen came back to the garden to plant a fresh host of plants that would bloom later in the year. He told me their names but I forgot them as soon as he had finished talking. Obviously I was nowhere near ready to learn gardening.

Alexander drove me to the hospital for my next appointment because I was beginning to find getting in and out from behind the steering wheel a struggle. All my aches and pains also made it difficult to drive. He was taking me to lunch afterwards and I'd made him promise not to let me give in to any of my cravings. I was dreading my meeting with the scales at the doctor's office. I felt as though I was inflating like a balloon. The night before I'd woken in a panic thinking that I was breathing in too many calories. Thorin kept coming up to me and putting his head on my lap. He looked at me as though he was the one who was supposed to be taking care of me, instead of vice versa. His daily walks were agonising.

'Are you okay?' Alexander asked. 'You seem a little distracted.'

'I'm okay, I'm just tired. I'm tired of being pregnant, I want to move on to the next stage.'

'Being a mother?'

'Yes.'

'I think you'll be a fantastic one.'

To my great relief the doctor didn't yell at me for my weight gain. Instead she tied me up to a monitor for twenty minutes so I could do nothing but lie quietly and listen to my baby's heartbeat. I closed my eyes and listened to the rhythmic sound echoing through the room. My breathing slowed and I relaxed. When I opened my eyes Alexander was staring at the monitor with what seemed like an almost terrified expression on his face.

'Look how much he's grown,' I said.

'Sorry,' my doctor said, 'now it's time for the internal exam.'

'You've never needed to apologise for those before.'

'A lot of mothers find that they hurt towards the end. So just be prepared and try to relax as best you can.'

'Great,' I said, 'what's another ache to add to the list?'

'Can I hold her hand?' Alexander asked.

'Sounds like I might need that,' I laughed. Then I nearly screamed.

'I'm sorry,' she said. 'Try to relax.'

I gritted my teeth and squeezed Alexander's hand.

'Okay, you're all done now. You can breathe again.' She patted my arm and I exhaled while Alexander winced and flexed his fingers. 'I want to monitor your blood pressure, you seem a little stressed. Also, I recommend long walks to get your baby to drop. Massage your breasts and have lots of sex if you can.' She looked at Alexander and then winked at me. We blushed.

When we got home after a long, leisurely lunch I made tea and Alexander said he would take Thorin for his afternoon walk.'

'Oh thank you. I know she said long walks but I just can't right now. I don't know what she did to me but it still hurts.'

'So all that sex will have to wait a while?' I laughed so hard that tea came out of my nose. 'But you're right, she did say that you needed to take long walks, so you really should go,' he reminded me.

'All right. But can we go together? I'm afraid I'll get cramp or sciatica and fall over. Thorin isn't quite big enough to drag me back. But I'm big enough to squish him.'

Alexander nodded and sipped his tea. 'You got it.'

'Okay, I'll ... Hold on, that's my phone.' I went into the hallway to get it out of my bag. Two minutes later I came back into the kitchen, beaming. 'That was Aksel. The local TV news want to come out the day after tomorrow and do a segment about me and the hotel.'

'That's great!'

'It is.' I sighed and then laughed. 'If I can last that long.' He gave me a big hug and I slumped against him. 'But can I have a nap before we go for that walk?'

When Sara came over to clean the next day I told her about the news crew coming to film us and she was thrilled.

'I'll make sure the place looks fabulous,' she said. 'You just concentrate on not going into labour in front of the camera.'

'That might give us good publicity,' I laughed.

I spent the next hour making up a list of bullet points so I'd have intelligent things to say to the journalist that would hopefully make people rush to the website. Martin and Caroline had done a fantastic job and it looked more inviting than even I could have imagined. My business cards had arrived and I made sure that my desk in the hallway was a welcoming reception area. I called the florist to ensure that we'd have fresh flowers delivered. Everything had to be absolutely perfect. It was an unexpected opportunity for the business and I was determined to make the most of it. Then I took Thorin out for a long walk as per doctor's orders. Alexander was coming over again later to help me follow the rest of them.

Next morning the house was filled with the warm scent of oatmeal and raisin cookies. I'd woken up in the night with an urge to bake and clean which I took as a good sign. According to my pregnancy book the nesting urge meant that my baby might finally be on his way. The florist was arriving just after ten and I was expecting the news crew around noon. I was going to use every estate agent's trick in the book to make the place look welcoming, restful and all that the website promised it would be. Émile was squirming inside me, trying to adjust to the reduced amount of space and I was ready to do anything and everything I could to lure him out.

Alexander took the cookies out of the oven because I was having trouble bending down. I waddled over to the kettle and made us a cup of tea.

'I can't take much more of this,' I said. 'Why won't he just come out?'

'He's just waiting for the perfect moment to make his grand entrance,' Alexander said and smiled at me. 'And those cookies do smell delicious. So round about now would be a good time.'

We both looked down at the floor, as though we were expecting my water to break.

'Anything?'

'Nope,' I shook my head. 'Nothing. Pass the cookies.'

He laughed and handed me one. 'I don't think I'll be the one to blame if our kids get fat.'

'I guess not. But I suppose that's something we should talk about.'

'Fat kids?'

'No. But what shall we do when Émile comes and I open the hotel? How do you think the guests will feel about you being here?'

'Meaning?'

'Well,' I smiled, 'if you come here to get over heartbreak a couple in love with a new baby is probably the last thing you want to see.'

'It's not like I live here.'

'You practically do.'

'True.' He smiled at me and then looked out the window. 'I guess I do. Maybe I shouldn't be here so much.'

'What?'

'I mean when the guests are here. Maybe you have a point.'

'I know. But we'll have to work it out somehow.'

'Maybe.'

'Maybe?'

'I mean, we should think …'

At that moment the doorbell rang and I heard Aksel's voice outside. I looked at Alexander for a long moment and then went to open the door.

The day was warm and it really seemed like spring. I served the news crew coffee and cookies while Aksel made the introductions and took notes for his next article. They filmed all over the house and then set-up in the garden. Thorin walked regally up the steps to the terrace and lay down to watch. They wanted to interview me walking through the trees but after I'd stood around waiting for half an hour a wave of nausea almost brought me to my knees.

'Are you all right?' Alexander asked.

'I feel sick. I need to sit down.' I grabbed hold of his hand and slowly lowered myself onto the terrace steps. My head was spinning and I cursed myself for having eaten all those cookies. 'Could you get me some water, please?'

'Of course.'

I tried to breathe deeply but I felt myself go pale. I started to shake and Thorin planted one of his giant paws on my leg. I smiled at him and raised a limp hand to try and scratch his ear. Alexander came running from the kitchen with my water. He rubbed my back while I breathed deeply and resisted the urge to throw up.

'Thank you,' I said and drank deeply. 'I needed that.'

Alexander nodded, looking at me with a strange, distracted look on his face. Then he took the empty glass back inside.

I sat on the steps with Thorin while the TV journalist asked me questions and I told him about all the work that had been done to the house and what the plans were. Most of what I said was a repeat of what Aksel had already written. I told him about the website, the yoga classes and the photography course that I had suggested to Caroline. The wave of nausea passed as I smiled and laughed and grew animated and started to gesture. I saw the hotel rise up before my eyes again and I was happy and optimistic and ready to take on anything the future could throw at me. Alexander was watching me from the kitchen as I spoke, the same distracted look on his face. They told me it would be a two-minute segment. It seemed like a lot of effort for something that would be over so quickly.

Later that afternoon, when everyone had driven away, I walked through the house and looked at the flowers in every room. I stood in the doorway to the kitchen and smiled at the cookie crumbs on the table. Alexander had gone home and wasn't answering his phone. Thorin and I were alone in the house. I felt my baby squirming again and I decided to move my hospital bag from the bedroom to the front door. There was a strange feeling in the air, like something waiting to happen. For the moment I wasn't sure whether it was good or bad. I was quite looking forward to seeing myself on the news. Hopefully I wouldn't look like a woman who had just fought down the urge to throw up all over the terrace. I felt impatient, anxious, like I was stuck in a waiting room with no idea of when my bus was even scheduled to arrive. Restlessly I wandered out into the garden and enjoyed the song of the birds and the fresh green of the grass. I'd had enough of being pregnant now. For nine months I had watched myself getting bigger and more ungainly. I'd fought through aches, pains, nausea, worries. I'd missed out on all my favourite foods, I'd bravely resisted most of my cravings. I'd bought a pram, a cot and Alexander had installed a car seat for me since I was too big to wiggle my way around in the back seat. This week, next week, the week after, I would meet my baby. So why did I feel so anxious?

Alexander and I sat together in front of the television that night. We watched how the house materialised on the screen and my dream began to take shape in front of all the people watching the local news. I leaned against Alexander but he didn't put his arm around me like he usually did. We sat like that for a long time, saying nothing. Then he moved away from me and sat alone at the other end of the sofa. When I got up to make some tea I looked at him and knew that he was going to tell me something I didn't want to hear.

'What is it?' I asked.

'Nothing,' he said and gave a wan smile.

'Yes, it is. I can tell.'

He looked at me like someone who didn't know which way was up. I sat back down again and tried to take his hand, but he pulled it away from me. Ever so gently, as though he didn't want to disturb me.

'I ...' He looked at me and bit his lower lip. 'I'm so sorry.'

'For what?'

'I ... I can't be a stepfather.'

'Sorry?' I stared at him, not able to find words.

'I just can't. I'm not ready. I'm not ready to move in with someone and have children. I just can't do it.'

I could still only stare. 'I ...' I began. Part of me, for some strange reason, wanted to laugh. 'I ... I know you're not ready for those things. I've not asked you to move in with me. I'm the one who's been telling you to take it slowly. Remember? You're the one who's been talking about trophy wives and children. But now,' I stopped as the reality of what he was saying dawned on me, 'now that you finally made me believe you really meant everything you said about getting married and having a life together, you're ... you're *taking it back*?'

'I ...' He just stared at me. 'I'm sorry. I ... I do love you. I don't want to say goodbye. I just ... I can't ...'

'So you just woke up this morning and decided that you'd changed your mind and this wasn't for you after all?'

'No!' he said. 'I mean ... When you were so sick this afternoon I just ... I kind of panicked. When you talked about me living here I just ... Please, can't we ...'

'Can't we what? Forget you said anything?'

'No ... I mean yes. I mean ...' He moved towards me.

'Don't.' I held up my hands and got up from the sofa. 'Just don't. I told you this would happen, didn't I? I told you from the very beginning that you would do this to me. And all your talk about being so different from every other guy turned out to be just a load of crap.' I found myself getting shrill. 'Actually, forget it. Just go.'

'I …' He looked up at me and stood, taking a step towards me, and I could see that he was crying. But I couldn't cry. I was numb. 'Please, I'm so sorry.'

'Don't. Don't be sorry. Please just go.'

'Can we …' He put his hand on my arm.

'Don't touch me.' I shook his arm off. I turned away from him and tried to take deep breaths. In front of my eyes I seemed to see the life I had imagined unravelling as I spoke. 'Do you remember that day on the beach? Do you remember when I said this was what would happen? I spent so many months holding back, trying not to let myself really fall for you because I was so scared this would happen. But you just wouldn't let go and you made me believe it. Was it just a game to you? Just seeing if you could make the silly woman fall for your lines?'

'No!' He put his arms around me and I could feel the tears coming.

'No,' I said. 'Please don't.'

'I'm sorry, I just … Can't we just forget this ever happened and go back to where we were?'

'Changed your mind again? Ready now?'

'No. But I can't lose you. But I just … I'm just not ready for all this.'

'But you always knew there was "all this". You always knew I was pregnant. And when you kept talking about our future, how could you not know that meant living together at some point? How could you not expect me to … Forget it. Please, just go. I can't look at you right now.'

'I don't want to lose you.'

I sighed. 'You can't have it both ways. You can't make me believe we have a future, change your mind and then expect me to forget everything you said about going. Don't you see? You can't go backwards in a relationship. It doesn't work that way. I could never sit with you again, never hear you say you love me, without wondering if it was really true. I'd never be safe with you, never trust you again.' He looked like he was about to say something but I shook my head. 'You've said what you wanted to say. Now please, just go. Like you said when you wouldn't talk to me about my apartment, it's my life and my decision. You don't want to get involved. I guess should have known then. Now please, just go.'

He let me go, turned around and walked towards the hallway. I wanted to call him back but I wouldn't let myself. In the doorway he stopped and looked back at me. His eyes were red. I bit my lower lip and shook my head. 'Please, just go.'

His footsteps seemed so loud on the floorboards. The sound of the door closing echoed through the house. I walked over to it like a sleepwalker and locked and bolted it. Then I went back to the sofa and curled up with Thorin beside me. Then I cried. Alone in my enormous house, while my baby squirmed inside me, I tried to grieve for the love I had just lost and for the man who had just rejected not only me, but my child.

Everything happens so quickly, I thought. My life had fallen apart this afternoon and I hadn't even known that it was happening. There would be no more babies, no rock star father, no more mornings waking up with him next to me. He'd never figure out how to work my coffee machine, he'd never take Thorin for another walk, he'd never hold me so close and make me feel so cherished. I don't know when I finally fell asleep, but when I woke up it was still dark, Thorin was resting his head on my legs and Alexander had called twice and sent three messages.

Week Thirty-Nine

I couldn't face the thought of being alone in my house after that. Not for a moment would I stay under the roof that he had fixed, shower in the bathroom he had installed or sleep in the bed where he had lain next to me night after night. The only thing I could think to do was run. Somehow, some way, I had to get out. So I packed Thorin into my car and we drove off.

We left Langeland and found a hotel on the west coast of Jutland. We walked along the beach for hours. Away from prying eyes, I sat on a large stone and cried for the future I had lost while Thorin lay at my feet. How could I ever have been so stupid? How could I have let myself be swept away by another set of empty promises? Never ever again, I said to myself as I stared out across the water and brushed away angry tears. I'm done. Done with the lot of them.

But I couldn't stop the memories of our time together. The afternoon before my birthday when Alexander found me on the beach in Rudkøbing. Our first weekend together when we drove to the other side of Langeland and walked along the beach there. All those nights we lay in each other's arms and watched the stars. The music he played for me. The teddy bear he bought for Émile. The little girl I had dared to imagine would follow him one day. I thought about how hard I had fought against the memory of you because it stopped me from trusting him. How unbelievably liberating it was when all the walls came down and I was simply free to love him. My house was filled with him. Not just the memories and the photographs behind my desk, but the very bricks and the kitchen cupboards. How could I bear it without him? This refuge I had designed, thinking never to need it again, would never be a haven for me. But how I needed it right now! Well, I thought with a wry smile and a shrug of my shoulders, there'd be no happy couple to make the guests feel awkward now.

At night I couldn't sleep. Instead I sat by the window, looking out across the dark sea and listening to the waves breaking against the shore. I pictured Alexander alone in his house, maybe in his studio or on the sofa where I had covered him with a blanket when he was ill. He had said he would write a song for me. I'd never hear it now.

For the first time in months I missed you and I saw clearly the path I had trod all these years. It would be so easy. So easy to turn my thoughts towards you and away from Alexander. Away from the life I had allowed myself to believe would be mine. There was a ready-made romantic dream just waiting for me to fall into again. You were out there and I was having your baby. It would be so easy.

But what would happen then? You would disappoint me again. Or I would run even further away and fall for someone else's lies. I'd already let you drive me out of one home, now I was letting Alexander drive me out of another. All that was missing was the coffee cup cooling by the sink. I had always run away. I'd run from your marriage and from our past. After every failed relationship, I had let myself get drawn back into the web of your dreams because it was easier than dealing with the pain. The pain of you was easy to deal with, like an old and familiar enemy you've been fighting so long they are practically a friend. But this time I didn't want to go back. Alexander had shown me a world far beyond the one you had imagined for us. But he had still left.

Despite everything that had happened between us and everything he had said, I had been right all along. He had been just another dreamer. The life he dreamt of was far in the future, he had had no concept of the reality of the present. Maybe that was who I was to the men in my life — a dream that couldn't be transferred to reality. Maybe there was just something fundamentally wrong with me. Obviously, once men were faced with the reality of life with me, their immediate reaction was to run away screaming.

The doctor had told me to go for long walks. If only she could see me now.

Alexander called and wrote at least once every day but I still didn't want to talk to him. Right now I never wanted to see him again. I didn't care that he had cried, didn't care that maybe his heart was breaking too. All I remembered, again and again, was telling him not to go so fast. That he was young and that we had all the time in the world. If he had just let our intimacy come naturally rather than try to cement us into some kind of pattern, this would never have happened. I didn't know what would have happened, but I knew it could only have been better than this.

Week Forty

We went home again because I couldn't stand people's endless questions about where the father was and what I was doing here so close to my time. I didn't want to run away anymore. I wanted the house I loved and the home I had created. I had promised Sara and Nikolaj I'd be a good landlord, not an absentee one. Langeland had healed me once, it could do it again. I had to believe that.

I got through the days by smiling politely whenever someone spoke to me, feeling for my baby's kicks against the hand I put on my stomach and walking up and down every street in Rudkøbing until I could feel the cobbles through the soles of my shoes. Food was still repulsive to me. My due date was Sunday. My parents were arriving on Friday. I could hold it together until then.

One thing did was confirmed for me amidst all the chaos. My house. When I opened the door and saw the familiar rooms, I was glad to be back. It really was home. Even if the memories made it unbearable right now. And I knew that what I had created was exactly what I needed, what others would need. Somewhere to rest when the world has collapsed. Somewhere people ask you no questions. Somewhere they just look after you and feed you chocolate and leave you alone.

After I got back the previous Friday afternoon I'd suffered five hours of regular contractions hoping for a labour that never materialised. On the Sunday it was two hours. I kept my fingers crossed and hoped for my baby to make his entrance early, but now it was Monday and I was still pregnant. I wanted chocolate again and was so unhappy now that I didn't give a damn what I looked like. Thorin loved his early morning walks in the clean spring air and bounded along happily beside me, amazing all the little children in town with his size. Nobody was willing to believe that he was a puppy. He made me smile when everything else seemed hopeless, and when we walked in the garden together no one saw me crying.

    I hadn't seen Alexander since the night I'd asked him to leave and not seeing him and not talking to him seemed like a bereavement. I hadn't told him that I'd gone and I pretended I didn't care if he'd come looking for me. I didn't want to talk to him right now. I'd either scream something I didn't really mean or I'd take him back and regret it. There was no way to save what we had had together. I welcomed the aches and pain I had previously loathed because they took my focus away from the heartache of his words. I couldn't think about the pictures he had painted of our lives together, the way he'd promised to love my son as though he were his own, the life I had allowed myself to imagine. It would never be a reality now. I would read about his career in the newspapers, I'd see him on talk shows, but he'd never be part of my life again. Each time that thought hit me, I had to stop myself from driving out to his house. I knew now that he wasn't ready for a life together, but he had made me ready for it and now we were too far apart.

On Tuesday I could barely move, I was so stiff. I managed two short walks with Thorin but mostly he roamed around the garden. Sara came over to get everything ready for my parents' arrival. She told me that after talking to people in town about the segment on the evening news, she now had two more cleaning jobs and at least one other inquiry. She was considering starting her own company. So maybe my own life had turned out to be a mess but at least I was helping make things right for others. We spent a lot of our time together discussing different ways to improve and renovate my grandparents' house. I started going over there a lot and every time I went, I was wrapped up in memories. Sara didn't ask any questions but she knew something was wrong.

    I was sitting in the kitchen that afternoon with a cup of tea and a novel that I couldn't concentrate on. Thorin was in his basket chewing on a doggy toothbrush with a rapt dedication that made me smile. The first pain surprised me. It was similar to the ones I had experienced in such regular succession on Friday and Sunday, and yet different. I breathed as the doctor had told me and got my phone out to measure the intervals, just as I had done before. There was another text from Alexander telling me he wanted to come and talk to me. Half of me just wanted him to leave me alone while the other half thought that if he really was so damn sorry, he should come and tell me in person rather than hide behind unanswered calls and messages. The poor guy couldn't win and that thought made me want to laugh. I gave up on my novel and got up, hoping moving around might make the pain go away.

When the doorbell rang, I was standing by the garden door looking out at the trees. Thorin leapt up and started barking. I wasn't expecting anyone and the thought that it might be Alexander made me both angry and happy at the same time. Life would be so much easier if falling out of love was as easy as falling into it. Thorin barked again but his tail wasn't wagging the way it normally did when someone he knew showed up. Maybe it wasn't Alexander.

The pains stopped as I walked into the hallway to open the door. I was only sorry I no longer had the strength to throw it open with a big dramatic gesture, just in case it was Alexander.

But it wasn't.

It was you.

'Hello, Anne,' you said. 'Can I come in?'

And, just like that, you walked back into my life.

We sat in the kitchen while a myriad questions ran through my mind. What were you doing here? How did you find me? And, most importantly, had you realised that it was your baby who was squirming away inside me?

'What are you doing here?' I asked.

'I saw you on the news.'

'The news?'

'Yes.'

With everything that had happened after the broadcast, I had tried to forget as much about that day as I could.

'But I was on the local news. How did you see that?'

You sighed and then smiled at me. 'We'd gone away for a few days. An early birthday celebration.'

We.

'Of course,' I smiled. 'Happy birthday.'

'Thanks. We were at a hotel not too far from here. On Funen. I was watching the news while waiting to go to dinner. Then I saw you.'

'I see.'

'Why didn't you answer my messages?'

'I did.'

'No, you didn't.' You looked at me and took my hand. 'And the ones you did, you didn't answer properly.'

'Why did you send them? You got married,' I went on before you could answer. 'That is supposed to mean goodbye. As in no more. No more messages, no more sex, no more confused emotions. The end. And I left because I had no intention of hanging around to watch your new beginning.'

'You didn't even tell me you were going. I just turned up at your apartment to find a strange woman there.'

I nodded and took my hand away. 'You weren't supposed to turn up. But having found that strange woman, you didn't call or write to me to ask where I was. Not for weeks. Why are you here anyway? Feeling lonely?' I could hear the sarcasm in my voice.

'I wanted to see you.'

'You're married. You shouldn't want to see me. Not while you were engaged, never again. You came to me the night before your wedding and we made love and the next day you stood up in a church with another woman, right around the corner from my building, and promised to love and cherish her forever. You never offered me any of those things except as a pipe dream that you ran from the next morning. What have I ever been to you except a body you could come to when you had an itch you couldn't scratch on your own?' I knew the tears were building up behind my eyes. I wouldn't let you see me cry. God knows I'd wasted enough tears on you. I'd come to terms with all of this during my pregnancy. I'd moved on. Just because the one I'd thought I was moving on with didn't want me didn't mean that I should run back to you. You were just my old safety net. You were not my true love come back to me at the last minute for some romantic, dramatic climax.

You looked at me. 'Is that what you think?'

'What do you expect me to think?'

Somewhere in the back of my mind a memory stirred. We'd had this conversation before. On a wet day in June, five years before. And it had ended with promises and tears and one of the most passionate nights we'd ever spent together. The next morning you'd kissed me goodbye, promised to see me later and I hadn't heard another word from you until Christmas.

Another pain hit me and I looked at my phone. Five minutes since the last one. I breathed deeply and you looked at me strangely.

'You didn't tell me you were pregnant.'

I shook my head and kept exhaling quickly. 'It doesn't matter. We've been here before. We've already said all this and I am tired of saying it and tired of hearing it. Go back to your wife, have a nice life, thank you for coming.' I winced and you took my hand again.

'Are you all right?'

'I don't know yet. I could be in labour.'

'Oh God! Right, let's get you to a hospital. You just keep breathing. Should I ... is there someone I should call? A boyfriend?'

I shook my head and bit my lip to stop the tears from flowing. 'No, no boyfriend.' Oh God, how did it get so mixed up? When I'd wanted you to be the one beside me during those first few months, Alexander had been the one there. Now you were here and all I wanted was him.

'Anne, I have to ask. Is this just an amazing coincidence or is this my baby?'

'Does it matter?'

'No.' You smiled at me. 'I didn't come because I saw you were pregnant. I came because I wanted to see you. When I saw you on television something finally clicked. I had to see you. I should have come for you a long time ago. Whether it's my baby or someone else's doesn't matter. It's yours and I want you.'

'Yes,' I nodded, 'it's your baby. But you married someone else the day after he was conceived and I didn't want to ruin that for you.'

'He? It's a boy?'

I nodded again.

Your mouth fell open and you tried to speak but I could see all words deserting you. So you did what you had always done. You took my face in your hands and kissed me. Then you just held me in your arms while I let myself cry. I felt your arms tighten around me and you kissed the top of my head.

'Why didn't you tell me?'

'I thought about it. I thought about it so many times. But I didn't want you to feel obliged to do anything. I didn't want to ruin your marriage and your new life. And,' I sat up and looked at you, 'I didn't want you to do the honourable thing. I wanted you to want me for me, not because I had your baby. And you didn't want me. Not enough.'

'Oh, Anne, it really wasn't like that. I ... I love you.'

'Don't say that.' I disentangled myself and shook my head. 'Don't say it now just to vanish into thin air again tomorrow. You don't have to say what you don't mean. I'm not asking you for anything.'

'I do mean it. I love you. I've always loved you, since the first moment I saw you.' You gently pushed my hair away from my face and kissed me again. 'I know it's been messed up and we've made so many mistakes, but I do love you. Always have. Always will. I should never have got married. It was a mistake. If I'd really loved her, I wouldn't have been so desperate to see you one last time. After you were on the news, we had a long talk. Then we went home and talked a lot more. She told me she'd seen you sitting in the café. I did try. I tried to make it work. I tried to pretend you were out of my life forever. But you never will be. This ends now. No more running away, no more broken promises. I swear. It's you and me and our baby.'

You held me close and I smelled the familiar scent of your cologne. I tried to keep breathing deeply but it hurt too much. So I looked up and smiled at you through my tears. Then I felt another pain and something wet washed down my legs. 'Then do something for me.'

'Anything.' You laughed and kissed my hand.

'Drive me to the hospital. I'm definitely in labour.'

'Oh my God!'

Our son was born six hours later. You held my hand through it all and smiled at me. I breathed through the pain, through the muddle of my thoughts and the worry that I would wake up to find this had all been a dream and my baby was still nowhere near being born. I couldn't think of you or of Alexander, I could only cling to the belief that this was real and that I would get to meet my son. I didn't know if you meant what you said, I didn't know why you'd come to find me or if your wife even knew where you were.

When Émile took his first breath, when I heard him cry and they put him in my arms, I felt the most overwhelming sense of love I'd ever known. At that moment I didn't care if he was perfectly healthy or not, didn't care what the future held for us. When I looked at him for the first time, I knew he could have every problem in the world and I'd still love him as passionately as I did. I knew, at last, the meaning of unconditional love and I knew that we could manage on our own. Then you kissed me and asked to hold him.

'We need to talk,' you said. I nodded but was suddenly overwhelmingly tired. You stroked my hair and I watched as the midwife handed the little blue bundle to you. Then they wheeled us out of the delivery room and back to our ward. I called my parents to tell them that their grandson had decided to arrive ahead of schedule. They'd be on the next flight out. I left a message for Lisbeth and told her Emma now had a little baby boy to play with. I called Sara and asked her to take care of Thorin for me till I got back. The one person I did not know if I should call was Alexander.

When we got back to the room I sat down and the midwife helped me feed my son for the first time. You kissed us both on the top of the head, said you'd be back soon and then vanished out of the door. Half of me didn't expect you to come back. Part of me didn't even care if you didn't. After all I had been through over the last few months, I would rather see you walk away now than come back and make promises and make me believe in a future which would never materialise. While I waited for us be sent home, I sang to my baby. I held him in my arms and I knew that from now on he was the centre of my world. This beautiful vulnerable little baby who needed me to love him, protect him and to build a safe future filled with every opportunity I could offer him.

When the midwife told me I could go home, you still hadn't come back so I asked her to help me phone for a taxi. My car was still in Rudkøbing and my parents were still en route from Paris, due to arrive later that night. She didn't look too happy about the idea of the two us driving off on our own but I didn't see that I had much choice. I slung my bag over my shoulder and picked up my son. He was asleep and I kissed his forehead. I could gaze at him for hours. When he slept I wanted him to wake up because I missed him so much, even though he was right next to me. I'd heard of postnatal depression, but no one had told me about postnatal euphoria. Lisbeth had been right, you do fall in love with your children. There was no other way to describe everything he had made me feel in such a short space of time.

All these months I had waited to meet him. All these months I had endured aches and pains, cravings and revulsion, all for the sake of this tiny little creature now lying peacefully in my arms. I'd do it all over again for the sake of that first moment when he opened his eyes and looked into mine. They were my eyes, so dark blue they were almost black. Yet he looked so much like you. I wanted to take him home, let Thorin sniff him, and get on with my life. The three of us had a whole new life to build and I couldn't wait to get started on it.

We walked out into the reception area to wait for the taxi and I noticed two men sitting by the coffee machine in the far corner. Each of them was holding a ridiculously enormous stuffed animal. When they heard my footsteps they both stood up and turned towards me. I looked at them. Both were men who had loved me and hurt me. I knew how you had got here. I wondered vaguely how Alexander had known to come and decided Nikolaj must have called him. The two men looked at me and they looked at each other. They smiled at my baby. I couldn't think of a single thing to say to either one of them. So I adjusted my bag, smiled at them and at my son and walked out into the sunshine to where the taxi was waiting for me.

I heard running footsteps but I didn't turn around to see which of them was coming after me.

Author's Note

This is a work of fiction, although Anne's house may be easy to identify if you know your way around Rudkøbing.

I have been so touched by all the support and encouragement I have received while attempting to live this dream. There's no doubt that people asking me, 'When do we get to read it?' has kept me going through those times when it seemed as though the real world would never let me escape from it long enough to finish this. Thank you all, you've been amazing.

Special thanks to my son Matthew O'Reilly for giving me the title that made the idea come together - all I needed after that was to write it. My parents, John and Merete O'Reilly, have been amazing as always and supportive beyond anything I could have hoped for. I could never have done any of it without you behind me. The Barflies were always there with encouragement or much needed distractions - first round is on me. And Daniel Brown, I still need to read your book. For countless cups of coffee, great advice and the strange conviction that I could actually do this I owe so much to Thomas Østergaard, Michael Brorsen and Joachim Ardelt, and I promise to bring cake. Thanks to Marloes Gesman de-Witte and Sophie Egede-Schröder for reading an early stage of the manuscript and telling me I really was an author. Lastly thanks to my editor, Catherine Fitzsimons. She did an incredible job and I would recommend her to anyone.

Printed in Great Britain
by Amazon